Smith m

down a

Street v

'So don't sod about, my son, ...

one agent for the job. And tha' knows it.'

'She's in the cooler.'

'Then bloody get 'er out.'

Smith turned from the window. 'The psychiatrist said she's dangerous.'

'I should bloody well 'ope so, after all the training we give 'er.'

'He also said she was suffering from battle fatigue.'

'Aye, it's a tiring business is war.'

'And that she needed treatment. Which is one reason the Board of Inquiry recommended a spell in the cooler, where they have a resident psychiatrist.'

'Bugger the Board, son, I want 'er out.'

'Even if she's a psychopathic killer?'

'Especially if she's a psychopathic killer.'

RYFKA

Patrick Alexander

ARROW BOOKS

Arrow Books Limited
20 Vauxhall Bridge Road, London SW1V 2SA

An imprint of Random Century Group

London Melbourne Sydney Auckland
Johannesburg and agencies throughout the world

First published in Great Britain by Century 1988

Arrow edition 1989
Reprinted 1989

Printed and bound in Great Britain by
Courier International Ltd, Tiptree, Essex

ISBN 0 09 961810 9

To Anne

When fishes flew and forests walked
And figs grew upon thorn,
Some moment when the moon was blood
Then surely I was born;

G K Chesterton, *The Donkey*

Sweet day, so cool, so calm, so bright,
The bridall of the earth and skie:
The dew shall weep thy fall tonight;
For thou must die.

George Herbert, *Vertue*

Most secret
MEMORANDUM

TO: CD
FROM: Head of F Section
DATE: 15 February 1944

DISTRIBUTION:
SO
V/CD
D/CD (Ops)
D/R

Ref: FWS/EP/F1134

Attached is a copy of the interrogation of Agent F107 (field name Ryfka), requested by the Board of Inquiry investigating the incident at Alençon, in which three F Section agents were killed, including their organizer (field name Gerard). The only survivor was Agent F107.

NOTE: In the attached documents F Section agents are referred to by field names, circuits by codenames in capitals. Gerard was organizer of HORSEMAN, based on Rennes, Louis of COLUMBUS, based on Alençon.

(Frank W. Smith)
Head of F Section

Ref: FWS/LR/FS1102

Interrogation of F107 (RYFKA)
by Lt Col. F. W. Smith

SMITH: On the night of January the third you set out with
Gerard, Antoine and Philippe for an appointment with Louis.

RYFKA: In Samarra.

S: In Alençon, you mean.

R: Sure. Alençon.

S: What was the object of the meeting?

R: To discuss plans for a new subcircuit where
HORSEMAN and COLUMBUS overlapped.

S: Who asked for the meeting? Gerard?

R: Louis. He was setting us up.

S: How do you know?

R: The Gestapo were waiting for us.

S: That could have been a snap control.

R: Controls only operate on main roads.

S: They could have picked up a rumour about resisters
using forest roads at night.

R: It wasn't a rumour, it was a tip-off. The bastard
shopped us.

S: You mean Louis?

R: How did you guess.

S: I still say it could have been a routine control.

R: You think Otto Raab would get out of his warm bed
and his fat whore for a routine control? Mitten in der Nacht?

S: Let's keep to English. Raab was there?

R: And his sidekick, Blech.

S: How could Louis have known your route?

R: I'd driven him that way before. To *avoid* main road
controls.

S: Who else knew the route?

R: Gerard, Antoine, Philippe ...

S: So there could be other suspects?

R: Gerard's dead, Antoine's dead, Philippe's dead. Which leaves a nationwide shortage of suspects.

S: How did they die?

R: It was all in the signal I sent in mid-January.

S: We'd like more details.

R: What details? I mean, Antoine and Philippe were knocked off in the firefight with the Gestapo. The bastards were spraying us with Schmeissers, Sturmgewehr, every automatic weapon they'd got, including an MG 42. Ever heard an MG 42 blasting off at twelve hundred rounds a minute? Makes a kind of tearing sound, like tearing canvas, only louder. Scares the shit out of you. It sounded like they were cutting trees down with it. It's a wonder we weren't all killed.

S: Yes, it is, isn't it?

R: What are you getting at?

S: Simply quoting something Louis said.

R: That bastard'll say anything, he's under pressure.

S: From whom?

R: Whom? Ah, we're so kultiviert. Well, *whom* the fuck do you think? The Gestapo. They must've found out he's got a wife in Alençon.

S: You're guessing.

R: But guessing good. Listen, when he was working with us he was always cheerful and confident. Even strangers noticed it. Who's the big smiling man, they'd say. But after he went to Alençon and picked up with his wife he changed. He was scared.

S: How do you know?

R: I could smell it. I've lived with fear.

S: Did you tell Gerard?

R: No. He had enough on his plate. But I was against that bloody appointment in Samarra.

S: You mean Alençon.

R: Yeah, Alençon.

S: You had misgivings?

R: Like Romeo ... My mind misgives Some consequence yet hanging in the stars ...

S: But you went along. And in the forest of Perseigne, was it, you ran into the roadblock?

9

R: In the bit they call the Vallée d'Enfer. Hell of a place it is, too. Narrow, steep, twisting. We came out of a tight bend and there they were, waiting for us: a one-ton halftrack and an armoured troop carrier across the road. Then searchlights came on, blinding us, and someone shouted Halt.

S: Raab?

R: Blech. Raab never shouts. Anyway, I put my foot down and drove straight at them.

S: Wasn't Gerard driving?

R: He hadn't driven since the Gestapo hung him up by the thumbs and ruined his grip. But he taught me some of his racing techniques.

S: And what were the Gestapo doing all this time?

R: Nothing. I think they were stunned. Till I pulled the wheel over and went into a one-eighty-degree skid and threw mud and shit all over them. That woke 'em up. And they let fly with everything they'd got.

S: And hit you?

R: Hit a front tyre. I lost steering, slewed across the road and clouted a tree. Gerard and I scrambled out and flattened ourselves on the ground. Philippe jumped out of the back and Antoine started to follow, but seemed to hesitate in the doorway. You know, like a shy boy at a party. Then he shuddered and fell on top of me. I tried to shove him off but he weighed a ton and his blood was soaking me like warm rain. In the end Philippe pulled him off and gave me a handkerchief and said: Here, wipe your bloody face.

S: Antoine was already dying?

R: Antoine was dead.

S: And then?

R: We made for the forest. Not before time. As we dived into the scrub there was this terrific explosion and the car went up in flame and smoke. We'd borrowed it from a reluctant black marketeer and I kept worrying – I must have been in a state of shock – what the hell we were going to tell him. Sorry, old cock, 'fraid we bent the jaloppy a bit . . .

S: Once in the forest, who led the way?

R: I did. I was the only one who knew it.

S: You were armed?

R: Philippe had a Sten and a Smith & Wesson. I had a Sten and my Walther P38. And the little special I always carry. Gerard was unarmed.

S: Did the Gestapo follow you?

R: It was dark in the forest, apart from a splash of moonlight here and there in the breaks, and they got jumpy. They'd stop and listen, then loose off at any old noise. Once, when we were crossing a glade, we flushed some animal and it crashed away through the undergrowth and they opened up with just about everything, including that MG 42. It was like half the forest was being torn down. Gerard and Philippe flattened themselves against an oak tree and I crept round the edge of the glade – to rake them from the flank when they stepped into the moonlight. Then, all of a sudden, it was over. And they started to pull back. Probably scared of getting in too deep. It's easy enough to get lost there during the day, never mind the night. I could hear them blundering around and cursing, but they were getting fainter all the time. So I crept back to the others, and saw the oak tree had been cut down in the firestorm. Philippe was lying under it, dead.

S: Shot or crushed by the tree?

R: Don't know. I just made sure he was dead, then turned to Gerard, who was sitting on the ground in a patch of moonlight, leaning against the remains of the tree. I said: Well, come on, for Christ's sake. But he only smiled and shook his head. Then I knew he'd been hit.

S: Where?

R: In the gut. There was an old maison forestière nearby – the local maquisards used it as a hiding place sometimes – and I half carried, half dragged him there. At least it was dry and there were straw palliasses to lie on. I even found half a bottle of brandy in a cupboard. I took a swig but didn't give him any because of the gut wound. I used some of it to clean the wound though. It wasn't bleeding much, but he could have been bleeding inside.

S: Did he complain?

R: Complain? He wasn't a baby. I made him as comfortable as I could and was wondering whether to slip away and try to find a doctor, when I heard them coming back. With dogs.

S: The Gestapo?

R: No, the Salvation fucking Army. Ever heard Dobermans when they scent blood?

S: Was that when he asked you to shoot him?

R: He was dying anyway, but with a gutshot it could take a week or more. And he reckoned he had enough pain, without any help from the Gestapo.

S: Why didn't he do it himself?

R: He couldn't hold a gun properly.

S: He told *us* his hands were better.

R: He wanted to stay in the field. He said you'd bring him back if you knew how bad he was.

S: Was he in much pain?

R: He was wriggling a bit. Maybe the shock was wearing off. Anyway, he asked for the brandy and I gave him the bottle.

S: But you just said –

R: By then I'd decided to kill him.

S: Because he asked you to?

R: Sure.

S: Or because he was an obstacle to your own escape?

R: There was no point in both of us being caught. So it was a question of leaving him alive or leaving him dead.

S: And you chose to leave him dead.

R: He was the one who did the choosing.

S: Nevertheless, it was a cool decision on your part.

R: I've been trained to take cool decisions.

S: Were you sleeping with him?

R: Yes.

S: In love with him?

R: No. Just fucking good friends.

S: But –

R: Most of the time you're either bored or scared. Fucking lessens the boredom.

S: But you didn't find it difficult shooting him?

R: Shooting people's easy. Bang bang, they're dead.

12

S: I was merely trying to establish if there was a bond between you.

R: We'd both been tortured by the Gestapo. That always establishes a bond, you know. Actually, you don't know, do you, you lucky bastard.

S: I must put Louis's accusation to you: that you shot both men because they were hindering your own escape.

R: What the fuck does *he* know? He wasn't even there.

(NOTE: Interrogation discontinued in view of subject's mounting hostility and physical weakness)

10 February 1944

Interrogation abandoned on medical advice. Subject, however, volunteered a brief statement, copy of which is attached. It adds nothing material to the interrogation. What really happened in the forest may never be known. The SOE psychiatrist thinks her war experiences have triggered psychopathic tendencies in her personality. One result (he says) is that her version of the truth, even if she believes it herself, may not *be* the truth. A more beneficial result is that her war activities give her a sense of mission, and direct her energy and zeal, typical of this personality type, into acceptable channels. Acceptable in wartime, that is.

Raab's success in smashing HORSEMAN led to his promotion to Standartenfuehrer (full colonel). He is now in operational control of the Gestapo, SD and SS in Normandy and the Pays de Loire north of the river.

SIGNED ... F. W. Smith. ...
(Head of F Section)

SIGNED ... Ryfka. ...
(Agent 107)

WITNESS ... Aeronwy Jones. ...
(Warrant Officer, WAAF)

14 February 1944

Voluntary statement by Agent 107

I wanted to bury him to stop the dogs getting at him. But there was nothing to dig with. And the dogs were getting nearer. So I put a match to the straw palliasse he was lying on. It went up with a whoosh, and turned the whole place into a funeral pyre. Then the Gestapo arrived with the dogs. I gave them controlled bursts with the Sten till I was out of ammo, then chucked the gun and dived into the forest. The cool clean forest. I ran along a stream to throw the dogs off the scent and made for a farm where I'd been given shelter once before.

By now the alarm had been raised and the area was stiff with SS and Gestapo. In a lane near the farm I was challenged by an SS control. I ran off into a field and they opened up, but it was still dark and they just blazed away on the off chance. And got lucky. Suddenly, I found myself flat on my face. It was only a flesh wound, as it turned out, but it felt like I'd been hit by a truck. I managed to crawl into a ditch of freezing water. I could hear them crashing about and there was a lot of shouting and barking, but the freezing water was killing the scent. It was also killing me and I passed out.

When I came to it was dawn. And there was the farmer, staring down at me with a surprised look on his face. Then I must have passed out again. The next time I came to I was in bed and there was this doctor telling the farmer's wife I hadn't got a dog's chance and he must be bonkers to waste the last of his precious sulphanilamide tablets on me. A week later I was sitting up and he said the freezing water must have cauterized the wound. Which sounded crazy to me. A few days later I was strong enough to contact what was left of the local resistance and ask them to get a message to London.

The rest you know.

SIGNED.... Ryfka....
(F107)
WITNESSED BY.... F. W. Smith....
(Head of F Section)

WITNESSED BY... Aeronwy Jones....
(Warrant Officer, WAAF)

1

Dog minus 17

To most people, including Flight Lieutenant Meadows, it was Friday 19 May.

But then most people didn't know about Dog Day. Or D-Day, as it came to be called. Those who did were given the codename Bigot, which became the highest general security classification of the time. Since the previous December they had been secretly planning the invasion of Hitler's Fortress Europa (declared impregnable by Hitler himself). Meanwhile they were banned from operations involving risk of capture.

Flight Lieutenant Meadows was commander of C Flight and skipper of D-Daisy in a force of fifty Lancaster bombers that had taken off from their Lincolnshire base for a routine operation over France. The target was an ammunition dump at Le Mans, headquarters of the German Seventh Army, and between them the Lancasters should have been carrying 350 men. But on Friday 19 May they were carrying 351. And the odd man out was the only one who knew it was also Dog minus 17.

Meadows took D-Daisy in straight and level at his assigned bombing height of 19,500 feet, then said over the intercom: 'Right, Bluey, she's all yours.'

The Australian bomb aimer, lying on his body rest in the Perspex blister in the nose of the Lancaster, called back: 'Right a bit, Skip . . . Okay, that'll do . . . Nice and steady.'

Meadows kept her nice and steady. Then four black stars appeared in a neat line ahead, and exploded. He'd already started to get her nose up when the shock waves hit her underbelly. She bucked like a wild horse, but he managed to get her straight and level again. From the pattern of the flak he guessed it was radar controlled and probably 10.5

16

centimetre. Bluey's voice twanged over the intercom: 'Left a bit, Skip . . . Hold it.'

He could see the target ahead and below, already burning, though it seemed hardly more than a garden bonfire from that height. He could also see, in his mind's eye, Bluey reaching up to press the tit that would release the bombs in their preselected order. Bluey's voice, when it came, made him jump.

'Bombs gone.' Daisy, free of her burden, gave a little leap like a spring lamb. 'Bomb doors shut.'

He continued to hold her steady till Bluey said 'Okay for pix', which meant the automatic camera had taken the aiming point photograph. Then he banked and climbed rapidly to port to get above the flak.

By now the sky was full of exploding black stars, pretty as a picture, but they made Daisy pitch and roll like a fishing smack in a running sea. He pulled the control column back, pushed the throttles wide open and felt her climb like a bird. Soon he'd be above all that shit.

Then there was a tremendous jolt on the starboard wing and all the 55,000 separate parts Daisy was made of shuddered in sympathy. Well, not quite all. Some parts were missing, including six feet of wingtip and the starboard outer engine. Where the engine used to be was a fire. He didn't remember hearing an explosion but his ears were ringing and all his teeth felt loose. Then Daisy went into a screaming dive to starboard.

At 15,000 feet, with the flight engineer helping him yank back the control column, he managed to level her out and fly straight but lopsided. Then the starboard inner engine started to splutter. He feathered it and noted that the fire extinguishers were having bugger-all effect.

'Well,' he said over the intercom, 'at least the bitch is flying straight. More or less.'

'Don't call her a bitch, Skipper,' said the flight engineer. The rest of the crew joined in: 'Take it back, Skipper. Take it back.'

He knew how superstitious aircrew were. 'Okay,' he said,

'she's a bloody angel. But now her starboard inner's on fire.'

There was a deep religious silence, then someone said sadly: 'Oh, shit.'

'Number two tank's registering empty, number one has less than twenty gallons.' He paused to let it sink in. 'Guess what we're going to do now.'

The pilot of another Lancaster counted the parachutes as they blossomed out of Daisy's escape hatches. He counted eight, but they were some way below him, swaying like windblown snowdrops, and he could have been mistaken. So he asked the bomb aimer to check through his clear-view panel. The bomb aimer also made it eight. A Lancaster's complement was seven.

Back at base the pilot, who was from the same squadron as D-Daisy but in a different flight, reported the presence of the eighth man to the Intelligence Officer, who sighed irritably.

'Some brass hat from Group, I expect,' he said. 'Bloody joy riding.'

The IO and the pilot were sitting on opposite sides of a trestle table in the Briefing Room, sipping coffee spiked with rum. The pilot nodded. He'd wondered if it was something like that. It was known that desk-bound senior officers sometimes went on a raid to relieve their boredom. Unofficially, of course. If it came to light they got a dressing down from AOC at Group.

'Any idea who it might be?' the pilot asked.

'Haven't a clue. Group's full of chairborne charlies. And his name won't be in the Operations Record Book or on a five-forty, will it?' The IO had all the contempt of one chairborne officer for another. 'Anyway, we'll soon find out. Let's see now . . .' He looked across at the big operations board that took up most of one wall. 'Meadows was commander of C Flight. One of his pals should know.'

Later, when debriefing another C Flight pilot, the IO said: 'You're a pal of Bunny Meadows, aren't you? Know if he was carrying additional aircrew?'

An innocent-sounding question and it got an innocent answer. 'It'll be in the ORB if he was.'

'I'm not talking about an official passenger, I'm talking about a bloody joy rider.'

'Then you'd better ask Bunny himself.'

'His kite was shot down west of Le Mans. Crew baled out.' The IO paused for effect. 'All eight of them. Someone counted the parachutes. So if you know who the extra bod was you might as well say.'

The pilot shrugged. 'Mad Harry.'

Air Commodore Harold Romaine was the station commander. He was also a fighter ace of the First World War, in which he collected a DSO, a DFC and the nickname Mad Harry.

'Very funny, old son,' the IO said wearily. 'What a comedian was lost in you. Now tell us who it really was.'

Later that evening a report of the raid was telexed from the orderly room at the base to Air Ministry in London. It gave the names of the missing aircrew, including that of Air Commodore Harold Romaine. Since it was a Friday and most of the senior staff had left, the report spent a quiet weekend in a group captain's in-tray.

Dog minus 14

On Monday morning when the group captain drifted in after a heavy night at the American Officers' Club in Grosvenor Square and settled down to read the report, the shock of an air commodore's name on the manifest of a missing aircraft almost cured his hangover. He unlocked his safe with a shaky hand and took out a folder stamped MOST SECRET. It contained an alphabetical check list of all Bigots. His eye went immediately to the names beginning with R. Then he picked up the phone, his hand still shaking, but not from the hangover.

Within minutes Churchill had been informed, Eisenhower had been informed. To Churchill, chewing on a dead cigar in the underground war bunker beneath Storey's Gate in Westminster, it seemed the realization of a recurring

19

nightmare: that Hitler might somehow learn of the Allied invasion plans.

Only a few days before he'd growled to Eisenhower: 'I am haunted by a vision of the Channel tides running red with Allied blood . . . of beaches choked with the bodies of the flower of our manhood.'

2

Dog minus 14

Major General Mossop put the red telephone down and said 'Bloody 'ell' in the kind of northern accent in which aitches are silent. Like the pee in bathing, his father used to say. The accent faded after he went up to Oxford as an exhibitioner, but came back when he was provoked or the mood took him. He had cultivated a reputation for bluntness to camouflage a subtle and calculating mind.

The red telephone was on a direct line to Downing Street and it usually rang with trouble. But this lot, Mossop thought, must be at least eight on the Richter scale. And rising.

Albert Mossop was the chief (CD) of Special Operations Executive, a secret agency whose job was to organize resistance and sabotage against German forces in occupied territory and, in Churchill's phrase, 'set Europe ablaze'. It was so secret even its own agents didn't know the headquarters' address, except that it was somewhere in London. And the name plate outside 64 Baker Street was no help. It simply said:

Inter-Services Research Bureau

'One day,' Frank Smith, who ran the French Section, had told him, 'some poor old Jewish refugee is going to wander in and ask the way to Finchley Road in a heavy Cherman accent, and they'll take him out the back and shoot him.'

'Very funny, my son,' he'd said. But he didn't think it funny at all.

He pressed a switch on the desk intercom and asked his secretary to find Colonel Smith, then swivelled his chair round and pulled the drawstring of curtains on the wall behind him. They slid back to reveal a map of Europe

21

dotted with white labels fixed by insecure pins. The labels gave the codenames of SOE resistance circuits and sometimes an indication of their fate.

He stared at a label between Le Mans and Rennes. On it was written in his own clerkly hand:

HORSEMAN (fragment)

A fragment could be anything from a subcircuit with dependent cells to some poor bastard crouching in a hayloft, hoping to God the Gestapo wouldn't find him.

He was still staring at the label when Smith came in. Mossop waved him to an armchair, into which Smith slumped with the grace of long practice. He was tall, handsome in a willowy greyhound sort of way, and public school. This last grated on Mossop, who came from a working-class background and had clawed his way up the educational and career ladders by brains and grit. Despite their obvious differences they shared an understanding about the job in hand, though not always about methods.

Mossop lowered his grizzled head and stared over his glasses, looking like a small elderly bull about to charge. 'A Bigot was shot down over 'orseman territory on Friday.'

'A Bigot? What the hell was he doing over there?'

Mossop shrugged. 'I've no details. My orders are to bring 'im back. Before the bloody Germans get 'im.'

'With two days' start,' Smith said, 'the bloody Germans may've already got him.'

Mossop spoke slowly and clearly, without an accent. 'In that case, eliminate him.'

Smith sat up. 'On whose authority?'

'Downing Street's. Over the red telephone.' He smiled sourly and his accent came back. 'But tha' mustn't expect it in bloody writing.'

Smith studied his manicured nails. 'Don't think I like this.' A taxi hooted outside. 'Who is he?'

'Harold . . .' Mossop squinted at a scrawl on his blotter. 'Romaine. Air comm. With a DFC and DSO from the last show. Air Ministry are sending over 'is personal file.' He looked up. 'Well, it's your section, son. Who d'you reckon?'

Smith got up, wandered over to the wall map, studied it. 'It's a suicide job.'

'Someone with local knowledge,' said Mossop. 'Or the Gestapo'll 'ave 'im for breakfast.'

'There's only a fragment of the circuit left. And even that may have been penetrated. The Gestapo'll be sitting there like spiders, waiting for the next poor bloody fly.'

'We could lose ten divisions on D-Day if they pick this chap up and put 'im to the question.'

Smith moved over to the window and stared down at the sparse wartime traffic of Baker Street without seeing it.

'So don't sod about, my son, there's only one agent for the job. And tha' knows it.'

'She's in the cooler.'

'Then bloody get 'er out.'

Smith turned from the window. 'The psychiatrist said she's dangerous.'

'I should bloody well 'ope so, after all the training we give 'er.'

'He also said she was suffering from battle fatigue.'

'Aye, it's a tiring business is war.'

'And that she needed treatment. Which is one reason the Board of Inquiry recommended a spell in the cooler, where they have a resident psychiatrist.'

'Bugger the Board, son, I want 'er out.'

'Even if she's a psychopathic killer?'

'Especially if she's a psychopathic killer.'

The intercom on his desk buzzed and his secretary announced the arrival of a group captain from Air Ministry with a package to be signed for by the CD himself.

'All right, Jean, send 'im in.' He switched off the intercom. 'That'll be the personal file.'

The door opened and a group captain came in with a heavily sealed package. After the brief formalities had been completed and pleasantries exchanged, he left.

'A group captain as messenger boy,' said Mossop, undoing the package. 'Shows the size of the crisis.'

Smith went back to the armchair, dropped into it. 'I

thought Downing Street said something about bringing him back alive.'

'When Downing Street says summat, my son, you 'ave to read between the lines. And between the lines they were saying: Chop 'im. Bloody chop 'im. And that she'll do. And no messin'.'

'The odds are dead against her. She's known to the Gestapo, remember.'

'Aye, they beat 'er, scarred 'er, Christ knows what. But never broke her.'

'Maybe she's broken now,' said Smith.

'Bollocks, my son, she's as tough as old boots. And fit as a flea, accordin' to Colonel Webb.'

'I'm not talking about her physical condition. Did you read the psychiatrist's report?'

'Aye, bloody marvellous. All that stuff about adrenaline triggers and killing patterns and their similarity to predator feeding patterns. And 'ow some o' them big sharks can get into a frenzy and rip the side out of a boat. Lovely stuff, but what's it got to do with Ryfka?'

'She's unstable and ... well, she's killed quite a lot of people.'

'Aye, mostly Germans.' Mossop stared over his glasses. 'What 'ave you got against sending 'er?'

Smith hesitated, shrugged.

'Don't tell us you fancy the ugly cow,' Mossop said. 'Or 'ave you gone soft?'

'Aye,' said Smith in a passable northern accent. 'Like all bloody southerners.'

Mossop grinned and opened the personal file. 'Seems this Romaine chap's an expert on the movement of airborne troops. That's why 'e was at the planning meetings for Overlord. So 'e'll know all about our troop movements on D-Day.' He was about to shut the file when something caught his eye. 'Recently put in charge of a top-secret air formation for pinpointing German radar stations, measuring wavelengths and gathering other information that may lead to their being destroyed or jammed during the invasion.'

He looked up. "'e really would be God's gift to the Gestapo, wouldn't 'e?'

He snapped the file shut and switched on the intercom. 'Jean, ring our liaison bod at Air Ministry and tell 'im we want an aircraft to fly Colonel Smith to Perth in the next couple of hours. And no arguments. Then ring Perth, give 'em the ETA and tell 'em to 'ave a chopper warmed up and on standby to take 'im to Eagle Mountain. Then get me through to Colonel Webb.'

He switched off. 'There,' he said. 'QED. Which stands for Quite Easily Done. Any questions, my son?'

'What if she says no?'

'Make 'er say yes,' said Mossop. 'And I don't care 'ow tha' bloody does it.'

3

From the window seat in the lounge she had a perfect view
of Eagle Mountain. The crag perched on top looked like
the silhouette of a great black eagle mantling its wings over
the escarpment side of the mountain, which dropped 3,000
feet sheer to the valley. The eagle seemed to be leaning
over, as if about to swoop.

She spent a lot of time looking up at it. Hoping one day
to see a real live eagle sailing up on the thermals with a
lazy grace that seemed the embodiment of freedom. And
freedom was what she dreamed of. She'd been told there
were eagles in the mountains but she'd never seen one,
except in dreams. If she ever did perhaps it would be a sign
of her own freedom. It seemed ironic that she should end
up in a kind of prison camp, like her family. No, not like
her family. They were in a concentration camp. Or what
was left of them.

Eagle Mountain disappeared from her mind's eye and
she saw instead her mother and her younger sister and
brother, waving goodbye to her as the train pulled out of
Epinal. Her brother and sister were smiling, her mother
crying, which surprised her because they'd never got on.

'Always remember you're Jewish.'

'I'm English. I have an English passport and an English
father.'

'But a Jewish mother. And by Jewish law you're a Jew.'

'I don't even look Jewish.'

'So you think you can pass for white?'

'If you're so Jewish how come you married out?'

A painful silence. Then her mother said: 'I was in love.'

That was the last conversation they'd had, apart from
awkward banalities to cover emotion – have you got this,
have you got that – as they drove down rue d'Alsace to the
station. And then the goodbyes and tears on the platform.

Her most vivid memory was the feeling of relief and excitement as the train pulled out and she sat back and smiled at her father, who was taking her to London to stay with his brother's family for two years. To complete her education, as he grandly put it.

Though she was born in London she remembered nothing of it. When she was two she was taken to Alsace-Lorraine, where her parents settled. She grew up bilingual in French and German with a smattering of Polish and a bit of Yiddish. But her English was less than fluent, despite her father's efforts. He was the only one she could practise it with and he was away on business much of the time. She had always had an obsession about England and the English, nourished by ignorance and distance, a combination that often lends enchantment. The reality was something else. The English seemed cold and unresponsive and the food even worse than the climate. But after a time the place and the people, especially the foul-mouthed Cockneys with their pasty faces and bad teeth, who taught her to swear like a bargee, began to grow on her. The food, like the climate, never did. However, when the two years were up she got a job and stayed on. Ten years later she was still there, except for brief returns home for holidays.

Then the war broke out and she felt guilty about being safe in England. Shocks followed swiftly: the fall of France, the death of her father, the deportation of her family. She wished she were a man and could join a fighting regiment. Then she saw an advert for a bilingual secretary at the War Office and applied. At least she'd be doing something for the war effort, even if it was only banging away at a typewriter.

But the advert was deceptive. What the War Office was really looking for was prospective agents. And a few weeks later she was banging away with a Sten gun at one of SOE's special training schools. After three months' intensive training she was parachuted into France one moonlit night.

Well, that was the past. What jerked her back to the present as she stared through the window at the great crag above her was a black dot coming out of the evening sun, gradually growing larger. An eagle. At last. An eagle, soaring over Eagle Mountain.

The flight to Perth in an old unheated, unpressurized, noisy transport plane was cold, bumpy and frightening. Frank Smith hated aeroplanes. Train, with restaurant car attached, was the only way to travel.

When he arrived at Croydon and saw a clapped-out transport plane warming up on the tarmac his heart sank. A young and frail-looking WAAF officer got out and saluted. 'Colonel Smith?'

'We're not going in that thing.'

'The only crate available, sir.'

Smith sighed. 'Where's the pilot?'

'I'm the pilot, sir.'

He did a double take, saw the wings on her uniform.

'The only bod available,' she added apologetically. And saluted again. 'Pilot Officer Spriggs, sir.'

She was all of five foot tall and looked as if she'd have trouble flying a kite never mind a plane as big as a barn.

They climbed aboard and she revved up till the whole airframe vibrated. He winced, waiting for it to fall apart.

'Don't worry, sir,' she shouted. 'I've had over a thousand hours on these old crates.'

'It's not you, it's me,' he shouted back with belated gallantry. 'I'm a bloody coward when it comes to planes. Correction. I'm a bloody coward, period.'

To his surprise they took off like a bird, climbing quickly through low cloud, before levelling out. Then they were sailing over a sunlit sea of cotton wool.

The skies were clear over Scotland and it wasn't long before Pilot Officer Spriggs was in radio contact with Perth and given permission to land.

'Perth airport at one o'clock, sir,' she shouted over the engines.

Frank Smith looked down at a field the size of a matchbox. It contained two tiny huts and a windsock.

'Christ,' he shouted back, 'you can't land there.'

'It gets bigger up close, sir.'

'Jesus,' he said, for variation, 'it better had.'

The landing was so smooth he hardly felt the contact with the ground.

'Good show, Spriggs,' he said, overcome with relief. 'You've a touch like a midwife.'

'I think that's your helicopter over there,' she said, taxiing to a halt.

'I'd sooner walk,' said Frank Smith. Helicopters were the end, the *anus mundi*.

She decided to give dinner a miss. The food was excellent – no wartime shortages here – but she wasn't hungry and could always have a snack later. She made herself comfortable on the window seat and ordered a glass of Fleurie from the morose barman, who gave an affirmatory grunt without looking up from the racing page of his paper. She liked it that he never got matey.

He brought her the Fleurie and she sipped it, then leaned back, staring at Eagle Mountain and wondering about the eagle that had turned out to be a lousy helicopter. She knew there was a helicopter pad near the main gates but had never seen it in use during the two months she'd been there. Supplies came in by road once a week. There were no telephones, except in the colonel's office, no leave and no mail. No contact with the outside world at all, other than newspapers and the radio, which was permanently tuned to light music or *Forces' Favourites*.

Lieutenant Colonel Webb was in charge of the Special Training School at Eagle Mountain. But what they were being trained for remained a mystery. Meanwhile they took so-called refresher courses in close-quarter combat and weapons drill, were lectured on explosives, radio-telegraphy, map reading, Gestapo interrogation techniques and so on. Everything, in fact, that they'd done in the SOE training schools, apart from cross-country running. No cross-country running. They were confined to ten acres or so of parkland that might have been landscaped out of the wild valley by Capability Brown. Except for the chainlink perimeter fence, twelve feet high and topped by rolls of

29

barbed wire. 'To keep nosey locals out,' as Colonel Webb smoothly put it. 'After all, this is a prohibited area under War House regulations.'

The Victorian mansion that was their living quarters was like a luxury hotel. As well as the lounge and bar, there was a dining room, breakfast room, reading room, card room and library, plus a conservatory running half the length of the south front. The study had been turned into an office for Colonel Webb. When the Inter-Services Research Bureau requisitioned the place in 1941 squash and badminton courts and a gymnasium were added.

In fact, it had just about everything you could wish for. Except freedom. She took another sip of the Fleurie, but it seemed to have lost its fruit.

Then Frank Smith walked in. Well, that explained the helicopter. She tried not to look surprised.

'Hallo,' he said. 'Long time no see.' And sank into an overstuffed armchair. He had a tan leather briefcase, shiny with age and elbow grease, which he put carefully on his knees. Then he signalled the barman and asked for a malt whisky.

She waited till he'd been served and the barman was back behind his newspaper. 'What am I here for, Frank?'

'You know very well,' he said easily. 'A rest and a refresher course.'

'In prison?'

'And now we think it's time you were back on active service.' He raised his glass. 'Cheers.'

'And you've flown all the way from London to tell me. Isn't that kind?'

'Anywhere here we can talk in private?'

'My room.'

'Is that allowed?'

'Anything's allowed. Drinking, gambling, fornicating, anything. Except breaking out.'

He finished his whisky in silence. 'Perhaps we could take a drink up to your room.'

'We can take a whole bloody bottle up.'

It was a big room with a double bed and a bay window

30

that gave on to a balcony. Most of the bay was taken up by a round table and a couple of easy chairs.

Frank Smith put his briefcase and whisky bottle on the table, then poured himself a drink. He offered her one, but she declined and took a piece of knitting out of a drawer. He couldn't have been more surprised if she'd taken a gun out of the drawer.

She sat in one of the easy chairs and started to knit with steel needles that flashed in the dying sun.

'Slip one, knit one, plain one, purl. What the hell's purl?'

'A plain stitch done backwards.'

He sipped his whisky. The needles clicked rhythmically, peacefully. 'You still carry that little forty-five tucked down the front of your pants?'

The needles stopped. 'What do you want with me, Frank?'

'We lost an airman the other day. Friday, in fact. In a raid over Le Mans. We understand he parachuted to safety, somewhere between there and Vitré.' He paused. 'We want him back.'

'Get him into an escape line. The one to Quimper.'

'We think it's been penetrated.'

She shrugged, went back to her knitting.

Frank Smith sipped his whisky. 'It's your territory. Nobody knows it like you. Nobody.'

'Louis knows it.'

'He's . . . disappeared.' Another sip of whisky. 'This airman's rather special. With rather special info.'

'About what?'

Frank Smith gestured vaguely. 'Military matters.'

'You mean our future plans, that sort of thing?'

'I'm afraid I can't be more precise.'

'I did sign the Official Secrets Act, you know.'

'That's not enough to give you clearance for this stuff. The point is, if he's picked up by the Gestapo – '

'Why should they think he's got special information?'

Frank Smith took a deep breath. 'Because he's a bloody air commodore.'

She stopped knitting. 'Maybe the Gestapo have already got him.'

'In that case he must . . .' He swigged some whisky and shuddered as it bit him. 'Be eliminated.'

'Why don't you say killed?'

'I was using the word Downing Street used. They said – and I quote – he must be recovered or eliminated.'

'Downing Street? That must be some information he's toting around.'

She got up and went out on to the balcony for some fresh air. The sun had almost gone, but she could still see Eagle Mountain, bare and majestic. It would be there when they were all dead and gone, which comforted her. She went back inside.

'So you're looking for a psychopathic killer.'

'I *beg* your pardon?' Frank Smith said, trying not to sound surprised.

'That's how your high-powered shrink described me.'

'He didn't say anything of the kind.'

'Oh, he wrapped it up in a lot of bullshit about feeding patterns and killing patterns and adrenaline triggers or whatever. But that's what he meant.'

Frank Smith picked up the whisky, put it down again. 'How the hell do you know what was in a confidential report?'

'Confidential? Stuck in a filing cabinet with a spring lock? You people taught me to blow *safes*.' The scar twitched her face into a crooked smile. 'I probably read it before you did.'

He opened his briefcase, took out two unmarked buff folders containing the personal files of Ryfka and Harry Romaine. He glanced through the instructors' reports in Ryfka's file. He felt his memory needed refreshing after what he'd just heard. It was nearly three years since he'd read them. He remembered they were good. He'd forgotten how good. Phrases caught the eye . . . For unarmed combat: 'Swift, brutal, intelligent.' For initiative: 'Imaginative, resourceful.' Weapons training, including shooting at moving targets: 'Fast and accurate, even under pressure.'

Under mock interrogation: 'Cool, hard to shake.' And when it came to explosives: 'Blew the front off a safe quicker than anyone.' Go on, Frank Smith thought, surprise me. Bloody surprise me. Her conducting officer summed it up: 'One of the most resourceful agents we've had.'

Perhaps that old sod Mossop was right after all . . .

Then he came to the psychiatrist's report, but he didn't need to read that again. And didn't want to. As if *they* knew what made people tick. There were stranger things in the heart of man than were dreamt of in their little philosophies.

He closed the file. 'Will you take the job on?'

'Recover or eliminate? What do they really want?'

Frank Smith hesitated, searching for exact phrasing to define the deliberately inexact. 'They want him recovered. If it's not too difficult.'

'If it wasn't too difficult you wouldn't need me.'

'Then kill him.'

She got up and stared out of the bay window, as if transfixed. 'I think I saw an eagle,' she said, 'soaring over the mountain. Up and up, into the wide blue yonder. Then he just tipped a wing and slid down the sky.'

She turned away from the window. 'Marvellous. It's the first one I've seen.'

'Did you hear what I said?'

The scar on her face started to twitch.

'I get shot in an ambush, brought back to England, interrogated like a traitor and finally shoved into a high-class prison camp. Then you get in a jam. And want to send me on a suicide mission to get you out of it.'

'I'm not in a jam,' Frank Smith said quietly. 'It's our country that's in a jam.'

'Are you trying to appeal to my better nature?'

'We thought you might want to get out of this place.'

'And end up hanging by the thumbs in some Gestapo cellar? Or dead in a ditch? Whose brilliant idea was this?'

'The CD's.'

'Then you go back to the CD and tell him to get stuffed. With full military honours.'

Frank Smith sighed. 'All SOE missions are voluntary, of course. And I respect your decision.'

'Like fuck you do.'

Her anger revived his original doubts about her temperamental fitness for the job. In a way he was relieved.

'What will you do?' she said.

'Send in some other poor sod, I suppose.' He picked up the two buff folders, slipped them in his briefcase. As he did so a photograph fell out.

She picked it up and wondered if a face from the past was mocking her. But it was just a faded picture of a young RAF pilot leaning against a biplane, grinning his head off. With faded words in faded blue ink at the bottom. *All my love, Harry.* She wondered if the love had faded too.

'Harry,' she said. 'Is he the one?'

Frank Smith nodded. 'We're trying to get hold of a more recent picture.'

'I knew a Harry once,' she said, and the scar twitched again.

Mossop sent his secretary home at six, but stayed in the office, waiting for Smith's call from Eagle Mountain. The longer he waited the more gloomy he got. If it was taking that long to persuade her, Smith was in trouble.

Time dragged and the light faded till the office turned as gloomy as his thoughts. In the end he couldn't stand it any longer and took a cab to his club in Pall Mall, leaving the number with the SOE switchboard.

But the club was even gloomier. The only other occupants of the enormous lounge, with its fluted pillars and Adam fireplace, were three octogenarians asleep in their armchairs and making a variety of noises.

'It's like a geriatric ward,' he said to the club servant who brought him a large whisky sour. 'Sounds like one too. I think Sir George needs a bedpan, if it's not too late.'

He was on his fourth whisky before the call came through and he was directed, swaying like a mandarin, to the appropriate booth. After reminding Smith that they were on an open line, he said: 'I suppose she said no.'

'You must be psychic,' Smith said.

'Didn't you put pressure on her?'

'You think I'd succeed where the Gestapo failed?'

Mossop usually left his northern accent behind when he went to the club. Now it came back strongly. 'Art tha' tellin' me tha' didn't even bloody try?'

There was a soft laugh at the other end. 'No is rarely a woman's last word, but you have to pick your time. Anyway, I was hungry and went into the dining room, which was deserted by then. Halfway through the meal I looked up and there she was, standing by the table. She asked if she could join me. I said of course and she sat down and ordered a coffee. Then put her head in her hands and stared at the tablecloth while the coffee got cold. Well, it was her move. I just chatted on about bugger-all. Then, suddenly, she said: "I'll do it." I was so taken aback I said: "What?" And she said: "The job. I'll do it." '

'Any idea what made 'er change 'er mind?'

'Who knows what makes them change their minds? Listen, I'm flying her back to London tonight. I want to put her up in our best flat, the one at Orchard Court. Can you fix it?'

'Aye, always give 'em soft lights and sweet music before dropping 'em int' shit. Ah'm a great believer in that.'

The ruins weren't smoking and should have been, the sun was shining and shouldn't have been. It was all wrong. She stared numbly at the rubble of smashed brickwork and burnt black timbers, still damp from the fire hoses and giving off that scorched smell you can't mistake and never forget. Half the street, a tall frowning terrace of Victorian houses on the edge of Peckham Rye, had been flattened and burnt by a mixture of HEs and incendiaries. The house that had been a second home to her had gone. And her uncle and aunt and her three cousins with it. She stood there dry-eyed, staring at a heap of rubble with bits of broken furniture and torn underwear sticking out of it.

She turned away, her feelings too deep for tears. Then she went to a neighbour's house to phone Aunt Lottie, her only remaining relative apart from those in concentration camps. Lottie lived in the Cotswolds, near the little market town of Tetbury, and was easily upset. She didn't tell her what had happened, just asked if she could come down for a few days.

The night train from Paddington was full of troops with bulky packs and webbing equipment, and the air already acrid with cigarette smoke and male sweat. Ignoring the usual remarks, she made her way along the crowded corridor checking the compartments, but there wasn't a seat to be had. When she reached the last compartment she wondered whether to try the next carriage or give up and stay in the corridor with the licentious soldiery.

Then a man got up and offered her his seat. She thanked him and sat down. He was tall, in mufti, but of military bearing. His face was little more than a hazy outline in the half-dark compartment with its regulation blue masked light. At least he wouldn't be able to see much of hers. Anyway she was wearing her hair long to cover the scar.

After a time a Royal Marine sitting next to her got out and the man sat down beside her. She offered him a cigarette and he thanked her and took one. She took one herself and he leaned across to light it. In the flare of the match he wasn't bad-looking. Or perhaps it was the way the shadows fell. Then he leaned back and was lost in the shadows again. And attractive, she thought, and yawned. On her other side a fat sweating corporal of the Pay Corps spread his thighs and crowded her. She moved closer to the stranger. In the end, lulled by the rocking train, she rested her head on his shoulder and dozed off.

A metallic screech woke her as the train pulled up with a jerk and pitched her out of the seat. The stranger saved her from falling. From somewhere came the banshee wail of an air-raid siren.

There was a lot of noise and shouting and everyone was trying to get out. She got out into pitch darkness, then realized the train had stopped in a tunnel. The stranger was beside her. He took her hand and pulled her along. They came out of the tunnel into moonlight and she heard the ear-splitting whistle of falling bombs. She flinched and put her hands over her ears. She'd never been in an air raid before. She'd faced death on the ground before, but that was different. Especially if you had a weapon in your hand. Against death from the skies you were helpless. And it was so completely random, like drunken gods tossing bombs over the balcony of heaven . . . They kill us for their sport.

'They're after the railway,' the stranger shouted. 'It shows up like a river by moonlight.'

He took her hand again and they ran across a field white with frost to an open barn and threw themselves on the straw-covered earthen floor. The bombs shrieked down and the earth shook as if in convulsions. *Nor any voice to mourn them save the choirs, The shrill demented choirs of wailing shells* . . .

Through the wide doorway she saw the tunnel explode with a flash that lit the whole sky. The shrill demented choirs grew louder, the crump of bombs shook her to the bones. Then came a shower of fire bombs, raining fire from the sky. A shed next to the barn burst into flames and made her scream. She looked at the bales of straw around her and in her mind's eye saw them turn into snakes of fire. She got up and ran out into the white field to get away from the snakes.

'Come back!' the stranger shouted. 'You're crossing their bombing run!'

She heard his footsteps behind her, but ran blindly on, till the earth suddenly rose up and flung her backwards into darkness. When she came to she was being carried over his shoulder like a sack. Then she was back in the barn, lying on a heap of straw, half naked – the blast had ripped part of her clothing off – and he was leaning over her. From above came the sinister throb of a plane. He looked up.

'Heinkel one eleven,' he said.

Then the fire bombs started again, raining more fire from heaven. She tried to get up, but he pulled her down into the straw, held her fast.

'Let me go!'

37

'You'll get killed out there.'

His body was over her, protecting her. Suddenly she stopped struggling and clung to him.

Then the whole sky was throbbing with the Heinkels and a storm of HEs and fire bombs seemed to be bursting overhead.

'Oh, shit,' she half-sobbed.

He held her tight and she put her arms round him, burying her face in his neck, clinging to him as if his body were both a shield and a hiding place. She felt safe and warm under him and became calm enough to be aware of the straw tickling her naked back. Fire bombs rained down and Very lights lit the scene briefly and eerily before dying. Intermittently the crump of HEs shook the whole world. But she felt safe. A marvellous feeling. She relaxed her grip on him and snuggled back into the straw.

Then an almighty crump lifted the very earth she was lying on and she clung to him again, suddenly afraid.

'It's all right,' he said. 'It's all right.'

And she relaxed and sank back and stared at the stars framed by ragged holes in the roof. Then she became aware of the silence. The raid was over and she was lying half naked under a stranger. He rolled off her, got up and took his overcoat off, then settled down beside her in the straw, slipping an arm round her and using the coat as a blanket to cover them. She snuggled up and rested her head on his chest, feeling warm and indolent, and not inclined to move. It would be nice to lie there all night and wake up with his arm around her. But then, with daylight, would come disillusion. He'd see her ugliness and her scars. She wished she could disappear with the dawn, like a dream you try to remember. She sighed. She was being childish.

He was sleeping, breathing easily. Her head was still on his chest, and after a time its gentle rise and fall had a lulling effect and her fears began to subside. She became drowsy.

It was light when she woke up but it wasn't the light that woke her. It was his fingertips tracing the scars on her back, delicately as a fly walking. She flinched.

38

'What happened?' he said.

'I got drunk and fell on some barbed wire,' she said.

'Funny sort of marks to be made by barbed wire,' he said.

'You reckon.'

Till then she hadn't realized it was light – and that he was staring at her. She tried to turn away, but he put a hand under her chin and turned her head till she was facing him again.

'You're not beautiful,' he said.

'You don't say.'

'But you have beautiful eyes . . .'

'Yeah,' she said. 'Like pools of Guinness, some drunk told me.' She pulled away from him and tried to get up, but discovered her ankle was swollen and too painful to stand on.

'I must have turned it when the blast knocked me over.'

'I'll get an ambulance,' he said.

He got up and tried to brush himself down with his hands as best he could. What had once been a well-cut lounge suit in grey herringbone now looked like something a tramp might have rejected. It was torn, rumpled and caked with dirt. By daylight, she saw that he was even better looking. Her heart sank for some reason.

Outside the winter sun was trying to break up the early mist. She shivered, wondering if she'd ever see him again. He covered her with his overcoat.

'I don't even know your bloody name,' she said.

'Harry,' he said. 'And yours?'

She hesitated, then gave her field name. 'Ryfka.'

'Strange name,' he said. 'Strange girl. What sign were you born under?'

'You don't believe in that stuff, do you?'

'I just wondered.'

'I don't know my sign.'

'When were you born?'

She gave him a crooked smile. 'Some moment when the moon was blood.'

39

He nodded. 'And figs grew upon thorn.' He stooped and gave her a kiss. 'I'll be back.'

But he never came back. She knew he wouldn't.

Only the ambulance came, bumping over the icy field. The two men who got out found her swearing and trying to stand on her swollen ankle. They assumed it was the pain that was making her swear.

Dog minus 13

They landed at Croydon after midnight, but she got no
feeling of freedom till they were in the West End. The
helicopter to Perth and the plane to Croydon were like
prison vans with wings. And the drive into London through
bleak and blacked-out streets, empty apart from the
occasional newspaper van, wasn't much better. She still felt
like a prisoner in transit. But the West End was different.
Cruising cabs and midnight whores, soldiers and sailors on
the town. GIs everywhere. Piccadilly was alive, even in the
blackout. She wound down the window and heard a girl
laugh and a drunk singing 'Roll me over, lay me down and
do it again'. She laughed too.

As the car turned into Park Lane she said: 'Would you
mind stopping?' She'd hardly spoken since leaving Eagle
Mountain and Frank Smith wondered if she was feeling ill.

'Are you all right?'

'I want to walk.'

'But we're nearly there.'

'I want some fresh air.'

He told the driver to stop and she got out and went into
Hyde Park. He followed and they walked up Lovers' Walk
in the moonlight. She took a deep breath and felt free at
last.

'Did you know they call this Lovers' Walk?' she said.

'You sure you're all right?'

At Marble Arch she said: 'Tyburn Tree was around here.
I wonder if Raab will ever dance on air at the end of a
rope.'

At Portman Square she said: 'I thought we must be
heading for Orchard Court. Do I get the flat with the black-
tiled bathroom? Or is that for Men Only?'

They went up in a gilded lift, along a deep-carpeted corridor and into a flat that had everything, even a couple of bottles of Chablis, ready chilled, and a plate of smoked salmon sandwiches on the glass-topped coffee table in the lounge. And, of course, a black-tiled bathroom.

'I bet a few blondes have been lovingly bathed in there,' she said.

'How did you know about it? From another agent?'

'From the Gestapo. Who no doubt got it from some poor bastard they broke. "We know all about Orchard Court and the black marble bathroom," they said. "And about Major Smith. So we'll know if you're lying." '

'And what did you say? That I'd since been promoted?'

'That if they knew so much, why ask me.' She sipped the Chablis, bit into a smoked salmon sandwich. 'Bit of all right, this. Never think there was a war on, would you? Who fixed it?'

'The CD.'

'It's beginning to feel like the Last Supper.'

They ate and drank in silence. Then she said: 'How long have I got for the job?'

'How long will it take to find him?'

'If he's still in my territory . . .' She shrugged. 'Couple of days.'

'That would be marvellous.'

'Frank, if there's a deadline, I must know it.'

He drank some Chablis. 'Deadline. That's rather good, isn't it, in the circs?' He dabbed his mouth with a clean handkerchief pulled from his cuff. 'A fortnight today we're mounting a combined operation with the Yanks. If the Germans get wind of it, find out exactly where and when the attack's coming – if they get even forty-eight hours' notice, it could cost us . . .' He spread his hands. 'Fifty thousand men. Maybe more. And put several years on the war.' He paused. 'Our missing airman has this information. In some detail.'

So that was it. The Second Front. Had to be. The papers had been shouting about it for months. 'Tell us about him.'

'Air Commodore Harold Romaine. Forty-five. Flying ace

42

in the last show. Won the DFC at nineteen, dicing with Richthofen's circus and all that. Quite a chap.'

'And now you want him knocked off.'

'Latterly commander of a bomber base in the Lincolnshire Wolds. And of a secret air formation whose job is to overfly German radar defences in northern France and measure wavelengths and so on.'

'Then perhaps he was just doing his job when he was shot down.'

'Bigot is a codename for people with certain top secret information. And all Bigots are strictly forbidden to undertake any operation where there's a risk of capture. Air Commodore Romaine was a Bigot.'

'Then why did he do it?'

Frank Smith sighed impatiently. 'Who knows? According to Bomber Command, senior officers sometimes get bored flying a desk and wangle themselves on a raid. As "additional aircrew", so called. Heavily frowned on by the top brass, of course. Anyway, his motives don't matter now.'

She took another sip of the Chablis, rolled it round her mouth, then let its clean fresh fruit slide over her palate and die away like the end of a slow movement.

'Any luck with a recent photo?' she said at length.

'Trouble is he doesn't have a proper home. His place in the country was requisitioned for evacuees when the blitz started. All he's got now is a sort of pied-à-terre in Kensington. I sent a man round there to look it over.'

'You mean break in.'

'No pictures of him, plenty of her.'

'Her?'

'His wife, I suppose.'

'He has a wife then.'

'Well, presumably. I mean, he has a son. Also in the Air Force.'

He opened his briefcase, took out the old photograph, dropped it on the glass-topped table. 'You can give it back to me tomorrow.'

She couldn't see it properly because it was the wrong

way round, and she resisted the temptation to twist her neck or pick it up.

'Have you got me a decent wireless op?'

'A first-class chap.'

'Sooner have a second-class girl.'

'What's wrong with a chap?'

'They resent working for a woman, especially if she's young. Beg your pardon, youngish. How old is he?'

'Mid-thirties, I think.'

'Then he'll resent me even more.'

'Oh, balls.'

'Yes,' she said, 'that's probably the trouble. Let's hope they don't get trodden on.'

They went on drinking and talking about operational details, then Frank Smith said: 'It's nearly two o'clock. You'd better get some sleep. I'll pick you up around midday and we'll see how the document people and the tailors are getting on. The poor bastards'll be working all night. Hope your measurements haven't changed. You look thinner.'

'I had to have this uniform taken in when I came out of hospital.'

'That's going to cause problems.'

'If you give it to them they can get the measurements from it. Half a mo'.'

She disappeared into the bedroom and came out a couple of minutes later in a dressing gown and handed him her uniform jacket and skirt.

'I'll take it straight round to them,' he said.

She hardly listened, just waited for him to go. Then she picked up the photograph and studied the smiling young face. The face of Harry twenty years ago? Might be. And might not. By the time she'd finished the Chablis the face was blurred and life itself was blurred, pleasantly for once.

'Hooray fuck,' she said, an expression she'd picked up from a bomber pilot called Willie at a *thé dansant* at the Grosvenor House. It was in the middle of the afternoon and he was drunk as a monkey. She had to support him as they swayed round the dance floor. From time to time he said solemnly: 'Hooray fuck.' And she said: 'Okay, what does it mean?' And he looked at her, eyes not quite focusing, and said: 'It means . . . You really wanna know what it means? I'll tell you what it means. It means . . . What it *really* means is . . . Hooray fuck. Unnerstand?'

'Perfectly,' she said.

They made a date to meet again a week later. But he never showed up. One of his friends showed up and said Willie couldn't make it. He'd gone for a burton over Germany. And she said: 'Hooray fuck.' And the friend said: 'You're okay. What are you drinking?'

She woke up to sunshine and the sound of hammering. The sunshine was coming in the bedroom window, the hammering came from the front door. At first she thought it was in her head. She wrapped herself in a sheet, stumbled to the door and opened it to Frank Smith.

'Midday, you said. It's not half-past eleven.'

'Ladies never take less than an hour to get ready.'

'Why didn't you let yourself in? You've got a key.'

'Politeness, my dear. And discretion.'

'Shove your discretion,' she said and went into the bathroom.

Their first visit was to a tall Victorian house in Kilburn, where Sophie and Angelique, who always made her French clothes, had sat up all night with two other seamstresses cutting and sewing together another set for her. A difficult task anyway, made more difficult because the clothes had to look worn. When they saw her they were shocked at her thinness.

'Thank heavens for the uniform,' said Angelique. 'We had to take in everything we'd run up.'

'You have disappeared to nothing,' said Sophie.

'Pauvre agneau,' said Angelique.

The fitting there was a success. All that remained was the finishing.

'We'll be back around three,' said Frank Smith.

The next call was at a Camden Town basement, where the forgers worked. They had the documents ready. All they needed was a signature for the *carte d'identité* and a

45

couple of index fingerprints in purple ink around the date stamp.

'Camille Brossart?' she said. 'Who's she? Sounds like a murderess out of Zola.'

'A bookseller's representative,' said Frank Smith, 'looking for rare editions.'

Under *Signature du Titulaire* she wrote in a bold sloping hand, *Camille Brossart*. Under *Empreinte digitale* she pressed the two index fingers, making sure their tips pointed towards the date of issue.

She stared at the flat front-lit photo on the *carte d'identité*. 'I even *look* like a murderess.'

'Let's go and have a smashing lunch at Fortnum's,' said Frank Smith cheerfully. 'Maybe saddle of lamb and a bottle of Volnay, if we're lucky.'

'I feel a bit like a lamb myself,' she said. 'The kind that goes to the slaughter.'

The lunch was excellent and the Volnay smooth as silk, though she only allowed herself one glass. She was always too nervous to drink before a mission, especially if it meant a night drop.

Over coffee she said: 'What about the messages I gave you? Will the BBC be putting them out?'

He nodded. 'After the nine o'clock news. If anybody's listening.'

'The Dugards will be, if they're still around.'

'And if they're not?'

'We'll end up sleeping under a hedge.'

'Or with the Gestapo. How do you know the Dugards weren't pulled in with the others – and turned?'

'They were an isolated cell. Their only contacts were with Gerard and me. And Gerard's dead.'

'I'd still prefer to drop you blind. That way nobody'll be waiting for you.'

She leaned back and gave him a lop-sided grin. 'If the Gestapo are waiting with the Dugards they'll be in the wrong field. And on the wrong side of the river.'

Frank Smith, who was finishing the last of the Volnay, put his glass down and grinned back. 'That's more like it.'

46

It was after three when they took a cab back to the Kilburn workshop, where she tried on her French clothes. They fitted perfectly. The clothes were packed into a battered French suitcase and at four an SOE car and driver picked them up for the fifty-mile drive to the market town of Sandy, near Bedford. And even nearer SOE's secret airfield at Tempsford.

As they settled themselves in the back of the car Frank Smith offered her a brown paper parcel. 'Your uniform.'

'You shouldn't have bothered,' she said. 'I'll be in France in a few hours.'

'You might like to wear it for those few hours,' he said with a sideways glance. 'You've been breveted lieutenant colonel.'

She was staring out of the window and didn't even turn her head, just gave him the two-finger sign.

'Well,' he said, dumping the parcel in her lap. 'I'm glad you're not letting it go to your head.'

'Another of the CD's brilliant ideas? To give the poor cow a bit of a lift if her morale flags at the last moment?'

The car dropped them at an eighteenth-century manor house set in open woodland a mile or two out of Sandy, and well hidden from the road. It was used as a staging post by SOE agents, commandos and other special forces leaving for occupied Europe.

She'd stayed there several times before and liked the place and the relaxed atmosphere that was really the calm before the storm. Her favourite feature was the magnificent staircase, which swept up from the main hall in the grand manner of a Hollywood set. All it needed was Bette Davis to come slowly down, eyes enormous in a dead-white face, one delicate hand holding the banister rail, the other holding a gun.

'Well,' said Frank Smith, 'the bar's open if you fancy a snifter.'

'I think I'll go up to my room,' she said. 'Join you later.'

It was a pleasant, high-ceilinged room with a double bed. Nothing fancy, but the familiar was always preferable. She unpacked the French clothes she was going to travel in and laid them out on one side of the bed, then checked her French identity card, ration book and clothing coupons, noting that some of the coupons had been carefully cut out. She also unpacked her guns and put them in a drawer. She'd check them later.

Then she undid the parcel, took out the uniform jacket and held it up. Though she was expecting it her pulse quickened at the sight of the new insignia on the shoulders. A crown above a single pip, the insignia of a lieutenant colonel. A full colonel would have a crown above two pips, a brigadier a crown above three pips. Which reminded her: a brigadier was the equivalent of an air commodore.

She put the jacket down, opened her shoulder bag and took out the photo of Harry Romaine. The young face smiled up at her. Sometimes it seemed familiar, sometimes strange. Now it seemed strange. She put the photo away, in the drawer with the guns, and picked up the uniform jacket and skirt, intending to hang them in the wardrobe. Then she caught sight of herself in a wall mirror and wondered what she'd look like with a crown above a pip on each shoulder.

There was a crowd of hard-looking commandos in the bar and a dozen or so men and women in the shabby clothes of various occupied countries. A faint smell of Gauloise, garlic and aniseed hung in the air, overlaying the moderato rumble of English, the lilt of French and the impossible sounds of Serbo-Croat.

Frank Smith was leaning on the bar with a handsome young captain of the Fourth Commando. When he saw her standing in the doorway he waved her over and introduced her. The captain glanced at the insignia on her epaulettes, came smartly to attention and saluted.

It made her feel uncomfortable, as if she'd caught herself showing off. She shouldn't have worn the dam' uniform.

'Can I get you a drink, ma'am?' he said.

She asked for a mineral water and then kept out of the conversation, despite the captain's efforts to draw her into it. After a few minutes she asked to be excused.

'Don't go,' said the captain. 'You look marvellous.'

48

She felt herself reddening and said she had equipment to check, which was true. She wanted to strip and clean her two guns, though it was hardly a matter of urgency.

Frank Smith watched her go and said: 'You embarrassed her. She can't deal with compliments. Only insults.'

'But I meant it,' said the captain. 'She looked terrific. Like a Barbary pirate with that scar. Only the black eye-patch was missing.'

She changed into the French clothes and hung the uniform in the wardrobe. Then she opened the drawer where she'd put the guns, but the first thing that caught her eye was the photo of Harry Romaine. She picked it up and studied it as she crossed slowly to the bed and lay down.

The smooth young face still smiled up at her, but remained an enigma. Of course it was beginning to look familiar. But the enigma wouldn't be resolved till she met him in person. Perhaps not even then. Not that it mattered. She'd have to kill him anyway.

In the end she got tired of staring at the picture and fell asleep.

It was getting on for nine when she joined Frank Smith in the half empty dining room, and gave him back the photo, which he put in his briefcase. She felt refreshed after her nap, but not hungry. She always lost her appetite before a mission.

'You must have something,' he said. He was at the coffee and brandy stage, which was mostly brandy.

'I'll help you out with the coffee.'

'It tastes bloody awful,' he said, pouring her a cup. 'You know, you shouldn't be using a Jewish field name the Gestapo already know.'

'You think they'd torture me any the less if I had a decent Aryan name?'

'I think we should change it.'

'You do?'

'I mean, what is it? A symbol? An act of defiance or something?'

'It's Hebrew for Rebecca.'

'Don't play silly buggers. If Louis *has* been turned I hate to think what he might have told Raab about you.'

'Not quite as much as Raab could've told *him*.' The scar twitched her mouth into a crooked smile. 'He had me strung up naked, remember.'

Frank Smith took a swig of the brandy. 'I don't know whether you've heard any of those stories coming out of Germany and Poland.' He took another swig. 'They're pretty horrible.'

'Atrocity stories always are. That's the idea.'

'Don't you believe them? After what the Gestapo did to you?'

'It's hard to believe that scum are representative.'

'But they're the ones you're up against. And using a Jewish field name . . .' He shook his head, then took a slip of paper from his pocket. 'Here's a list of alternative names. Any one you like.'

'The only one I like is Ryfka.' The scar twitched again. 'It happens to be my mother's name.'

He finished his brandy and let out a long breath. 'Oh, shit . . . All right. But listen. For communication purposes at least, you're Linnet and I'm Woodpecker. Okay?'

'Message received and understood,' she said, and got up to go. 'Any sign of my wireless op?'

'He'll be along.'

'Send him up to my room, would you?' she said, turning away.

'Hold it,' he said. 'Have you a plan of action?'

She shrugged. 'Find him, kill him, get the hell out.'

He reached for the brandy bottle, changed his mind and poured a coffee. 'Tell me,' he said, 'what's Raab like?'

'Dead ordinary,' she said. 'And no imagination. That's the hallmark of the torturer . . . When he put me in a bath and kept holding my head under water till I nearly drowned, a dozen clerks and typists crowded into the room to watch. They were ordinary people too.'

He thought about this but wasn't sure he agreed with the implications. He turned to ask another question, but she'd

50

gone. He went back to the coffee. It still tasted bloody awful.

Then a voice said: 'Evening, Colonel Smith.'

He looked up to see a stockily built man with blunt features and Brylcreemed hair. He was wearing shabby French clothes, but spoke English with a London accent.

'Michel,' he said, automatically using his field name, 'you've just missed your organizer. Sit down and have a brandy.'

'Make it a beer,' said Michel. 'Got me a decent set?'

'A brand new B Two,' said Frank Smith, and ordered a beer from a passing waiter.

'Sooner have a Mark Four.'

'None available. Production's slow. Anyway, what's wrong with a B Two?'

'It's a bloody sight heavier to lug around – and the Gestapo can recognize the case. What about a transmission sked?'

'There isn't one. Just follow normal procedure, transmitting by day, receiving by night. But if that becomes difficult transmit when you can. We'll have a couple of frequencies on twenty-four hour standby for you.' He took out a washleather bag, put it on the table. 'And here are the crystals to go with them.' Then he took out a bulky manila envelope and laid it next to the little bag. 'A one-time pad, various code letters, your bluff check and true check and so on. Take it up to your room and look through it. Any queries, let's know.'

The waiter brought the beer.

'What kind of mission am I going on?'

Frank Smith smiled. 'Your organizer will tell you what you need to know.'

Michel raised the glass of beer to his lips. 'Who is it?'

'Field name Ryfka.'

'A Polak?'

'A woman.'

'A woman?' He put the beer down untasted. 'I was told this mission was going to be a tough one.'

'Could be.'

51

'Well,' said Michel, raising his glass again, 'let's hope she's up to it.'

'Yes,' said Frank Smith. 'I'll drink to that.'

She was sitting on the bed reassembling her Walther P38, which she'd field-stripped and cleaned. Not an ideal gun for the battlefield because no semi-automatic was as reliable as a revolver, but fine for undercover work. Anyway, she was used to it. Its double action meant it could be carried with one up the spout. All you had to do was release the safety catch and pull the trigger. No stopping to pull back the slide. The long trigger pull didn't make for pinpoint accuracy, but that wasn't so important up close. As her weapons instructor used to say: 'The main thing is to hit the bastard and put him out of action.'

The other gun she always carried in the field was a small American special, crudely made from cheap stampings, tubing and screw machine parts. It was a single-shot pistol, so you only got one chance. And the barrel wasn't even rifled, but it fired a forty-five slug and was deadly from a few feet. It fitted into a neat wash-leather holster she'd stitched inside the waistband of various slacks and skirts. The Americans had issued the gun to resistance forces through their Office of Strategic Services and though it looked like a toy, it was said to have killed more men than all the service issue forty-fives put together. Only having one chance concentrated the aim wonderfully. To say nothing of the mind.

There was a knock on the door. She got off the bed, put the P38 away and said: 'Come in.'

A man came in carrying the type of suitcase that held the SOE wireless set.

'Ah,' she said, smiling, 'you must be Michel. I'm Ryfka.' She put out her hand. He shook it, perfunctorily. She indicated a chair. 'Do sit down.'

He sat on the edge of the chair, very upright, and stared at a point just above her head. She got out her knitting. That made him shift the focus of his vision.

'Are you with a circuit?' she said.

'I was two years with Pugilist.'

'In the south somewhere, isn't it? Run by Jules?'

He nodded. She knitted busily.

'And now?'

'I'm an instructor on the wireless course.'

'Very impressive. I'm lucky to have got you.' She smiled. He didn't smile back.

'Did Frank Smith brief you?'

'Only about codes and frequencies.'

She decided to follow security rules and tell him only what he needed to know. 'We're going to bring out an airman who was shot down near Le Mans last week.'

He nodded again and there was a brief silence. Then he said: 'What time's take-off?'

'After midnight. The pilot's waiting for a winds forecast from the met people.'

He nodded. 'I've been given a set, a one-time pad and some other bumf, but no written orders.'

'There aren't any. All you have to do is send London a code letter indicating our safe arrival. And any other messages I give you over the next few days. Then, with any luck, we'll be brought out by Hudson or Lysander. Did Frank Smith tell you there'll be a frequency open for us twenty-four hours a day?'

He nodded like a golliwog on springs, then cleared his throat and said: 'Am I allowed to know where we're going?'

'To a farm north of Laval, not far from the River Mayenne. An easy landmark for a pilot to spot by night. And plenty of big fields to land in. If you've got a half-million map handy I'll pinpoint it for you.'

He produced a map and she showed him. Another of those nods and he folded up the map and put it away.

'Tell me,' she said, 'do you like women?'

'Oh, yes,' he said.

'But not to take orders from.'

'I've never had to take orders from one before,' he said, deadpan.

'Then you'd better get used to it, hadn't you?' she said pleasantly. 'And fucking quick.'

*

53

Just before midnight Frank Smith drove them to Tempsford's carefully camouflaged airfield. It wasn't much of a place, she thought. Hastily built in wartime, like so many other RAF stations. Apart from station headquarters, the officers' mess and squadron offices, all the rest were temporary huts. Well, not quite all the rest. There was one permanent building, tucked away near the edge of the airfield, the farmhouse of the old Gibraltar Farm. That was the send-off point for SOE agents.

And that's where they were taken – and meticulously searched by a WAAF warrant officer to make sure they were carrying no English money, no theatre or bus tickets, no English or American cigarettes: nothing that could give them away to the enemy. Their dispatcher bandaged Ryfka's ankles tightly to lessen the risk of a sprain on landing.

'Mine don't need bandaging,' Michel told him. The dispatcher looked at him but said nothing.

Then they climbed into their bulky flying suits and stuffed the big zip pockets with commando knives, pistols, emergency rations, maps, compasses, even small shovels. Finally, the dispatcher strapped them into their parachutes.

No one spoke. Tension was beginning to build, as it always did before take-off. Some tried to joke it away, or talk it away. Others kept quiet. She kept quiet. And clenched her teeth to try and stop the shakes. But it was no good, she got them anyway. She always did before a drop, especially in the dark.

'Scared?' said Michel.

'Shit scared.'

For the first time he smiled. 'Good job you brought your knitting then.'

Frank Smith went with them to the runway where a low-winged monoplane was waiting to take off. Though it was dark she recognized the long tailplane with its twin pear-shaped fins. A good old Hudson. But the familiar shape gave her little comfort. She felt cold and scared.

At the door on the port side, aft of the wing, Frank Smith wished them luck and gave them each a present. For Ryfka a gold bracelet, for Michel gold cuff links.

'If you run out of cash,' he mumbled, 'you can always flog the stuff.'

That was the practical reason for the presents. But she suspected there was a ritualistic reason too. Some kind of oblation to the gods.

Frank Smith hugged her and whispered: 'Look after yourself, old girl.' Then he shook hands with Michel and went quickly back to his car.

They clambered aboard and made themselves as comfortable as they could, squatting down near the trap door and leaning back against their parachutes. She began to feel better. She always did once she was in the plane and committed to other people's decisions. The dispatcher grinned and gave them the thumbs-up sign. Then he produced his vacuum flask of coffee. Another ritual. The twin Cyclones were beginning to roar.

She shouted over them: 'I go first. You second. Then the luggage. And stay put. I'll find you. Don't answer to anyone else.'

Michel nodded. Further conversation would have been lost in the mounting roar of the Cyclones. Then they were moving, bumping rapidly along the runway. Then, suddenly, the bumps smoothed out and the big awkward machine became light and graceful.

'We're unstuck,' yelled the dispatcher happily and gave them another thumbs-up. He poured the coffee and handed it to them. They held the cups tightly, warming their hands. It was cold and noisy in the Hudson, the whole airframe shaking with the vibration of the engines.

They crossed the French coast at Cabourg, where light flak came up to greet them. The plane began to pitch and roll and they climbed quickly to 10,000 feet to get above it. Then the pilot set course for Laval and soon the Hudson began her long, slow, gentle descent.

5

Dog minus 12

At about the time the Hudson was crossing the French coast, Churchill was chatting to Roosevelt from a quaint telephone booth covered in blue damask that stood outside the conference room of his underground war bunker at Storey's Gate, Westminster.

He chatted freely but as always was circumspect about military operations, referring to them only by codenames, though the line was considered absolutely secure. First, it was a radio-telephone link and the operators continually changed frequencies. Second, the calls were routed through a Bell A–3 scrambler in New York.

In fact, the SS had been listening to the calls for two years by way of an interception station on the Dutch coast, built at gunpoint by Phillips' engineers. The SS interception staff were not only able to keep track of the frequency changes but also unscramble much of the conversation.

This was the crowning point in the career of the station commandant, who had issued a standing order that whenever a conversation between the Allied war leaders was being monitored he should be immediately informed. Obersturmbannfuehrer Krantz, who was fluent in English, liked to listen in. He had his own pair of earphones, hanging from his own hook, in the radio room.

In the early hours of Dog minus 12, however, there was trouble. First from interference by storms over the Atlantic, then by losing transmission completely just when the conversation had been unscrambled and Churchill was in full flow. When they got it back all they heard was Churchill growling: 'I've just been told this line may be insecure.' And the line went dead.

Krantz took off his headphones, turned to Grossbrenner,

his second-in-command and chief of the interception staff, and said: 'What the hell was that about?'

Grossbrenner shrugged dismissively. 'They get the jitters from time to time in case the wicked Germans are listening in. It's all fantasy.'

But Krantz was a worrier. 'You don't think they could have found out about this place, do you?'

'Not a chance,' said Grossbrenner.

'Oh well, send copies to the usual people. Perhaps Fremde Heere West will be able to make something of it.'

The garbled fragment of the Churchill-Roosevelt conversation was enciphered on an Enigma machine, then telexed to the Reichssicherheitshauptampt in Berlin. From there it was telexed to Fremde Heere West, whose job was the evaluation of western intelligence, then to various other security agencies, including the Paris headquarters of the SS in avenue Foch (otherwise known as avenue Boche), Gestapo headquarters in rue de Saussaies and the Abwehr at the Hotel Lutetia.

No one paid much attention to it, which wasn't surprising. Reports were coming in all the time and a brief message that didn't make much sense got pushed to the back of the queue, especially in the middle of the night.

She felt hungry and regretted missing dinner. She pulled out a half-pound slab of milk chocolate and ate the lot, then felt full and a bit sleepy. Despite the noise and vibration she fell into a waking dream in which she saw the young Harry Romaine smiling at her. Suddenly he spat in her face. She woke up and found the dispatcher had opened the trap in the floor of the Hudson and ice-cold air was being dashed in her face. Through the black hole she caught sight of a long silver snake winding over the land below. The River Mayenne.

'Running in!' the dispatcher yelled.

She got to her feet. The dispatcher hooked up her static line. She checked that he'd done it properly, then moved close to the black hole.

'Action stations!'

It was awkward to shove her legs through the hole with a leg-bag attached to one of them. But she managed to sit on the leading edge of the trap, gripping it with both hands while the slipstream whipped her legs and she wondered how much longer she'd be able to hang on. The dispatcher's arm seemed to be descending in slow motion. His mouth formed the word 'GO' and she took a deep breath and launched herself. The slipstream flung her head over heels into the night.

Above her she saw a flash of orange flame from the engine exhausts, then she was swinging down through darkness. The big umbrella had opened. But the moon had gone. She reached down, undid the leg-bag and paid out the cord, then wriggled out of the strap holding her backside, swung her arms up and grabbed the nylon ropes of the 'chute. She tried to see the ground but it was just a deeper shade of darkness without the moon.

Then the cord of the leg-bag went slack and she tensed her muscles for landing. As she felt the first bump she went into a Japanese roll. Then she was on her back and the parachute, caught by the wind, was towing her through a field of standing corn. She threw herself to one side and pulled on the ropes to spill the air out of the bag. The parachute collapsed. She lay on the ground breathing hard and listening for suspicious sounds. But all she could hear was the wind in the corn.

As she stood up the moon came out from behind a bank of cloud and she saw two other white blossoms drifting downwind. Michel and the luggage. She watched them land and marked their positions by taking a bearing on a poplar flickering in the moonlight. Then she pulled her parachute into a straight line and rolled it up, twisting the lines into the in-and-out pattern taught at Ringway. She climbed out of her flying suit, emptied the pockets and undid the bandages round her ankles. Then she rolled the flying suit and the bandages into the parachute. She picked up the lot and moved off, again checking her bearing with the poplar and keeping an eye open for Michel.

He was leaning against a silver birch near a hedgerow.

Hands in pockets, playing it cool. 'Find our luggage?' she said.

He straightened up. 'I put it in a dry ditch on the other side of the hedge, along with my parachute.'

It was a good place, overgrown by thistles, nettles and cow parsley. She pushed her parachute in with the other stuff.

'No reception committee?' he said.

'Our reception committee's likely to be one man. Over there somewhere.' She pointed vaguely over the hedge.

'You mean we landed in the wrong field?'

'That's right. Let's go.'

She started off at a fast jog-trot and he followed her through a maze of country lanes. Once they hid in a ditch as headlights approached. A black petrol-driven Citroën swept past.

'Gestapo?' said Michel.

'Miliciens, probably. Local men. Maybe they spotted the 'chutes.'

She rested a minute or two, glad of the breather, then set off again. When they reached the field where Pierre Dugard was waiting, she first made sure the Gestapo weren't lurking in the shadows behind him.

'What happened?' said Dugard. 'I heard a plane go over. Did they drop you in the wrong place?'

She nodded. 'Navigational error.' She introduced Michel and added: 'Our luggage is under a hedge in the dropping zone. It includes a wireless set, some clarinettes and ammo.'

Clarinette was resistance slang for a Sten gun.

Dugard's truck, a wood-burning *gazo*, was parked nearby. She warned him about the *miliciens* they'd seen. 'They might be somewhere around our dropping zone by now.'

But when they got there the moonlit field was empty and only the wind stirred, parting the corn like blonde hair. They picked up the luggage and drove back to Dugard's farmhouse.

As soon as they were indoors Michel opened the wireless case, rigged the aerial, put in the appropriate crystal and tapped out the code letter telling London of their safe arrival. He waited for an acknowledgement, then signed off as Cameron Red, the codename of his set.

In a big kitchen full of gleaming copperware, Dugard's wife, Louise, served them with a spicy vegetable soup, liver pâté, goat cheese, bread still warm from the oven and a pitcher of fuchsia-red wine that was young and a bit rough for Ryfka's palate, but not for Michel's. He drank several glasses and after a time began to lean forward as if his head were top heavy. Soon he was asleep.

Ryfka asked about La Geste – Gestapo – and the local resistance.

'It's been pretty quiet since you left,' said Dugard. 'There were a lot of arrests immediately afterwards, but I had no way of knowing how many were connected with the circuit, since my only contacts were you and Gerard.' He shrugged. 'Anyway, la Geste are always arresting people.'

'Any air raids in the last few days?'

'On Friday there was a raid on an ammunition dump at Le Mans. I was at Evron, looking at some cattle, and you could see the smoke from there. Big black column a mile high.'

'American bombers or RAF?'

'Some of the locals thought they might be Flying Forts, but Father Lefevre said they were Lancasters.'

'Any shot down, do you know?'

'Father Lefevre saw some parachutes coming down near Parennes.'

'Any idea what happened to the aircrew?'

Dugard shrugged. 'There are conflicting rumours. Some say they got away, others say they were all picked up by la Geste. If you ask me, nobody really knows. Except Father Lefevre maybe.'

'Who is this Father Lefevre who knows so much?'

'Parish priest. Not a sparrow falls without his knowledge, never mind a girl.'

From SS headquarters in avenue Foche a telex of the recorded fragment of the Churchill-Roosevelt conversation was eventually sent to Standartenfuehrer Otto Raab, in

Rennes. It reached the Hotel Abelard, which he had requisitioned for his headquarters, around three in the morning, when the duty officer was just dozing off. The clatter of the telex machine soon woke him. He didn't relish waking Raab at that hour or any hour. Raab was a very frightening man. So he took the telex to Blech, Raab's aide, who wasn't at all frightening, even when he tried to be.

Untersturmfuehrer Christian Blech spoke to Raab on the internal phone and was told to come up. The night porter took him up in the lift and escorted him to the double doors of Raab's magnificent Second Empire suite, then hurried back to the lift. The night porter was scared of Raab too. Everyone, including Blech, who towered over him, was scared of Raab. Physically, Raab was insignificant, a typically neat, immaculate staff officer who'd never seen action – and whom Blech despised. Blech had seen action on the Russian Front and had been wounded there.

He went in through the double doors, shut them quietly and stood by one of the windows. The blackout curtains hadn't been drawn and there was some light from the waning moon. He didn't dare switch the lights on. Raab was photophobic and habitually wore smoked glasses.

His mouth ached for a cigarette but he didn't dare smoke in Raab's suite without Raab's permission. He'd have to wait till Raab had dressed, put on his glasses and carefully slicked the remnants of his reddish hair over his bald crown. Like Caesar he was sensitive about his baldness. About other things too. He never appeared before Blech or anyone else in a state of undress. Only before his deaf and dumb mistress, Blech assumed. Perhaps that was why he chose her. Perhaps he was shy or deformed or, Blech speculated hopefully, had a miniature penis. Blech often speculated about Raab and his relations with Solange, who was big and blonde and beautiful. Magnificent. Like a guardsman with tits. Raab indulged her stupidly though, even dangerously. Allowing her to make friends with the little Jewess who made her dresses. Maybe it was because she was the only one who could chat to Solange in that strange ticktack language. But fancy allowing a Jewess to wander in and out of Gestapo headquarters. Raab was a law unto himself, of course. But one of these days he'd go too far. Blech trusted he'd be around to see the fall of Raab. Some crash that would be.

'Dreaming of those heroic days on the Russian Front, are we?' The rustling voice, the silent approach from behind made him jump. He should have kept his eye on the dam' bedroom door. He snapped to attention and saluted. 'Heil Hitler!'

'Heil Hitler,' Raab said, yawning and taking the telex. 'Let's hope it was worth waking me up for.'

Always the concealed threat. Blech smiled uneasily, in the forlorn hope that Raab was joking.

'You may switch the lights on,' said Raab and sat on an elegant chaise longue to read the telex. Blech switched the lights on and stood to attention. There was a dry sound, like a cough. Raab was laughing.

'At ease, Blech, no one's going to shoot you. Well, not yet. There's some mineral water and glasses on a silver tray in the armoire.' He waved towards a tall slender cabinet.

Three o'clock in the fucking morning and the cowson offers me mineral water, Blech thought as he went to the cabinet.

' "A Bigot was lost over France on Friday," ' said Raab, reading aloud from the telex. He rubbed his smooth chin and Blech wondered if he'd just shaved or was naturally hairless. 'Bigot sounds like a codename and "lost over France" like an air raid. Who knows how many raids there were on Friday? They bomb us all the time.'

Blech set the silver tray on an occasional table near the chaise longue. 'Doesn't it say farther on, "Somewhere near Le Mans", mein Herr?'

'So it does, Blech. How observant. Don't stand there like a wooden Indian, sit down. You may pour yourself a drink.'

He went back to the telex while Blech sat down and poured himself the mineral water he didn't want. What he really wanted was hot coffee laced with brandy and a lungful of cigarette smoke. He smothered a huge yawn.

'The rest is garbled through transmission breaks, caused

apparently by storms over the Atlantic. All we get is a few words from Churchill: "Sending in one of our most resourceful agents, who knows the area ... resisted torture and then escaped ... must be recovered or eliminated." And that is all. The rest of the transmission was lost. Through incompetence, no doubt.'

He dropped the telex on the silver tray. 'Why should avenue Foche send it to us?'

Blech, who'd been dreamily wondering, not for the first time, what Raab's Junoesque mistress looked like naked, recovered his wits and said: 'Presumably because Le Mans is in our area, mein Herr.'

'Well,' said Raab dryly, 'at least you're half awake. What about the resourceful agent who knows the area, resisted torture and then escaped?'

Blech was astute enough to look blank, and let Raab demonstrate his cleverness. His job as aide to the Standartenfuehrer was a sinecure. He wanted to keep it.

'How many agents do you remember who resisted torture *and* escaped?'

'Well, no one really ...' Blech stopped. He mustn't overdo it. 'Oh, you mean Ryfka?'

'I mean Ryfka.'

'Didn't we hear she'd been retired from active service? On health grounds?'

'Health grounds?' Raab gave another dry cough or laugh. 'We nearly killed her at Alençon ...' He popped two white tablets into his mouth, and drank some mineral water. 'If they're sending her back they must have some very pressing reasons. Very pressing.'

He picked up the telex, read it through again, then stared at Blech. The smoked lenses completely obscured his eyes. But Blech knew they were pale and white-lashed.

'Who – or what – must be recovered or eliminated?'

Blech shrugged. 'It makes no sense.'

'Not in truncated form. But I've a feeling it could be the key to the whole mystery.'

6

She could feel the heat from the iron on her face, hear the voice, rustling like dead leaves in the wind. 'We're going to brand you.' As the iron was about to touch her she woke up and found the sun warming her face.

She was in bed in a room with whitewashed walls and sloping ceilings. An attic room that brought back memories of Lottie's rambling cottage, of sliding under the bedclothes into the warmth and ignorance of childhood. Well, she was a big girl now and it was half past bloody seven. She got out of bed, yawned, shivered and started to dress.

Father Lefevre was tending his vines. He had a plot of half an acre on sloping ground near Voutré, a few kilometres from Evron. Dugard had driven her there after breakfast. She had dressed with some care, deciding on a skirt rather than slacks, and combing her hair into the pageboy bob that helped hide the scar on her face. Priests were usually conventional, even immoral ones. And there was gossip about Father Lefevre and his young housekeeper, according to Dugard.

'Some of it undoubtedly malice,' he added. 'We'll stop off at Evron and get him some eggs and a bottle of wine.'

'A bribe?'

'He's awkward. Won't talk unless he trusts you.'

'He'll trust me if I'm with you, surely?'

'Not necessarily. He thinks men are fools over women.'

Dugard introduced her by the name on her papers, Camille Brossart, said she was connected with the resistance and was anxious to trace the airmen shot down in Friday's raid.

Father Lefevre, who was small and round with a flat ugly face and eyes like black buttons, looked her up and down, then led them into a dilapidated house, grumbling about

64

the weather. 'The spring did the damage. Too wet and too cold. So the flowering was delayed and the fruit set small and uneven. We need plenty of sunshine, then rain. Only God knows what sort of vintage we'll get. And so far he's failed to inform me, despite innumerable requests.'

He took them to his study, a big room which looked small because it was crammed with books and dominated by a huge desk, itself covered with books, manuscripts tied with green ribbon, writing materials and bric-a-brac. The rest of the furniture, two tatty armchairs and a sofa with broken springs, was also piled with books. There were even books on the floor, a hazard for unwary guests.

'Pray sit down,' said Father Lefevre with a grand gesture, 'carefully removing any books that discommode you.'

Ryfka managed to find space on the edge of the broken-down sofa, but had to lean forward, which made her hair fall across her face. She found herself staring at the manuscripts with their small spidery writing in violet ink.

'I am the Balzac of Voutré,' Father Lefevre said by way of explanation. 'An artist and an éleveur of wine. Also a priest. Some priests are fools. I am not.' He was looking at her more like a man than a priest. 'And I have no knowledge of the fate of the airmen. If I had it would be my bounden duty to report it to the proper authorities.'

She felt a flush of anger mantling her cheeks and stared back at the button-black eyes appraising her with cynical sensuality. Dugard quickly produced the eggs and the bottle of wine. 'A small gift,' he said. 'From both of us.'

Father Lefevre shouted for his housekeeper, Marie-France, a peasant girl with big tits and knowing eyes. 'Take the eggs, leave the wine,' he said. 'She's a slut,' he said to the others. 'Hence the untidiness.'

Marie-France ignored this, picked up the eggs and went out.

'Why do you keep her then?' said Ryfka.

The little priest spread his arms in a Christ-like gesture of compassion and his voice took on the fruity timbre of a professional preacher. 'Pure charity, my dear. Nobody else would employ her. Though I speak with the tongues of men and of angels, and have not charity, I am become as sounding brass or a tinkling cymbal. Let's have a drink.'

He uncorked the bottle and rooted around till he found three clean glasses. He poured a little wine into one, swirled it round, sniffed it, tasted it. 'Not much nose, not much fruit. Too young, too acidic, but clean over the palate. Good colour. Might improve.' He poured wine into the other glasses.

'Your health,' he said, raising his glass to Ryfka.

She pushed her hair back and got up. 'Let's piss off,' she said to Dugard, and started for the door. The priest's next words stopped her short.

'The plane shot down on Friday,' he said, 'was a Lancaster. I saw them going over earlier, at least two squadrons, in the direction of Le Mans.' His hands made a small placatory gesture. 'Sit down and have some wine, madame.'

She turned, not sure whether the volte-face was genuine or sardonic.

'Perhaps we should listen,' Dugard said softly.

She re-balanced herself on the edge of the rickety sofa.

'Four of the men were picked up by the Gestapo within a few hours, at Sainte Suzanne, not far from here. The others, I believe, were arrested later, on the outskirts of Fougères.' He poured himself more wine, sniffed it again. 'It needs time to breathe.'

'Have you any idea what happened to them?'

'The four who were picked up at Sainte Suzanne were taken to Le Mans for preliminary questioning. They were the pilot, flight engineer and two air gunners. They were then entrained for a Luftwaffe holding camp in Germany. My informant was unable to say which camp.'

'Your informant?'

'Another priest, an old friend. A woman of his parish has a lover in the SS at Le Mans. A lover who is indiscreet in his cups and in bed. She feels guilty about the association and confides in my friend. He was here yesterday to try my home-made pâté with a little Sancerre.'

'And the other men?'

66

'I am not sure. But I've heard they are being held in the Gestapo prison at Rennes, pending transfer to Germany.'

'Well, that shouldn't be difficult to check.' She hesitated. 'Is there something else?'

'Do you know how many men were arrested at Fougères?'

'The rest of the crew, I was told. Which would be three, would it not?'

She nodded. 'Unless the plane was carrying additional aircrew. It happens occasionally, I believe.'

The little priest, who was lolling back, sat up. 'That might account for it . . . There were rumours that an airman had been seen near Jublains. And old Madame Thibaudier – she lives the other side of Parennes – said she counted eight parachutes. But nobody takes any notice of her. They say she has visions and can't count. In my experience of bargaining with her she can count like an adding machine. Only faster.'

As soon as they got in the truck she said: 'Why the volte-face?'

'He saw the scar when you pushed your hair back.'

'What could it mean to him?'

'Haven't you heard about la Balafrée, the Scarred One? Who was tortured by the Gestapo, branded with a red-hot iron, but never broken? Who escaped, half dead, from the prison hospital? And then got back to England – '

'By swimming the Channel?'

Dugard shrugged. 'All right, the story may have grown into something of a legend. But people need legends in wartime. And that legend could help you. Indeed, it already has.'

'So has my Walther thirty-eight.'

'Sometimes you talk like a man.'

'I've been trained like a man.'

They drove the rest of the way to Parennes in silence.

Madame Thibaudier, who was over seventy, lived with a quarrelsome collection of cats, goats, chickens, a backward son and a fat dog who got on with everyone. Her house, a converted barn, was on the south side of Parennes, near a little wood, once part of the Forêt de la Petite Charnie. It had small windows and a flagstone floor and smelt of animals and cooking.

'A bit off-putting to the fastidious nose,' said Dugard, 'but you get used to it. The backward son, by the way, interferes with little girls. Touches their bottoms. As if trying to remind himself of something. I've watched him.'

'How old is he?'

'Twenty.'

'And she's seventy?'

'He's her adopted son. Not in law, but in fact. He was a war orphan, hitch-hiking south to some relatives, when he was knocked down by a German military truck outside her front door. She took him in and nursed him back to physical health. Mentally he may be a brick short of a full load, but he's a great help to her. Grows the vegetables, feeds the animals, fetches and carries. And he's not stupid, just limited.'

They drove in through a gateway that had no gate. The fat dog barked to let you know he wasn't really scared, the chickens squawked, a gander honked, the goats stared. Madame Thibaudier, sitting outside in the sunshine, peeling potatoes, looked up in expectation of trade and gave them a wide toothless smile.

They got out of the truck and Dugard introduced Ryfka as an old friend of his and Father Lefevre's. Then he brought the conversation round to the events of Friday. Madame Thibaudier's beady eyes lit up. Ah, yes, it had been a great day. She had never seen such things before. Great white parasols like fleecy clouds, floating down from heaven. She thought it was a holy vision. She often had holy visions. One parasol flew right over the house and she could see a man swinging from it. For a moment she thought it was an angel, but it didn't have wings.

'Do you know where he came down, madame?' Ryfka asked.

'In the barley field at the back. Julien says it was an airman.'

'Julien?'

68

'My son.'

Ryfka nodded. 'Do you know what happened to the airman? Or the other airmen?'

Madame Thibaudier hesitated, looked down. 'No,' she said, 'I know nothing.' She looked up. 'Would you like coffee? It's only grain coffee, I'm afraid. Whatever happened to proper coffee? The war, people say. That's just an excuse. Or perhaps a glass of sherry wine? The only aperitif for a lady, I always think.'

Ryfka smiled. 'No thank you,' she said, wondering why the old girl had become wary at the mention of the airmen. 'I'd like to meet your son though, if I may.'

'Of course, of course. He's out the back, lifting potatoes. He's very intelligent, really. But sometimes . . .' Her face clouded, she made a little gesture of distress. 'The light goes from his eyes.' She cupped her hands round her mouth and yelled with a loudness that made Ryfka jump: 'Julien! Julien!'

A few seconds later Julien appeared round the corner of the house. Tall, lean, not bad-looking, with untidy fair hair, soft brown eyes and a tendency to smile. He wore a check shirt and corduroys tucked into gumboots. The clothes were old and patched, but clean. Introductions were made and Ryfka noted that his manner was shy, almost childlike. She decided to treat him as an adult, which was what she always did with children, apart from using the familiar address.

'You saw the parachutists come down, I believe?'

Julien nodded. 'Eight of them. Maman and I counted them.'

'Do you know where they landed?'

'To the north, most of them. Perhaps on the other side of the river.'

'The Vegronneau?'

Julien nodded.

'One man came down in the barley field at the back, didn't he?'

Julien hesitated, looked at his maman. His maman looked at him, impassively. 'Yes, that's right,' he said.

'Do you know what happened to him?'

Another exchange of impassive looks.

'No. I didn't see him again.'

The old witch was telling him what to say as surely as if she said it out loud.

'I'd like to see the barley field. Would you show me?'

'Of course he will,' said Madame Thibaudier. 'Won't you, Julien?'

'Of course, Maman.'

'Be careful, Julien. And look after the lady.'

'Yes, Maman.'

He led her round the back of the house, across a vegetable patch, through an orchard and a small wood, scant of trees but cool and shady. The trees ended abruptly and there, sloping down before them, lay the barley field, shimmering in the sun. They stayed in the shadow of the trees. It was quiet, almost silent, except for the summer sound of insects.

She asked him if he knew the names of some wild flowers at the edge of the field. He gave her both the vernacular and Latin names of every flower in sight.

Without looking at him she said softly: 'You're very observant and you know a great deal. You could help me if you wanted to.'

She heard him sigh, then felt a hand on her bottom. It stroked her gently. She didn't move, just stared at the wild flowers and the shimmering barley.

'Where is the man? Who is hiding him?'

The hand was withdrawn. She sensed fear.

'I wouldn't hurt you,' she said, keeping her voice soft and low. 'Or tell tales about you.'

The hand returned.

'Do you like dogs?' he said, stroking her.

'Better than I like most people.'

'You should see the dogs at Foucault. Their eyes speak to you. So do their ears. Such ears.'

It was getting on for noon and the sun was pouring through the window when Raab dismissed Blech and went back to bed. The bedroom was still in darkness, apart from a stray

70

shaft of sunlight slanting through a gap in the curtains, as he slid into bed beside Solange. He eased himself close enough to feel the warmth of her back. He was usually cold, she always felt warm. And he needed warmth or he wouldn't get to sleep. He had power of life and death over most of Normandy and the Pays de Loire, but not over sleep.

He decided to wake her, then realized she was already awake. She had an uncanny instinct for his needs. Then her arms were round him, the big warm milky breasts in his face, their bitter-sweet smell in his nostrils and in his ears the small animal sounds she made in lieu of speech.

He knew that one day, when he moved on or went back to Germany, he'd have to kill her. It would be in her own interests. Meanwhile, he spread her legs and mounted her.

'I must say,' said Dugard, as they drove into Evron, 'I didn't expect you to come back hand in hand with a chap that interferes with little girls.'

'I learnt something.'

'Interesting?'

'He interferes with big girls too.'

'Oh my God, he didn't try it on with you, did he?'

She smiled. 'He likes stroking girls' bottoms. Next on the right.'

'No, it's Montsurs we want, straight ahead.'

'I want Foucault. Do you know it?'

'Sure. Six houses and a church at the arse end of nowhere. Why do you want to go there?'

'To see a man about a dog.'

They turned off a narrow twisting road to go down an even narrower twisting lane, rutted, bumpy and unmetalled, hedges on either side. It ended at a gate after an abrupt right turn. A large hand-painted notice near the gate announced:

LE COURT KENNELS
GERMAN SHEPHERDS
BRED & TRAINED
Please shut gate

71

A hundred yards farther on there was another gate. Beyond it a patch of grass, then the whitewashed front of an old farmhouse. A path led from the gate to the house.

As they pulled up there was a sound of deep barking and at every window, upstairs and downstairs, appeared a handsome head, sometimes two or three, with pointed ears and big intelligent eyes.

'Don't they look lovely?' she said.

'From a safe distance,' said Pierre.

'You stay here,' she said, getting out of the truck. 'I won't be long.'

'Unless they eat you.'

She opened the gate and went up the path. Three or four big dogs came round from the back of the house and ambled towards her. A man appeared at the front door. He was tall and had only one arm. A war veteran and not bad looking. Pleasant smile. Mid-forties, she guessed.

'They won't hurt you,' he said.

'Monsieur Le Court?'

'Come in,' he said.

There were German Shepherds everywhere. Lying on the staircase, on the landing, in the hall. Some of them got up and started to go to her. Le Court told them to stay. They stayed.

'What are you looking for,' he said, 'a dog or a bitch?'

'A man, actually. British airman, shot down near Parennes on Friday.'

'I heard something about a plane being shot down. But why come to me?'

The wary type. She'd have to take a chance. 'Let me explain,' she said. 'I'm with the resistance.'

'So are a lot of good collaborators, now the war's going the other way.'

'This area was covered by one of the biggest circuits till a few months ago, when it was penetrated by the Gestapo. I'm trying to reorganize it.'

Le Court suddenly smiled. 'Well, as long as you're not an agent provocateur. There's been one around here lately, I believe. A woman, what's more.'

72

He opened one of the doors out of the hall and showed her into a sitting room. When she turned round she found herself looking down the barrel of a Luger.

He called over his shoulder: 'Marie, come here a moment. I think we've caught that Gestapo bitch.'

Light hurried footsteps and Marie Le Court came in, wiping her hands on her apron. Dark and pretty but on edge. Younger than her husband.

'I'm nothing to do with the Gestapo,' said Ryfka.

'She came with a man,' said Le Court. 'He's outside in a truck. I'll get a shotgun and deal with him.'

'The man outside is a local farmer,' said Ryfka. 'And when did the Gestapo ride around in a clapped-out old gazo?'

'It could be part of your cover,' said Le Court.

Marie, who was peering out of the window, said: 'That looks like Pierre Dugard's truck.'

'They're all much of a muchness, these old trucks.'

'He just wants to shoot somebody,' said Marie. 'To prove he's not a collaborator just because he sells dogs to the Boche.'

'I lost an arm fighting the bloody Boche. And the only reason I do business with them – ' He stopped abruptly, turned to Ryfka. 'Who the hell *are* you?'

'I was with the resistance group that got ambushed by the Gestapo at Alençon.'

Marie went to her, reached out and lifted the hair from the left side of her face. 'Put that stupid gun away, René,' she said.

Le Court hesitated, then pushed the Luger into the waistband of his slacks. 'How did you know about the airman?'

'Your wife was buying eggs from Madame Thibaudier on Friday. She saw the airman come down. Julien told me.'

'He promised not to tell anyone,' said Marie.

'He trusts me,' said Ryfka. 'And so should you. Do you know the airman's name?'

'Romaine. Squadron Leader Romaine. He said we should call him Harry.'

'Was he in uniform?'

73

'He'd buried his battledress blouse, along with his parachute, by the time we found him. And was just cutting the
leggings off his flying boots to make them look like ordinary
shoes. You know, with that special knife they give them.'

'And then you brought him back here?'

Marie nodded. 'René was furious. Said if the Boche
found out it could mean the end of our son, never mind
us. Then he calmed down and said of course we must help
him.'

'What worried me,' said Le Court, 'was all the other
nosey sods who might have seen him with her. Round here
they live on gossip.'

'And where is he now?'

Marie shrugged. 'He left after a couple of days. Suddenly.
Without a word.'

'Do you know where he went?'

'We're not sure. Come into the kitchen, I want to finish
kneading some dough while the oven's hot.'

'And I'll make you some real coffee,' said Le Court.

'Did you say real coffee?'

'Now she'll know you're a collaborator,' said Marie.

Le Court said sharply: 'My son is doing forced labour in
Germany and I'm trying to get him back.' He turned to
Ryfka. 'I supply Seventh Army headquarters and the
Luftwaffe with guard dogs. But it doesn't stop me hating
them. Or pinching their coffee, if I get the chance.'

'You see?' said Marie. 'He's touchy because he feels
guilty.'

They went into the kitchen, which was big and airy, with
an old-fashioned dresser, refectory table, racks of pots and
pans and a tiled floor. Marie stood at a worktop kneading
the dough with an excess of nervous energy while Le Court
made the coffee.

'After we got back,' said Marie. 'I phoned my brother in
Rennes. He's a doctor and one of his patients, a farmer at
Talensac, has some connection with the resistance. I was
hoping we could use the farm as a safe house for Harry till
arrangements were made to get him back to England. But
Jean – that's my brother – said the farmer had been taken

in for questioning by the Gestapo, and the place might not be safe any more.'

'And how did Harry take it?'

'He was restless. Impatient. He had a map of France made of silk – part of the standard escape kit, he said – and asked me to show him where the farm was.'

'That was Friday night?'

'And on Saturday he mooned around the house all day and played with the dogs. But he was on edge. I could tell.'

'He'd lost his nerve,' said Le Court.

Marie stopped pummelling the dough. 'He just wanted to get out.'

Le Court nodded. 'Because he'd lost his nerve.'

'Because he didn't trust *you*,' Marie said, pummelling the dough again.

Le Court turned to Ryfka. 'She won't hear a word against him.'

'Anyway,' said Marie, 'by Sunday he'd gone. I heard the dogs barking in the early hours, but thought it was a fox or something.'

Ryfka finished her coffee in silence.

'Was it nice?' said Le Court.

'Sensational.'

'Another cup?'

'Thank you, but I must go.' She turned to Marie. 'Last question. Can you give me some idea what he looks like?'

'I can do even better,' said Marie, taking a sketch book from a kitchen drawer. She opened it and pulled out a pencil sketch of Harry Romaine.

'Did you do this?'

'It helped to while away the time.'

Ryfka could see the likeness to the photograph, though the face was older and more battered.

'Can I borrow it?'

'You can keep it,' said Marie. 'Maybe it'll stop René being jealous.'

'Merde,' said Le Court. 'Merde, merde, merde!' And slammed out of the room.

*

She was mostly silent on the way back to the farm, wondering whether the rift between the Le Courts was really due to jealousy. Or to something else. Like his working for the Germans. Though you could hardly blame him for that with his only son on *Service Obligatoire du Travail*.

7

After lunch she changed into slacks and cardigan and screwed her hair up into a topknot. Then she put on a trenchcoat, jammed a black trilby on her head and bent the brim down at the front. She examined the result in the bedroom looking glass and wondered if she'd pass for a man. She'd done it before, but she always had the feeling that because she knew she was a woman other people would know. With her hair up the scar would be visible, but scars on a man weren't uncommon in the fifth year of the war.

Finally, she packed her two guns, the Walther P38 and the little forty-five special, twitched the black hat to a rakish angle and went down to the kitchen, feeling like a stage villain.

Michel, who was drinking coffee with Dugard's wife, stared at her. 'You look like Gestapo in that outfit.'

Pierre Dugard came in from the yard. 'I've stowed the suitcase in the back of the truck.' He hesitated. 'I still think you ought to let me drive you to Rennes.'

'We'll take the train from Vitré.'

'There'll be a police control at Rennes.'

'French police don't usually look for trouble.'

'There could be an SS control as well.'

'That's a normal war risk, like the pox. You can't insure against it.'

Ten minutes later they were on the road to Vitré.

Though it wasn't more than forty kilometres it took nearly two hours, partly because of the roundabout route Dugard took, partly because the old wood-burning *gazo* ran out of breath on the hills. Downhill she was great, with the wind behind her. But like most journeys it was more uphill than down. And Dugard was worried they might miss the 4.45 *voyageur* to Rennes, the last of the day. The rest would be troop trains or supply trains.

But they made it. Dugard dropped them in the Place de la République and they boarded the train with minutes to spare. It was crowded but they found seats, and even room for their cases under the seats. She was carrying the two smaller cases holding their clothes, Michel the hefty one with the wireless set.

She'd already given him instructions what to do if they got separated. He was to make his way to a house a few minutes walk from the Place des Lices, in the old quarter, find the back entrance, knock and say he had a message for Dominique, who would look after him till she arrived. On no account was he to go to the front entrance.

He wondered why but said nothing. He still resented her. He looked at her, mannish bitch, lolling back half asleep, hat pulled down over her eyes, and hoped they didn't run into trouble. Having a woman to look after could only make it worse, especially if she panicked. Then he realized her black sardonic eyes were on him.

'We're coming into Rennes,' she said. 'Get your case.'

He dragged out the transmitter case as the train hissed and clanked to a halt. They got out and started walking towards the barrier in a crowd of women and old men, plus a few German soldiers. The sun was shining and he felt happy to be in France again, to hear French voices again . . .

Then the crowd thickened, spread out and finally stopped. There was a babble of irritable chatter . . . 'What's up?' . . . 'What's going on?' . . . 'Hey, stop pushing, you pig.'

Ryfka gave her case to Michel. 'Look after this.' Then she disappeared into the crowd, shoving and elbowing her way through with a ruthlessness that took Michel's breath away. He tried to see what was happening, but people were milling around like cattle and little old ladies causing chaos with umbrellas.

Suddenly Ryfka appeared out of the crowd. 'Give me your case,' she said. 'You take mine.'

'It's too heavy for you.'

78

'Do as you're fucking well told,' she said through her teeth.

Michel took a deep breath, handed over the suitcase. Ryfka lowered her voice and said: 'Remember what I told you.'

'Hold it,' he said. 'What's going on?'

But she was already ploughing through the crowd again, cursing everyone out of the way in fluent German. Her voice was hoarse and sounded like a man's. 'Hau ab!' he heard her spit at a German soldier who tried to remonstrate with her. He wondered what it meant. *Up yours*, perhaps. Or *Get lost*.

He tried to follow her, but the crowd was impossible and he lacked her ruthlessness. Then, suddenly, unaccountably, the milling, swaying crowd parted. And he saw what she must have seen. And went cold.

Beyond the barrier, where French police were waving passengers through after a cursory glance at their papers, were two young SS officers. Everyone with a parcel or case, even a shopping bag, was being directed to the *consigne*, where more SS men, under the eye of a Scharfuehrer, were methodically searching every piece of luggage.

'Jesus,' he murmured, visions of being strung up by the thumbs in some Gestapo cellar suddenly before him.

With fear and fascination, he watched Ryfka walking to her doom. Then, as she neared the barrier, she held up the case with the wireless set for all to see.

Jesus Christ, she's SHOWING 'em the fucking thing.

He heard her shout in that hoarse mannish voice: 'Ein beschlagnahmtes Funkgeraet! Rufen sie einen Wagen, aber sofort!'

She brushed past the French police control – and came face to face with the two young SS officers. They looked startled and turned to consult each other.

'Sofort! Standartenfuehrer Raab erwartet mich!'

Immediately, as if by reflex, they turned and shouted at a Sturmmann, who shouted at an SS man, who shouted at somebody out of sight.

Michel didn't understand a word of it. The German

sounded brutal. But he could feel his heart thumping against his chest as he waited for her to be seized. He slipped a hand inside his coat, started to draw his Browning automatic.

Then a shiny black Citroën, with an SS driver, raced on to the station concourse and pulled up with a screech of tyres.

Ryfka began to breathe more easily. Then, out of nowhere, the local police *commissaire*, Loubain, appeared beside her – and she knew the game was up. He'd questioned her once before and was bound to recognize her . . . But all he did was open the car door for her. She threw the suitcase on the back seat and got in after it. She stared at Loubain's dour face. He stared back, dark eyes expressionless. She looked past him, waved to the SS officers, who snapped to attention and saluted. Then there was a sudden roar of high revs, another screech of rubber and the car raced off, horn blaring, pedestrians scattering like chaff before the wind.

Raab didn't get up till mid-afternoon, when Solange brought him coffee and rye bread. The room was still in darkness and she waited for him to put on his smoked glasses before pulling the curtains back.

He wondered, idly, how she always seemed to know when he was awake, and always had his coffee ready. The only explanation was that she was an animal. It was well known that animals had a sixth sense.

After he'd washed and dressed, had some coffee and nibbled at the rye bread, he went into the salon to read intelligence reports that had come in while he slept. Part of the huge salon was partitioned off with Chinese screens to make an office with a plain wooden desk, telephones and even filing cabinets. The whole setup looked incongruous.

He reread the fragment of the Churchill-Roosevelt conversation and had doubts about some of his deductions. There were other resourceful agents besides Ryfka who had escaped from the Gestapo. And the chances were it was one of them who was being sent back. The more he thought about it in the cold light of day the more it made sense.

Ryfka could hardly be fit enough to undertake an SOE mission, therefore it must be some other agent. It was logical.

Through an opening in the Chinese screens he watched Solange talking to the little seamstress, Bernadette, her hands fluttering and gesticulating in the strange language of the deaf and dumb. He talked to Solange freely – she was an expert lip reader – and at times, perhaps, indiscreetly, but whether she really understood was anyone's guess. Sometimes she nodded and smiled, while her brilliant eyes remained blank. At other times she seemed to understand everything. Not that it mattered: the only person she could talk to was Bernadette, who'd lost her speech through shock at the death of her mother. And her fate, like her father's, was sealed. They would have been deported a long time ago, with the rest of the Jews, if Bernadette hadn't meant so much to Solange, and if her father hadn't been the best cutter left in Rennes. He made all Raab's uniforms. Immaculately.

Another reason why Raab tolerated the Jew, as he called him, was his musical ability. He knew all the old German songs that Raab liked, and played them on the accordion with great feeling.

The Jew was whisked off to Raab's country house whenever Raab felt in need of musical diversion. Les Sapins Argentés, as it was called, was once a farmhouse. The farmer and his wife had been shot for sheltering resisters and most of the land sold off to collaborationist neighbours. Raab retained the house and a few acres for his own occasional use.

Soon after he took it over he allowed Solange's mother and grandmother to move in. They were all that was left of the family. Her two brothers had been killed in the current war, her father in the last. Her mother, Therese, had become silent and remote. Only the Jew and his music brought colour to her cheeks.

Grandma Tilly was ninety and most of the time didn't know there was a war on. And when she did she mixed it up with some other war. What she did know was that neighbouring farmers were constantly sending electric currents through the walls of her bedroom. And sometimes through the sitting room and kitchen. Even through the roof, not to mention the beautiful lavatory Colonel Raab had had built at such expense. But nothing was sacred to diabolism. She was afraid to undress at night in case electrical demons were hiding behind the curtains, waiting to subject her to unspeakable practices.

One of the phones on Raab's desk rang. It was an unlisted number on an outside line. He lifted the receiver, said 'Yes?' in his soft voice and listened intently. 'You're quite sure it was her? Excellent. I shall remember this.' He hung up, then rang Blech on the internal phone and told him to call local security chiefs to an immediate conference.

Then he turned to signal Solange to take Bernadette into another room. But she'd already done so.

The house was at the end of a cul-de-sac of big solid middle-class houses. The feature that made it stand out was its gleaming new paintwork. That of the others was flaking, though they still looked grimly genteel. Pumice-scoured steps led up to a polished oak front door. From inside came the tinkling of a piano, playing dreamy *thé-dansant* music.

He wondered why the front entrance was out of bounds. The sight of a couple of German officers strolling down the street cut short his speculations. He hurried into a passage at the side of the house, made his way past some dustbins to a gloomy back entrance and rang the bell.

The door was opened by a burly man in his late forties. He had a harelip and beetle brows, which gave him a murderous look. His collarless shirt was unbuttoned, showing a hairy chest and a silver crucifix on a chain. He asked Michel what he wanted in a voice as harsh as the face.

Michel said he had a message for Madame Dominique. From Ryfka. Without another word the burly man picked up the cases and led him along a dark passage to a parlour full of knick-knacks and old-fashioned furniture with anti-macassars. If monsieur would wait a moment . . .

Quick light footsteps and a handsome woman came in and introduced herself as Dominique. She was tall and elegant in a long Edwardian gown with puff sleeves and a military collar. Her hairstyle was elaborate and her perfume almost as powerful as her air of respectability.

A bit daunted, he mumbled that Ryfka sent her regards and expected to be along later. He wondered whether to mention the incident at the station, but decided not to. Let Ryfka tell the story herself – if she lived to tell it. He asked if he could stay there till she arrived.

'Of course,' said Dominique graciously. 'We shall give you a room. Leave the cases. Josef will bring them up.'

She led him into the dark passage and up some equally dark stairs. The back stairs for servants. From the front of the house drifted laughter and the tinkling of the piano.

'Is this a hotel?' he said.

'A quiet hotel,' said Dominique. 'With all the amenities.'

Raab read the transcription of the Churchill-Roosevelt conversation to the local chiefs of the SS, Gestapo, Milice and French police and waited for comments. All he got was silence. Not that he expected anything from Loubain, the commissioner of police, whom he didn't entirely trust. He looked around, wondering where Blech was.

'Any idea who the "resourceful agent" might be?' Another silence.

He smiled. He was in a good mood after that phone call. 'I have reason to believe it may be the woman known as Ryfka.'

A murmur of surprise.

'Yes,' he said, 'life is full of surprises.'

The double doors of the salon opened and Blech hurried in and made his way through the Chinese screens.

'Excuse me, mein Herr,' he said, breathless after running upstairs. 'An SS driver has been found shot dead in his car off the rue Gambetta. He'd picked up one of our men who got off a train with a captured wireless set.'

There was a frozen silence, broken by Raab: 'One of *our* men? Any description of him?'

'Shortish for a man, about five foot five or six – '

'But tallish for a woman?'

'High cheekbones, dark eyes – '

'Any distinguishing marks?'

Blech cleared his throat. 'A scar on the left cheek.'

'Well, fancy that,' said Raab. 'And no one recognized her?'

'I was at the station,' said Loubain. 'And I didn't recognize her.'

'How was that?'

Loubain shrugged. 'She looked like Gestapo. She *sounded* like Gestapo. And she was holding up a captured set.' Another shrug. 'She fooled a few other people too.'

Raab nodded. At least Loubain was honest. That was something. He went to the window, stared out over the rooftops. 'She's here ... Somewhere in the streets below ...' He turned back to the others. 'If you see her, leave her alone. I don't want her arrested. Is that understood?'

A buzz of bewilderment filled the little office.

'They think I'm mad,' Raab murmured to Blech, who thought so too.

She booked a room for the night in a small hotel near the Place des Lices, paying in advance, then managed to get a taxi to Dominique's place. She lugged the heavy case round to the back door, which opened before she could ring. The next thing she knew, Josef was hugging her.

'Ryfka.' he said. 'Are you well?'

She hugged him in return. 'Has my friend arrived?'

'He's in the room next to yours. I'll take you up.'

He picked up the heavy case as if it weighed nothing and led her along the passage to the back stairs.

'And Dominique?'

'At confession. She will join you later.'

Michel was sitting on the bed reading a paperback when

there was a knock and Ryfka came in with the transmitter case.

'You'll be wanting this,' she said, putting it down.

His mouth dropped open, he got off the bed. 'Christ, you actually made it.' He put the case on the bed, opened it and started setting up the wireless. Anything to avoid looking at her. 'Shouldn't we tell London we've got a lead on the airman?'

'I'll give you a message.'

He gave her a pad and pencil and she sat at the dressing table and started to write down the message in clear. 'Found a decent earth for the aerial?'

He didn't answer and she went on writing. Suddenly he said: 'What happened when you went off in the car?'

'I directed the driver into a side street. Said I had a call to make.' She took out a cigarette and lit it. 'Then I shot him while he was showing me a picture of his wife and kids.'

He uncoiled the seventy-foot aerial wire and earthed it to the stack pipe outside the window. She gave him the message, which he started to encipher. Then she got up, went to the door. 'Think I'll lie down for a bit.'

'War's war,' he said, still avoiding her eyes. 'And I don't care what you did. I mean – '

'If you're trying to thank me,' she said, 'forget it. I like killing people. Didn't Frank Smith tell you?'

In her own room she fell on the bed, suddenly exhausted. But within an hour she'd recovered like an animal and got up and changed into the kind of two-piece suit with long jacket and knee-length skirt that was fashionable in France at the time. She put on make-up and combed her hair into the long pageboy that hid the scar.

Then she called for Michel and they joined Dominique for dinner in her suite on the top floor. They were served by the taciturn Josef, who joined them at table, but still kept an eye to their needs, especially Ryfka's. He sat next to her, unobtrusively anticipating her wishes, refilling her glass, making sure everything was to hand. She sat straight-backed, eyes modestly lowered, saying little. Michel found it a disconcerting switch from the mannish striding figure yelling at the SS in hoarse German.

He also found the meal disconcerting. Its luxury seemed sinful after the rigours of wartime Britain: smoked trout with Chablis, crown of lamb with a Clos de Beze. And real coffee afterwards.

Perhaps sensing this Dominique said: 'This is a special meal for a special occasion.'

Both she and Josef were members of the Horseman circuit and Ryfka had already explained that she was trying to recover a shot-down airman and that Michel was her wireless operator. It was agreed he should use his room as a transmitting station.

'Transmissions will be few and short,' said Ryfka. 'So the Boche direction-finders won't have time to pinpoint the set. And with a bit of luck we'll be away in a week.'

Over coffee Dominique mentioned that the Place des Lices was buzzing with rumours when she came back from church. 'About a man who'd bluffed his way past the SS control, commandeered a Gestapo car – '

'An SS car,' said Ryfka. 'At least, it had an SS driver.'

'You don't say?' said Dominique. 'More coffee, my dear?'

The shop fascia said in white-painted letters, barely readable in the blackout: POMPES FUNÈBRES.

At the back of the window, in a blue satin niche, stood a small plaster saint, rim lit from behind to create the glow of a nimbus without breaking blackout regulations. The face, with its look of bogus innocence, reminded her of Luc.

The shop itself was in darkness apart from a pencil of light from under a closed door at the back. A card hanging on the glass entrance door said SHUT, but when she tried the door it opened. A bell tinkled as she went in. A sickly perfume hung in the air and she heard the sound of sawing. It stopped and a voice called out: 'I'm shut. Can't you read?'

'I'm looking for your cousin,' she said. 'Luc.'

'My wife's cousin. So he says.'

86

The light in the workshop was switched off and someone came out and shone a torch in her face.

'Don't you recognize me, Victor?'

'I thought you were dead,' said Victor, slipping the catch on the entrance door. 'Come into the workshop.'

They went in and Victor switched the light on again. The place was littered with partly built coffins and there was the typical coffin smell of varnish and pine.

'How's business?'

'People still die.'

'It's not all bad then.'

Victor started planing one of the partly finished coffins. 'Achille Leblanc gets the best business.'

'He's in with the biggest collaborators.'

'He's even got the Jean-Paul Truchet funeral.'

'Didn't know the bastard had died. Somebody shoot him?'

'Nobody shoots the mayor. And I don't even get to bury him. His wife is my wife's second cousin, and I was *promised* that funeral.'

'Where's your wife's other cousin?'

'Luc?'

'I tried his old address but he must have moved.'

A gloomy nod from Victor. 'Right next door to us. I never was lucky with cousins, especially my wife's.' He shook his head. 'His black market deals will get us all arrested.'

He had dark thinning hair, hollow cheeks, mournful eyes and an undertaker's stoop from carrying all those coffins.

'Listen,' he said, 'I don't know what you've come back for. And I don't want to know. I don't want anything to do with the resistance. I just want to go on making coffins and burying people decently. It's a service. Not heroic. But necessary. So do what you have to do, but don't involve me.'

All the time he spoke he was working: planing, polishing, mitring. And worrying. 'Just don't involve me.'

'Of course not,' she said, knowing all the time she would if she had to. She had a soft spot for the little undertaker, who was often taken advantage of by those he trusted, including his pretty wife.

*

87

There was no answer from Luc's apartment, which didn't surprise her. She tried Victor's apartment and in due course Luc answered the door, in shirtsleeves and out of breath.

He flung his arms round her. 'Ryfka baby, you look great!'

To Luc all women looked great, though some looked greater than others. 'So you made it, huh?'

'What are you talking about?'

'The ambush, baby, the ambush. We thought you'd been rubbed out. But you made it.'

Luc was obsessed with everything American and his French was peppered with the slang, often inappropriate.

'And how's Luc?' she said as he led her into the salon.

'Getting by, making a buck. Take a seat.' He indicated a big comfortable-looking sofa.

She sat down, looked around. 'And Cousin Bette?' That was Victor's wife, Beatrice.

Luc gave an exaggerated shrug. 'Rustling up some coffee, I guess. Victor rang to say you were on your way.'

'The good Victor.'

'Sure, the good Victor.'

'And his good cousin. Or rather, his wife's good cousin. Some cousin.'

He spread his hands. 'Can I help it if he doesn't make her happy?'

Bette came in with coffee on a tray. She was wearing a housecoat and nothing much under it. Her hair was untidy, her face shiny, but she had the kind of moist voluptuousness that spoke straight to male loins. Soon she'd run to fat.

She exchanged greetings with Ryfka, sat on the sofa and served the coffee in silence. She wasn't a chatterer. Ryfka didn't care for her but trusted her. Except with men.

Luc sat proudly between the two women, like a cock sandwich, certain he was the object of their joint desires. In fact they both used him, in their different ways.

Ryfka said: 'I want a car, Luc. Something that can move. A traction avant. Not some old gazo. And by the morning.'

Luc nearly fell off the sofa. '*Tomorrow* morning?'

'Tomorrow morning.'

'Impossible, baby. Impossible.'

*

Blech was drunk, but not stupidly. He had a girl on his knee and was feeling her casually while talking to Loubain, with whom he was sharing a table. Loubain was alone, though several girls had offered to join him. In the event of an Allied invasion Blech had orders to arrest him because Raab didn't trust him. If that were the only reason most of France would have to be arrested.

The place was full of German officers, mostly SS, though there were some Wehrmacht officers and a Luftwaffe pilot on crutches. Most of them had girls with them. The Luftwaffe pilot, leaning on his crutches, started singing *Lilli Marlene* to piano accompaniment. At first he could hardly be heard in the general hubbub, but gradually it died down as the clear tenor voice rose through the cigar and cigarette smoke that hung in the air like blue mist.

Aus dem tiefen Raume,
Aus der erde Grund,
Hebt sich wie im Traume
Dein verliebter Mund...

'What the hell's it supposed to mean?' said the girl on Blech's knee.

'Learn German, you cretin,' said Blech.

' "Out of deepest space, out of the very earth," ' said Loubain, ' "there rises like a dream your beloved mouth." '

'Ah, lovely,' said the girl. 'Isn't that lovely?'

'Actually,' said Blech, 'it's all about a whore who doesn't give a shit for love.'

The song ended to applause and uproar as a drunken young SS officer clambered on to a table and started to sing an obscene song. Almost immediately Dominique appeared. 'Come on, Willi, get down.'

'Go to hell,' said Willi, trying to keep his balance.

'Please, Willi, be a good boy.'

'Get down, Willi,' roared Blech, 'or I'll have you clapped in the bloody guardhouse.'

Willi got down, with some help.

'Thank you, gentlemen,' said Dominique. 'We don't want the authorities to think we run a disorderly house, do we?'

Ryfka stuck to side streets and alleyways, where possible, to avoid main road controls. But near the Place des Lices a black Citroën shot out of a side street and pulled up alongside her. Two SS officers jumped out.

Part of the street was bright with moonlight and involuntarily she shrank back into the shadows like a frightened girl, slipped a hand into her pocket and cocked the Walther P38, then touched the floating pin above the hammer to reassure herself there was a bullet in the breech.

'Where are you going, madame?' said the taller of the two, shining a torch in her face. 'Curfew starts in ten minutes.' He was close enough to jump her if she tried to draw the gun. She could shoot through the pocket. But only once. 'After that,' her sergeant instructor used to say, 'it's a pound to a pinch of shit the slide will catch in your coat lining and jam. Unless you happen to be in a movie, dear.'

She gave him the address of the hotel where she'd registered. It was an old trick of hers to have a legitimate address, even if she didn't use it.

'Your papers, please.'

She took her hand out of her pocket, opened her shoulderbag and produced her *carte d'identité*.

'Camille Brossart. Bookseller. Born in Colmar. That's in Alsace, isn't it? You speak German, then?'

'Natuerlich,' she said, not knowing what else to say. She felt sure he'd recognized her and was playing games.

He smiled. 'Read any good books lately?'

She slipped her hand in her pocket again, felt for the P38. She might as well try a shot through the pocket. At least she'd have the advantage of surprise. And one good shot.

Then he snapped to attention, saluted. The other officer followed suit like an automaton.

'Gute nacht, Fräulein.'

'Gute nacht,' she said faintly.

90

8

Dog minus 11

God, it was cold. The dawn wind went through her slacks and sweater with icy fingers and the Place des Lices was empty apart from a couple of bums asleep against a *pissoir*. Like the opening of that Hemingway story. *You know how it is there in Havana in the early morning with the bums still asleep against the walls ... before even the ice wagons come by* ... It ended in death and disaster, she remembered. The thought depressed her. So did the black Citroën waiting for her like a hearse in the courtyard of the block where Luc and Victor lived.

Next to it was Luc's old van with Luc sitting inside, hunched over the wheel, smoking a cigarette and looking nervous. He got out when he saw her.

'Something wrong?'

'No deal,' he said. 'The man wants sixty grand.'

'For a day's hire? Does he think I'm buying it?'

'There's a refund of forty thousand if you bring it back alive. And it includes a tankful of black market petrol – at fifty francs a litre.'

'For sixty grand he throws in the petrol.'

'I told him,' said Luc, 'I told him. No deal, baby, I said. No deal.'

One side of her mouth lifted. 'What was your cut? Baby.'

He spread his arms. 'Would I do a thing like that to you?'

'Not twice. So stick to screwing your so-called cousin.'

She took the road for Montfort, turned left at l'Hermitage, through Cintré and on to Talensac. Tournier's farm was on the other side of Talensac, close to the Forêt de Montfort, which was really more of a *bois* than a *forêt*.

It was in an isolated position, at the end of a long narrow lane and hidden by trees. She drove up the lane, through a gateway, then saw the farmhouse and outbuildings ahead of her. A track to her left led through a screen of trees and bushes to other outbuildings. Garages for the heavy farm vehicles, judging from the ruts in the track.

She pulled up in the farmyard, switched off. Silence. Not a dog barked, not a hen clucked. She got out, looked around. Still no sound. Only the sudden *tak-tak-tak* of a worried blackbird. And the wind walking through the trees. All it needs, she thought, is a creaking door and I'll bolt.

Behind her a door creaked. She spun round, going for her gun. But it was just the wind swinging the door of a dilapidated barn. And that dam' silence, playing on her nerves like an unseen presence. She went to the barn and kicked the door open. Empty. A few bales of hay and an old coat hanging on a nail. She let out a long breath and put the gun away.

But where was the farmer? Still in Gestapo hands? And his family? And the dog? No dog. That worried her.

As she crossed to the farmhouse she noted a footpath at the back leading in the direction of the garages. *Always look for possible escape routes, the instructors said.*

She gumshoed along the side of the farmhouse, peering in at the windows. Comfortable and clean with a lived-in look. Not a soul about though till she came to the kitchen window. She looked in and saw a man in an RAF pullover sitting at a table drinking coffee. She couldn't see his face and didn't want to. She didn't want to look at him. Just creep up behind him and get it over with. Then get out. She put her hand in her pocket, felt for the P38, pushed back the safety catch, checked the floating pin with her thumb. But she needed positive identification. Something more than just an RAF pullover.

The kitchen door was unlocked. She opened it quietly, stepped inside.

'Air Commodore Romaine?'

He swung round. The stranger on the train. It was like a kick under the heart. She waited for a sign of recognition, but he stared at her blankly. A nasty little doubt jabbed her. After two years could she really be sure?

'Who are you?' he said. Another kick.

So he didn't even recognize her. She pushed her hair back to reveal the scar. Still no sign of recognition.

'I thought . . .' She stopped, confused, unsure.

'Yes?'

'I thought perhaps I'd . . . met you before somewhere.'

He looked at her blank-faced. 'I'm afraid you have the advantage of me.'

She felt a sudden flush of anger. She'd spent a night in his arms – well, more or less – and he didn't even *remember*.

'Where's the farmer?'

'Tournier? Went to visit his old mother in Rennes. Took his wife along. And the dog.'

'When's he coming back?'

'Yesterday, he said. But maybe he decided to stay over.' He paused, his eyes examined her. 'You must be from one of the special forces.'

'The Le Courts took you in, looked after you. Then you upped and left them – in the middle of the night – without a word. Why?'

He shrugged. 'Didn't trust *him*. She was all right, but . . .' He shook his head. 'There was something funny about him.'

His eyes held her. 'What exactly is your mission?'

'To get you back to England.'

'Who sent you?'

'I must ask you to follow my instructions.'

'And if I don't?'

'I'll blow your head off,' she said and drew the gun.

'Of course. The old fail-safe clause.'

She raised the gun, sighted along it, aiming at the heart. Her own felt like a shard of dry ice. She could hear a clock ticking, yet time was standing still.

Then she heard something else. And whipped round towards the window. 'What was that?'

'What?'

'A noise. Something.'

She moved to the window, peered out from behind the curtain. The farmyard was empty but she still couldn't get

93

rid of the feeling she'd had all along: that someone was out there.

'Didn't you hear anything?' she said, turning from the window.

'Like what?'

'A sort of click. Maybe a gun being cocked.'

'Or the wind rattling something.'

She moved quietly to the door. 'Wait till I give you the all clear. Then come out.'

She opened the door an inch at a time, then put her head out. Nothing. She stepped outside, gun in hand. Still nothing.

She turned and called softly: 'Okay, all clear.'

Nothing happened. Then she heard him say in a low voice: 'Come back inside.'

She kicked the door open and saw him standing by the window.

'Come on out,' she said. 'With your hands up.'

She'd do it outside. It would be easier outside. She'd suffocate in that kitchen.

He put his hands up, shook his head. 'You should have listened to me', he said quietly as he stepped out into the farmyard.

Then she realized he was staring straight past her. She spun round. There were SS troops and Gestapo all over the place. And more coming out of the woodwork. All with guns pointing at her. Some were leaning on the bonnet of her car to steady their aim.

'Drop your gun!' A harsh German voice. Blech.

If only she'd told Romaine to step out ahead of her. A pull of the trigger and her mission would have been over. Now if she tried anything she'd be dead before she could blink.

'Drop it!' Blech again.

She dropped it. It hit the ground with a thud exaggerated by the stillness.

Then Raab's voice: 'I'm coming out.'

Her eyes made a quick tour of the farm buildings. The

94

creaking barn door was pushed open and Raab came out and made his way through the crowd of SS and Gestapo.

Everything was suddenly clear. They couldn't have moved into position till after she'd gone into the farmhouse. They must have parked their transport with the farm vehicles at the end of the rutted track. And waited for her – in those bloody outhouses around the farmyard. Including the barn she'd searched. But of course the bastards didn't move till she went into the farmhouse.

They were waiting for her. She'd been set up

Raab was standing before her, smiling. He rarely smiled, either from disinclination or because he had bad teeth.

'Ryfka. Meine kleine Ryfka,' he said, softly as a lover. Then he hit her in the face, and the farm buildings went upside down and she was looking at a blue sky with cotton wool clouds, slowly revolving above her. She felt blood come into her mouth and a boot go into her kidneys.

Then there was a commotion, an explosion almost. Harry Romaine was coming to her rescue. He disappeared under a scrum of SS men. Raab ran towards them, screeching: 'I want him alive!'

Everyone's attention was on the struggle. And a struggle it was. Romaine fought like a madman, managed to wrench a pistol from an SS holster and started pulling the trigger. Before they overpowered him one man was dead, three were wounded.

And Ryfka had vanished.

Neatly parked at the end of the track were several Gestapo cars, a troop carrier and Raab's personal transport, an armoured car. After the seventh attempt on Raab's life in two years the SS general in overall charge of security in France had insisted he travel by armoured car.

She wondered if she'd be able to drive it. She'd driven one once, during a training exercise . . . No, that was crazy. Take one of the *traction avants*. They were fast and easy to handle.

*

95

The moment he saw she was missing Raab knew she must have taken the short cut from the farmhouse to the garages.

'She's after the cars,' he called out to Blech. 'Take her car and cut her off before she gets to the road.'

Blech and three Gestapo piled into the Citroën and went off in a cloud of dust. Raab ordered a detachment of SS to follow on foot.

Blech kept his foot hard down and the car bucketed along the rough track, raising more dust. He rounded a sharp bend and shrieked: 'Jesus Christ!'

Coming straight at him was Raab's armoured car. He pulled the wheel hard over to get off the track, but wasn't quick enough. The armoured car ploughed straight into the side of the Citroën with a terrible graunching sound, knocked it over and into the bushes – and ploughed straight on.

Blech and the Gestapo man in the front, though badly shaken, managed to clamber out. The armoured car was just turning off the track into the lane. The Gestapo man whipped out a pistol and started firing wildly at it. 'You might as well try a pea-shooter,' said Blech.

It was quite an experience, almost enjoyable but for the noise and the fact that she wasn't quite sure what she was doing. It really was awfully noisy. But you felt awfully safe. And as Raab's command vehicle it was equipped with a powerful radio. The SS truck and at least one of the Gestapo cars would also be equipped with radio. And by now Raab would be calling for roadblocks. She switched on and listened to the babble of German, regularly punctuated by *Achtung! Achtung!*

Well, it would take some roadblock to stop this baby. She leaned forward and looked through the front observation slit. The road ahead was clear, but there'd be a roadblock at the first junction. She could hear the instructions going out.

Raab never shouted. But he spoke into the transmitter of

96

the SS troop carrier with an acidity that would have etched a steel plate.

'Then get some heavy vehicles. Tractors, trucks, anything. But stop her. Yes, I know it has a ninety millimetre cannon – it's my personal transport – and a light machine gun. No, you idiot, you can't. By the time they got there she'd be back in England. Over and out.' He turned to Blech. 'She's crashed through one roadblock, shelled another, machine-gunned Gestapo cars. And now they want to call up the SS Panzer division at Redon for a couple of Tigers.'

She went through two more junctions with no sign of a roadblock, which made her suspicious. At the third junction she realized why. They'd been busy setting up the big one: three heavy trucks across the road and three more behind. She couldn't smash through that lot. She slowed down saw a turning on the right and took it. Almost immediately she had to cross a wooden bridge over a stream. It collapsed as she drove over it. The supports had been sawn through. A trap. And she'd fallen right into it. Then her head hit a metal bulwark and blackness pierced by a thousand shooting stars descended on her.

She came to in the back of a car, wedged between a couple of Gestapo men. In front, next to the driver, the young SS captain who had set the trap was speaking over a two-way radio.

'Hier ist Hauptsturmfuehrer Pohl . . .' He was having a hard job containing his pride.

She looked down at her hands. They were lying in her lap, handcuffed. The Gestapo men on either side of her were looking out of the window. Nobody was paying attention to her, probably because they thought she was still out.

She thought of trying to ease a hand inside the waistband of her slacks to reach the little single-shot pistol . . . But it was too difficult and it wouldn't work anyway. The driver, who was driving very fast, had a fat white neck that folded over his tight collar. A ridge of short silky hair divided the nape vertically. An inviting target. She imagined a black

97

hole appearing in it, the car going out of control and crashing . . . At that speed they'd probably all be killed. Though you'd stand a better chance if you were expecting the crash . . . Six months ago she'd have tried it without hesitation. Now the thought of it made her shake. But thought of the coming torture made her shake even more.

'Marvellous,' said Raab, who wasn't given to extravagant language. 'And like all the best plans, simple. Young Ernst Pohl is due for promotion. I shall see to it.'

He was being driven by Blech to the village outside Rennes where Ryfka had been captured.

'Did she put up much of a fight?' said Blech.

'She was knocked out in the crash. Anyway, we have her gun.' He held up the P38. Then his expression changed and he reached for the radio. 'When *we* caught her and stripped her . . .'

'We found she had a hidden gun,' said Blech, trying not to smile. 'Good job you remembered, mein Herr.'

But Raab wasn't listening.

'Achtung!' he was saying with a quiet but steely urgency into the radio transmitter. 'Hauptsturmfuehrer Pohl! Achtung! Achtung!'

The car swerved violently, hit something and turned over. The world was spinning and she heard a faraway sound of rending metal, then blacked out. The next thing she knew the car was upside down. Steam was hissing from a broken radiator, someone was moaning. The hissing died, the moaning went on.

Then the radio spoke: 'Hauptsturmfuehrer Pohl! Achtung! Achtung!' But Hauptsturmfuehrer Pohl, whose head was resting on the radio, was no longer listening. She had a strange feeling. As if she were watching something she wasn't involved in, like a film. The driver had a black hole in the back of his neck and the lower half of his face was missing. The windscreen in front of him was shattered.

One of the Gestapo men was still moaning, the other was unconscious or dead.

She knew her head was cut because blood ran down her face, half blinding her. But she didn't feel any pain. She didn't feel anything. Perhaps it was all a dream. What was she holding a gun for? One of the rear passenger doors must have burst open on impact. She ought to try and clamber out, but couldn't make the effort. Besides her hands were manacled.

Then she found herself outside the car. But she couldn't remember climbing out. Which proved it was a dream.

The car was partly on its roof in a ditch and leaning drunkenly to one side. Ludicrous. Pathetic. Poor little car. She felt like weeping.

As she walked unsteadily away the radio crackled on. 'Achtung! Achtung!'

The young priest at the church of Saint Sauveur, on the western outskirts of Rennes, had finished hearing confessions. The church was empty apart from three or four whiskery crones in black bombazine, publicly at prayer in a front pew before retiring for coffee and scandal. He remained alone in the confessional, as he often did, for one of those sessions of sweet silent thought and remembrance of things past. Remembrance wasn't always sweet, though, as a sudden roar of low-flying aircraft reminded him.

It brought back memories of a Blitzkrieg wedding of 1940. The groom, a boy of eighteen or nineteen in a uniform that fitted where it touched, was about to depart for the front, leaving behind a heavily pregnant bride. Only their peasant families and nearest available relatives were at the ceremony, hardly more than a dozen people. And all as stolid as the ruminants in their fields.

He was about to declare them man and wife when an air-raid warning sounded, followed by anti-aircraft fire, machine-gun fire and then that sudden roar of aircraft. And bombs falling, falling, falling, each one nearer than the last. Till the whole church was shaking. And the young priest with it.

The couple and their ruminant relations stared stolidly up at the roof.

'Fokke-Wulfs, I think,' said the groom.

The bride smiled up at him. She always knew he was a clever boy.

The young priest suddenly couldn't take any more. 'Please excuse me,' he muttered and got hastily down on hands and knees to crawl under a pew. The peasants watched him with round dispassionate eyes.

The raid was over as abruptly as it began. The young priest got to his feet, dusted himself down and completed the ceremony as soon as he decently could. The married couple and their peasant relations thanked him kindly and left. But he felt diminished in their eyes. And in his own.

When everyone had gone he sat down in the empty church and wept. That was nearly four years ago, but the feeling of shame came back as hotly as ever. The boy never came back at all.

He became aware of a disturbance in the church, heard the crones twitter like frightened birds. He sniffed back his emotion, went quickly out of the confessional and into the nave.

A woman was coming towards him, swaying like a drunk, her face covered in blood, her hands manacled in front of her. She looked on the point of collapse. He went to her, put an arm round her. Up close he could hear the rasp of her breathing.

'Gestapo,' she said.

The twittering of the crones rose to a crescendo. The young priest turned on them. 'Go to the café as you always do. And breathe not a word of what you have seen to anyone. *Anyone*. You hear me?' He lowered his voice to little more than a hiss. 'Or I shall put a most unholy curse on every one of you.'

As they started to promise and protest he pointed to the big double doors of the west front. 'Go!'

They went, squeaking and twittering like black mice.

He turned to Ryfka, put his arm round her again, and led her to the south door of the church.

'There were people outside who saw me come in,' she said. 'Someone may talk to the Gestapo.'

'My house is close by,' he said. 'You'll be safe there.'

Raab and Blech reached the scene of the crash as stretcher-bearers were carrying Pohl and the Gestapo men to the ambulance.

'Two dead, two injured,' said Raab, staring at the over-turned car. 'One with a broken leg, the other with a broken back.' He turned to Blech. 'And *she* walks away.'

'Perhaps the gods of war are on her side,' said Blech, who was mildly superstitious, but not to the extent of believing in *Blut und Boden* and all the other hocus-pocus of Nazi mythology.

'Shit,' said Raab. 'You talk shit. She's handcuffed and she must have been hurt – there's blood all over the place. She can't have got far. I want the area flooded with SS, Gestapo and local milice. I want her found.'

Mathilde, the priest's leathery old housekeeper, bathed her face with surprising gentleness, wiping away the blood and revealing the scar, livid against her pale skin. The priest stared at it in surprise. 'Are you . . .' He stopped, too embarrassed to add, 'the Scarred One?'

'Of course it is,' said Mathilde. 'Who else?'

'That cut on your head will need stitching,' said the priest. 'I'll ring the doctor.'

'No,' said Ryfka, 'ring the Café Select and ask for Luc. And tell him to bring a picklock for Gestapo handcuffs.'

Luc was about to pour cognac into his coffee when Georges Belami came in and made straight for him. He took one look at Belami's white face and shaking hands and pushed the cognac across the table towards him. Belami gulped it down.

'Christ,' he said, 'why didn't you *tell* me you wanted the car for that bloody woman?'

'What are you talking about, Georges?'

'That woman,' said Belami. 'La Balafrée. That's what I'm talking about. Driving my bloody car. The bloody Gestapo recognized it. And so they should. The bastards *sold* it to me.'

'Take a seat, Georges, and keep your voice down.'

Belami sat down opposite him but still had the shakes. Luc called to the girl behind the bar for more coffee and cognac. She was big and fat and slatternly, but he fancied her.

He turned reluctantly away. 'Now, tell us what happened.'

'All I know is they arrested her and some airman somewhere out of town,' said Belami. 'Next thing the bloody Gestapo are hammering at the door. I nearly shit a brick, I tell you.'

The fat girl served the coffee and cognac and Luc smiled at her. She ignored him. 'But you spun 'em a tale, huh?'

'Said I hired it out to a stranger for cash, didn't I? Which was near enough true. I've never met her, thank God. But if I'd known you wanted that car for something *illegal* –'

'You thought we just wanted it to go to church in. For sixty grand.'

'Listen, if the Gestapo start getting rough with me –'

'You'll keep your mouth shut,' said Luc quietly, 'or you'll find yourself at a funeral. With lots of flowers. But *you* won't smell 'em.'

'Don't threaten me, you bastard,' said Belami.

The slattern called out: 'Telephone, Luc, you slob.'

Luc went to the zinc-topped bar. 'If you were made of chocolate,' he told her, 'I'd eat you.' He picked up the telephone. "Allo? Luc here.' He listened deadpan. Then he said: 'I'll pick up Josef and be right over.'

Luc's ancient wood-burning van was stopped at a roadblock at the western end of rue de Brest.

'Where are you going?' said the young SS officer in charge.

'To the Bar Kazimierz,' said Josef. 'For a drink.'

'What have you got in the back?'

'A few bags of potatoes,' said Luc.

The SS officer poked his head in the driving cab, sniffed. 'Are you drunk?'

'Of course he's not,' said Josef. 'Bit pissed maybe, but not drunk.'

'Here,' said Luc, taking out a cellophane packet. 'Pair of nylons for your girl.'

'The only place you can get nylons is England. The Americans brought them over.'

'You can get them in Spain, in Switzerland. All over. If you have connections. I have connections.'

The young SS officer pocketed the nylons and turned to Josef. 'You have a funny sort of accent in French.'

'So have you,' said Josef.

'Where are you from?'

'Cracow. Came here in 'thirty-two.'

'Your papers.' He turned to Luc. 'And yours.'

They produced their papers. The SS officer glanced at them, handed them back. Then he said to two SS men: 'Have a look in the back.'

'Say,' said Luc, 'what are you really looking for?'

'A woman.'

'Ah,' said Luc. 'Aren't we all?'

One of the SS men called out: 'Nothing except some bags of potatoes, Herr Obersturmfuehrer.'

'All right,' said the SS officer. 'Fuck off.'

'Heil Hitler,' said Luc, sticking his arm out of the driver's window.

'Heil Hitler,' echoed Josef, sticking his arm out of the other window. 'And up the thousand-year Reich.'

The church of Saint Sauveur was still empty when the Gestapo sergeant and one of his men searched it.

'We'll talk to the priest,' said the sergeant. 'He's chicken. And if he's hiding anyone he'll soon squawk.'

Opposite the church was the street where the priest lived. As they crossed towards it Luc's old wood-burning van careered round the corner and nearly ran them down.

'Christ,' said the Gestapo man, jumping aside. 'They must've robbed a bank.'

'So what?' said the sergeant. 'The Fuehrer's robbed the lot.'

*

103

The priest was at his desk composing a sermon on the text that the meek shall inherit the earth, when the Gestapo called. The leathery housekeeper showed them into the book-lined study. The priest looked up and asked if he could help them.

'A woman we want to question was seen entering your church a short while ago,' said the sergeant. 'She was staggering and had blood on her face. Did you see her?'

'I spent over two hours hearing confessions and when I left the church it was empty.'

'I asked if you saw her.' The sergeant's cold eyes probed him.

'If I had,' said the priest, 'I should have given her immediate succour and comfort.'

'She's a criminal.'

'In the eyes of God or the eyes of man?'

'Don't chop logic with me, you pious bastard. Or I'll break your legs.'

'Blessed are the merciful,' said the priest, standing up. 'For they shall obtain mercy.' He folded his arms because they were beginning to shake and stared into the cold eyes. 'I hope, from the bottom of my heart, that you too will obtain mercy when the day comes. As come it must.'

'You're going the wrong way,' said Josef, and added gloomily, 'not that it matters. Whichever way we'll hit that goddam' roadblock. And then they'll find her.'

'Don't worry, we'll take her to see Charlot.'

'Who the hell's Charlot?'

'Someone who owes me.'

Luc pulled up in a street of mean-looking houses and knocked at a door that was opened by a mean-looking man.

'It's no good,' he said. 'I still haven't got it.'

'I'm after your advice,' said Luc, 'not your money.'

'My advice?' said Charlot.

'About drains,' said Luc.

They went into the kitchen and Charlot produced a sketch plan and spread it on the table.

'I drew it myself,' he said with some pride. 'Partly from old plans, some of which have since been lost.'

'You're a genius,' said Luc, leaning over the plan. 'What I want to do is get from here to here – without going through that bit there. Where there happens to be an SS control. Savvy?'

'That shouldn't be difficult,' said Charlot, also leaning over the plan.

'You mind not getting too close?' said Luc. 'You stink.'

'I bath twice a day. Sometimes more.'

'Maybe it gets into the clothes. Or your soul.'

'This part of the system isn't used any more and has been blocked off, apart from access manholes. Marked in red. You need a special tool to open them, but I can give you that. One other problem, the layout's a bit complicated and you could get lost.'

'We won't get lost,' said Luc. 'Because you're coming with us.'

'Oh, shit,' said Charlot.

'Quite so,' said Luc. 'But not too much, I hope. We have a lady with us.'

Luc had no trouble at the roadblock. After his men had searched the van the young SS officer said: 'And where's your friend?'

'Still at the Bar Kazimierz, I expect.' Luc mimed emptying a glass.

The young officer grinned and waved him through.

The street he was looking for was less than a minute away. He drove slowly along it till he spotted the manhole cover, then pulled into the kerb. Almost immediately the cover was pushed up and Charlot appeared, then Ryfka, then Josef. Ryfka had a bloodstained bandage round her head and leaned heavily against Josef. As she got in the van with Josef she looked terrible, Luc thought.

He drove quickly to the Place des Lices, which was packed with market-day crowds, and pulled up. 'It'll be quicker to walk across the square than try to drive through that lot.'

But walking was slow. She was weak and needed help. He and Josef, each taking an arm, supported her on either side.

'I think I'm going to faint,' she said.

'Try and hold on,' said Luc. 'We're almost there.'

But as they started to cross the Place des Lices an SS patrol appeared out of nowhere and yelled: 'Halt!'

Josef picked Ryfka up in his arms and plunged into the milling crowds. Luc pushed ahead, to clear a passage for them. The Germans tried to follow, screaming at the crowds and firing bursts in the air with automatic weapons.

The light was failing, she was losing consciousness, losing her bearings. She seemed to be on a dark heaving sea that was holding her up, yet holding her back. A mysterious white-flecked sea. She could hear its murmurs as plainly as a child holding a seashell to its ear.

And down the back garden the sound comes to me,
Of the lapsing, unsoilable, whispering sea . . .

She could hear Josef too, faint and faraway, shouting in his strange Polish-accented French: 'Résistance! Aidez-nous! Résistance! Aidez-nous!'

And Luc's voice, rising like a shrill wind: 'Résistance! Aidez-nous!'

And the murmurs rising, swelling to a roar. And the dark mass, flecked with white faces, suddenly parting before her like the Red Sea before Moses.

And then she was swept into the comfort of its darkness and her own.

9

In the enveloping darkness she became aware of hands undressing her. Two pairs of hands. And two voices, a man's and a woman's, talking about her. They sounded faint, perhaps because of the hammering in her head.

'How can men do that to a woman?'

A woman's voice that sounded familiar. Then a man's voice, irritable, nervous, less familiar. 'You mean the scars? Surely you've come across sadism? I thought it was quite commonplace in your business.'

'Not like this.'

'It's a matter of degree. And having a free hand. The Gestapo have a free hand.'

She opened her eyes, flinched at the evening sun flooding the room, and closed them again. But not before she'd caught sight of Dominique and a man she recognized but couldn't place. Small and untidy, dark hair streaked with grey, and a ragged edge of beard that gave him a piratical look at odds with his nervousness.

He must have gone to the window and pulled down the venetian blind, she could feel the dimming of the light through her lids. She opened her eyes as he came back to the bed.

'How are you feeling?'

Her memory came back. Charvet. Philippe Charvet, the resistance doctor.

'Stiff and sore. A headache. That's all.'

'You've had quite a bang on the head. It'll need stitching. I'll give you a local anaesthetic.'

'Save it for someone who needs it. I know you're short of the stuff.'

'That's my problem,' the little doctor said irritably. 'You will not suffer avoidable pain at my hands.'

He gave her the local anaesthetic, cleaned the head

wound and stitched it. 'You have some bruising over the kidneys. Were you kicked there?'

'I was kicked somewhere.'

'Have you passed water since you got back?'

'No.'

'If you see any blood in it let me know. You're also suffering from concussion and shock. Rest in bed is the only cure.'

She watched him put his things away in a black bag. 'I can't stay in bed. I've a lot to do.'

He took two pills from a box, poured water in a glass from a carafe on the bedside table. 'Take these now.'

'What are they? I hate taking pills.'

'They'll ease your headache.'

She swallowed them and made a face.

'They will also make you sleep,' he said. 'I'll see you in the morning.'

Then he said something to Dominque and they went out. She could hear them talking in low tones on the landing and tried to sit up and listen. But the effort was too much and she dropped back on the pillow. The darkened room soothed her. And the throbbing in her head was beginning to recede. Then, as if a blackout curtain had come down, she was asleep.

It was dark when she awoke. Diffused moonlight filtered through the slats of the venetian blind. Enough to see that her clothes were on a chair by the window. She got out of bed and fetched them, then sat on the bed and started to dress.

The door opened quietly and she saw Josef, silhouetted against the landing light.

'Are you awake?' he said, blinking into the darkened room, his eyes not yet adapted.

'Draw the blackout curtains, would you, and put the light on.'

By the time the light was on she'd pulled on a blouse and slacks, but was beginning to feel shaky. She got back on the bed and looked at her watch. Half past eight.

'How are you?' said Josef.

'Peckish,' she said.

'There's vegetable soup with chopped sausage in it.'

'Any news?'

'The Gestapo have pulled in Belami.'

'I thought that was a book by de Maupassant.'

'The one Luc hired the car from.'

'Will he talk?'

'Luc's not waiting to find out. He's moving into another pad.'

'Where is he now?'

Josef jerked his head. 'Downstairs.'

'Bring him with you when you bring me the soup. Michel too. But give me another ten minutes or so, I want to rest my eyes. They're beginning to hurt.'

'I'll turn the light out.'

When Josef had gone she put her head on the pillow and tried to rest, but couldn't. Twice Harry Romaine had come to her rescue, like a knight at arms. And his reward would be a bullet. Well, the days of chivalry were over. And plenty of men would die in this war and be forgotten, except perhaps by the girls they left behind them. *The pallor of girls' brows shall be their pall; Their flowers the tenderness of patient minds* . . .

She remembered the night of the air raid, his body over her like a shield . . . She still couldn't decide whether it really was the same man. Not that it mattered now. He'd have to die anyway.

'Have the Luftwaffe asked for him?' said Raab, leaning back in his swivel chair.

Blech, sitting on the other side of the desk, shook his head. 'They may think they've got them all. He was flying as additional aircrew, remember.'

'They'll find out when they question the others. Then they'll be on the phone, yelling for him. At least, the Graf von Kirchen-whatsisname will.'

'Von Kirchen-Wehbach.'

'How is the prisoner? Recovering?'

'Deteriorating, they think, mein Herr,' said Blech.

'They *think?*' said Raab. 'Don't they know? They have a doctor.'

'He's on leave, mein Herr.'

'Is he the only doctor in town?'

'The only one left who speaks English, it seems. And he's on his rounds.'

'The only one left?'

'There were three Jew doctors who spoke English, but they've been deported, mein Herr.'

'Perhaps we should have deported some of the others with them,' said Raab. 'For all the use they are. However, we can do without von Kirchen-Shitbags screaming down the phone.' He pressed the switch of his desk intercom. 'Get me the governor of Rennes prison.'

'Will you want to question the prisoner yourself, mein Herr?'

Raab shook his head. 'He was just an instructor at some RAF flying school, according to Le Court. Though it might be of interest to the Luftwaffe.'

The phone rang and Raab picked it up. 'Yes? Put him through. Good evening, Governor. I understand you're worried about the condition of the prisoner Romaine. So am I. And I want him to have the best attention before being handed over to the Luftwaffe. You can be assured of my co-operation.'

He hung up and stared into the distance. 'Why *did* they send her back?' He spoke softly, as if to himself, but then turned and looked directly at Blech.

'Local knowledge must have been a factor.'

'In that case what's so important about the former Horseman territory? It doesn't include any of the likely invasion areas. Yet I feel that at this stage of the war her mission must have something to do with the Second Front.'

There was a long silence, then Blech said: 'Perhaps it's something simple like . . .' He shrugged. 'Like getting the airman back.'

'A squadron leader? Hardly. No, the attempt to recover him was merely . . .' Raab waved dismissively. 'En passant. She's done that sort of thing before.'

'Perhaps we should ask avenue Foche or even the Haupt-amt to run a check on him. They'll have copies of the London Gazette on file and other information about British service personnel.'

'May as well go through the motions, I suppose.' Raab shrugged. 'But *she's* the key to the mystery. Find her and we'll find out what her mission is.' He rubbed his hairless chin. 'Or I'll show her things de Sade never dreamed of.'

Blech nodded, but he was no longer listening. Through a gap in the screens he could see Solange. She was on the other side of the salon, standing against the light in cami-knickers, being fitted for a dress. She towered over the tiny Bernadette. He tried not to look at her, but his eyes kept straying in that direction. Her hands, delicate for someone so big, fluttered like small birds.

'A penny for them, Blech.'

'Oh,' said Blech, 'I was, er . . . wondering what they were talking about, mein Herr.'

'I will tell you, Blech. They are talking about clothes or cooking. Or some cheap romance they've been reading. Trivia, Blech. To which they address themselves with the earnestness of medieval Schoolmen disputing how many angels can dance on the point of a pin.'

'I like the dress,' Solange's hands were saying. 'And the way it changes colour with the light. They are watching us. Do not look at them. One day he will kill me. Not from hatred, but to save me from my own people when the Germans withdraw from France. Or so he tells himself. But also because he likes killing. It's neat. And he's a very neat man.'

'He has talked to you about these things?' Bernadette's hands said.

'No.'

'How can you bear to stay with him?'

Solange smiled and her fluttering hands said: 'Habit. Besides, there is nowhere to go.'

'You can come to us. You can always come to us.'

A smaller, sadder smile. 'He will want to kill you too. But do not fear, he cannot hide his plans from me.'

*

111

'Where are they holding him?' Ryfka said between spoonfuls of soup. 'At the Hotel Abelard?'

She was sitting propped up by pillows, with the bowl of soup on a tray in front of her. Luc, Josef and Michel were gathered round the foot of the bed.

'In the hospital block of Rennes prison,' said Luc. 'So the guards told Jacques Lacaze. Seems he put up quite a fight.'

'Is he badly hurt?'

'Jacques says the prison doctor was worried about handing him over to the Luftwaffe – who play hell if their prisoners are beaten up or injured by the Gestapo.'

'Jacques still has the grocery shop opposite the prison?'

Luc nodded. 'That's how he keeps on good terms with the guards. Sells them wine for next to nothing. Which is about what it's worth. It has the bouquet of old drains.'

She finished the soup and pushed the tray away. Josef put it on a side table. 'I need more information,' she said. 'What about the Jewish tailor Raab uses?'

'Yaka Mnouchkine?' Luc shook his head. 'Stay away from him. The bastard's a collaborator.'

'That's how he survived, I suppose.'

'Plus the fact that his daughter's the only one who can chat to Raab's mistress in that deaf-and-dumb lingo. I tell you, between them they've got a nice little racket going.'

'Mnouchkine. Where does he come from?'

'Germany. His wife got killed in those riots that night in 'thirty-eight – '

'Kristallnacht.'

'So he took the kid and shoved off. To get *away* from the Germans. That's laugh, isn't it?'

'A killer. And you don't think they'd help?'

'Help to sell you down the river.'

'I've been sold once today already.'

'Who by?'

'Another collaborator, I suppose. Set me up nicely.'

'You want him dealt with?' Josef cut in.

'No,' she said. 'He's got enough trouble. And he's no longer a danger. Who's the local Luftwaffe commander?'

'Kirchen-Wehbach,' said Josef. 'The Graf Udo von Kirchen-Wehbach, no less.'

Ryfka turned to Luc. 'Hear you've got a new pad.'

'I always keep a couple in reserve. For emergencies.'

'A couple? You mean you have another pad?'

'Fully furnished. Everything you're likely to need.'

'And a back door?'

'Goes without saying.'

'Could I have it for a few days?'

Luc spread his arms. 'When do you want to move in?'

'In about half an hour, if that's okay.'

'Hold on,' said Josef. 'The doctor said – '

'I know what he said, and I haven't time. Is Nikki le Stephanois still operating around the Forêt de Chevré?'

'In a limited way,' said Josef. 'With about six men, a few pistols and rifles, no automatic weapons and no explosives – he used up the last of it derailing a troop train.'

She turned to Michel. 'You've got a list of dropping zones and landing fields. Find one handy for Nikki – I think there's one near Dourdain – and ask London to parachute him some canisters of Sten guns, ammo and plastic explosive with Cordtex, primers, detonators and so on. Soon as possible. Oh yes, and some drugs for Dr Charvet. Josef, give him a ring, will you, and ask him what he needs. And can you get in touch with Nikki?'

Josef nodded. 'Marius at the Bar Kazimierz can contact him.'

'Do you want to tell London anything about the airman?' said Michel. 'They're bound to ask if you don't.'

'Tell them . . . Yes, tell them we've lost contact. No, temporarily lost contact with him.'

'Anything else?' said Michel.

'A P38 for me, if they can lay hands on one.'

'There's one at the pad you're going to,' said Luc. 'I always keep a spare gun at a spare pad. You never know.'

It was over a run-down shopping parade and approached by narrow stairs between a hardware store and a café. Two rooms, kitchen and bath. And the back door opened from the kitchen on to an outside iron staircase, which led down to a service road with exits at either end.

'I like it,' she said. 'Out of the way, a bit ribby, nice and secure.'

'I think I ought to stay and look after you,' said Luc.

'I think you ought to piss off,' said Ryfka sweetly. 'I have things to do.'

Luc shrugged. She was an ugly cow anyway, and he'd have been doing her a favour. It would have been a feather in *her* cap.

Yaka Mnouchkine was basting the sleeve to a uniform jacket when he heard the knock at the door. He wondered who it could be. Gestapo? No, they'd be *hammering* at the door. And it would be three o'clock in the morning. A client? Not this late. A friend? He had no friends. A surprise, then. He hoped not. Surprises were always a letdown.

He stuck the needle into the cloth and went out into the dimly lit passage that led to the front door. He hesitated, took off his yarmulka and stuffed it in his pocket. This was no time to be Jewish. Then he opened the door.

It was a woman. Young, as far as he could make out in the weak glow of the masked ceiling light. Robin Hood hat, two-piece suit with long jacket, white blouse with military collar, high heels. As usual, he took in the clothes first. Then the face. High cheekbones framed by dark hair. Dark eyes. Fleshy lips. Strong jawline. That was about all he could make out. The hat, pulled down at the front, hid most of the face.

Ryfka saw a small, lean man with not much hair and shabby clothes. No advertisement for a tailor, she thought.

'Monsieur Mnouchkine?'

The voice was warm and pleasant, a bit husky. But he was apprehensive of strangers these days. 'What do you want?'

'A word.'

'What about?'

She shrugged. 'Clothes.'

'I make clothes for the Germans.'

'Your daughter too, I believe.'

'Who *are* you?'

A brief silence as the woman stood motionless in the darkness outside. Then the wind picked up and they both shivered.

'You'd better come in,' Yaka said, without quite knowing why. As he led her into his workroom she noticed he had a slight limp. 'Excuse the mess,' he said.

He picked up the uniform jacket and went on with his basting. The rhythms of work soothed him. There was something about the woman that made him nervous.

She looked around. There were four treadle sewing machines, half a dozen tailor's dummies, two cutting tables, one stacked with rolls of cloth, a long narrow wall mirror and a couple of free-standing mirrors. Two of the dummies were draped with unfinished uniform jackets, one of the SS, the other of the Luftwaffe, The rest were bare. On a row of hangers were other uniforms and suits in various stages of preparation.

'I used to employ six people,' he said.

'And now you work for the Germans.'

'And a few rich collaborators. Which are you?'

'Neither,' she said.

He looked up from his work. 'Are you . . .'

'From the resistance? That what you were going to say?'

'My neighbours tell me I'll be killed after the war. If the resistance don't get me first.'

She smiled. 'The resistance don't kill civilians.'

'They kill collaborators.'

'If they did, they'd have to do a lot of killing.' The smile became crooked because the scar was beginning to twitch her mouth to one side.

She went over to the blue-grey Luftwaffe jacket draped over a dummy. It had the collar patches and shoulder straps of a Hauptmann. 'That's the equivalent of a flight lieutenant in the RAF. Very smart.' She fingered the cloth. 'Nice bit of shmatte.'

Her odd manner and oblique speech made him even more nervous. He'd had trouble with his nerves ever since

115

the Kaiser's war. And postwar life hadn't improved them, especially since 1933.

'You want some clothes?'

'I'm not sure what I want.'

'Well, I could show you some pattern books.'

'I'm not talking about clothes,' she said. 'How do you get on with Raab?'

He put down his work. 'What do you mean? I just make clothes for him.' He hesitated. 'Well, sometimes in the evenings, I play old German songs for him. On the accordion.'

'Does he ever chat to you?'

'To a Jew? An Untermensch? He just gives me orders.'

'Does he talk freely in front of you, if other people are about?'

Yaka stared at her. 'You *are* resistance, aren't you?'

'You must know him pretty well. And your daughter's friendly with his mistress, isn't she?'

'Please leave my daughter out of it.' He took his yarmulka from his pocket and put it on. 'Have you come here to kill me?'

'Why are you so nervous?'

'I don't know.' He shrugged. 'I had shell shock once.'

She felt in her pocket. 'Would you like a cigarette?'

He shook his head. Then he said: 'You wouldn't have an English cigarette, I suppose?'

She smiled her crooked smile. 'It would be foolish of me to carry English cigarettes.' She took out a packet of Gitanes. 'These are all I have.'

'They're too strong. I shouldn't smoke at all, really. I got a whiff of gas on the Somme.'

'Will it upset you if I smoke?'

'Please,' he said. Her politeness was even more unnerving.

She lit a Gitane, breathed out twin streams of smoke. 'Is your daughter also deaf and dumb, like Solange?'

'Not like Solange,' he said and picked up the uniform jacket and started basting again. 'She saw her mother killed on Kristallnacht. In Frankfurt. They'd gone out together.

116

She came back alone. And couldn't even tell me about it. She'd lost her voice.' A deep breath. 'She was eight years old.'

'And she's never spoken since?'

Yaka kept his eyes on his work. 'Two years ago she started making dresses for Solange – and learned the language of the deaf and dumb. That's how they became friends.'

Ryfka smoked in silence for a while, then said: 'The other Jews were rounded up and deported, weren't they?'

Yaka nodded. 'About a year ago. We were rounded up too. There was this big SS raid on the Jewish quarter. Trucks rolling down the streets and SS men yelling: "Juden 'raus! Juden 'raus!" ' He looked up. 'I still hear them in my dreams.'

He put his work aside and started moving about the room, aimlessly tidying up, as if to occupy his hands.

Some months previously (he said) he'd built a false wall in an upper room for Bernadette to hide in the event of a round-up. There was no point in their both trying to hide because the SS would see the signs of occupation and tear the place apart. But he felt he might be able to persuade them that Bernadette had run away from home after a quarrel. Desperation must have lent his words conviction because the SS men believed the story – from what he heard them saying among themselves – but decided to beat him up anyway. He knew he mustn't cry out, for Bernadette's sake, and nearly bit his tongue through trying to keep quiet. Then a black curtain seemed to come down and he didn't remember any more. When he came to she was leaning over him, weeping silent tears.

They were driven to the station and herded into cattle trucks with other Jews. The sliding doors were pulled shut, the iron locking pieces rammed home, and they were left there in the dark, packed to suffocation, without food or water. Soon there was the stench of excrement.

Then a miracle happened. The doors were unlocked and pulled open and he heard the shout: 'Mnouchkine 'raus!' He fought his way out on to the platform, dragging Berna-

117

dette with him. They were told to go home. The other Jews were driven back with whips and gun butts.

His first feeling was one of unbelief. It was a trick. It must be. Then, as he realized they were free, came relief. Finally came guilt. Why should *they* be saved?

It seemed that when Solange heard of the round-up she became hysterical. Raab thought she was having convulsions. Then she gave him a note saying she would kill herself if Bernadette were deported. The mighty Raab shrugged, picked up the phone . . .

'And suddenly we were walking home, through the empty streets of the Jewish quarter. Like two ghosts.'

He picked up the basting needle, put it down again. He couldn't concentrate on work any more.

'Who *are* you?' he said.

She pushed her hair back from one side of her face. 'Does that mean anything to you?'

He stared at the scar slanting down from temple to jaw. 'I was in the Place des Lices when the SS tried to take you. La Balafrée. The name was on everyone's lips. And I prayed with all my heart you might escape. And now you come to . . . to kill me?'

'Mnouchkine sounds east European,' she said. 'Bessarabia, perhaps. Or the Bukhovina.'

'My family moved to Germany in the last century, and I was born there.' A small dry laugh. 'In 1914 I fought for Germany, bled for Germany. In 1938 I fled from Germany.'

'And sooner or later you'll be killed by Germany.'

'Or by good French patriots. Or by you.'

She shook her head. 'There are enough people killing Jews, without me.'

'Are you Jewish yourself?'

'My mother was.'

'That makes you a Jew under our law.'

'Not to mention German law.'

She wondered how far she could trust him. Nervous people weren't always reliable. Yet there was something about him . . . She took a deep breath. 'I need help,' she said.

'From me?'

'And your daughter.'

He hesitated. 'I'm afraid I haven't been entirely frank with you.'

'What do you mean?'

'Our rescue from the cattle truck was a miracle. It was also a shock. And the shock brought a second miracle. As we were walking home Bernadette suddenly said: "Papa! Ich spreche! Ich spreche!" And I took her in my arms in the middle of that empty street, and we wept. But I told her not to tell anyone she'd recovered her speech, not even Solange. You see, if you can't speak people forget you can still hear. They look on you as another deaf mute. And speak freely in front of you. I thought Bernadette might pick up information that might one day save our lives.' He shrugged. 'It was deceitful, perhaps pointless.'

Ryfka smiled. 'I think it was very sensible. And that's just what I need from you and your daughter: information.'

'Nothing easier,' said Yaka. 'She reports everything to me. What sort of information?'

'About a British airman in Rennes jail.'

'Ah, the squadron leader.'

'You've heard of him?'

'Of course. As you probably know, the Luftwaffe get angry if their prisoners are beaten up by Gestapo or SS. In fact, the local Luftwaffe colonel – '

'Graf von Kirchen-Wehbach?'

Yaka nodded. 'An aristocrat, from one of the old Kader Familien. You know, all duelling scars and punctilio. And a stickler for rules and regulations, including the Geneva Convention. Told Raab he'd come down and horsewhip him if another Luftwaffe prisoner is beaten up.'

'Have you ever met him?'

'I once made a dress uniform for him.'

'How did he treat you?'

'Very polite, very correct. It was always Herr Mnouchkine. With Raab it's just Jew. "Do this, Jew. Do that, Jew. Get the hell out of it, Jew." '

'Does Raab take the horsewhipping threat seriously?'

119

'I don't think so. But why not ask Bernadette? She'll be home soon.'

Suddenly she felt tired. The wound in her head was beginning to throb. 'I must go,' she said.

He saw her into the passage. 'It's a pity you can't wait. She won't be long. They always bring her back by car.'

'I've had quite a day,' she said. 'I'll call in the morning to see if you have any information.'

'One moment,' he said and took her into a gloomy little parlour smelling of mothballs and lavender. From a drawer in a rickety sideboard he took out what looked like a long jewel case and opened it. Inside, on worn and shabby velvet, lay the Knight's Cross of the Iron Cross with its black and white silk ribbon. In the lid of the case was a faded photograph of a frail-looking young man being decorated by a German field marshal, resplendent in the uniform and shako of a Death's Head Hussar. Despite the passage of time and the poor quality of the picture it was obvious who the young man was.

'I wasn't always nervous,' Yaka said.

Raab was working late in his office with an artist who had prepared roughs of a poster offering a reward of two million francs, twice the usual reward, for information leading to the capture of the British agent known as la Balafrée.

The dominant feature of the roughs was a charcoal sketch of Ryfka, based on a prison photo taken at the time of her capture, and before she was scarred. Like all prison photos the lighting was flat and harsh and the prisoner's face expressionless. Much of this, inevitably, had carried over into the sketch.

'No scar, no character,' Raab told the artist. 'And her face is far more alive than that, especially about the eyes.' He stood at the artist's shoulder as he sketched, driving him to despair with criticisms and rejections. 'Make the scar thinner. No, that's too thin. And why give her a Jewish nose? It might not be obvious from the photo, but it's shorter and straighter. Cheekbones higher, jawline stronger, lips fleshier. And the eyes . . . impossible to describe. But they're darker. And at times they . . . seem to *burn*.'

He stopped, shook his head. 'I could do better than that.'

Then why the fuck don't you, the artist wished he had the nerve to say.

'Right,' said Raab, 'let's start again.'

They worked all evening on the sketches, not even breaking for dinner. The artist was beginning to wonder if it would go on all night when Raab suddenly said: 'That'll do. You won't get much closer than that. In fact, it's not bad.'

He sent for sandwiches and a bottle of wine for the artist and had two white tablets and a glass of mineral water for himself.

Then he put the sketch on the artist's easel and studied it. 'At least it's got some character and some life.'

In fact, the likeness was very good. One or two more touches, Raab thought, and we're there. But it was wise to give the artist a break because he was clearly getting tired. Raab was an expert at pushing people to their limits – and sometimes beyond.

The artist was still eating his sandwiches and drinking the wine when Blech came into the office with a telex message.

He saluted and said: 'We have another report of a conversation between Churchill and Roosevelt, picked up by our interception station near The Hague.'

Raab, who was feeling good, pointed to a chair. 'Sit down and have a glass of wine, Blech, and tell us what it says.'

Blech remained standing at attention, staring straight ahead. 'Not very much, I'm afraid, mein Herr. After the usual polite exchanges Churchill says: "We've located our Bigot and hope to contact him shortly." '

'And?'

'That's all, mein Herr.'

'Don't tell me they lost transmission again.'

'No, mein Herr,' said Blech. 'It was the interception station they lost. The RAF blew it to bits.'

10

Dog minus 10

Thunder like the crack of doom woke her at dawn. She sat up and saw rain clouds pissing silver down a sullen sky, heard the wind rattling the window frames. She slid down under the bedclothes like a little girl, then told herself not to be such a baby and got up, washed in the tiny bathroom and put on slacks and a rollneck sweater. The flat was cold and lonely. Maybe she should have let Luc stay. He wasn't the danger to poor sex-crazed women he thought he was.

She went into the kitchen, made some grain coffee and sat at a whitewood table, warming her hands on the hot mug and trying not to look at the storm, especially the lightning. Fire from heaven or fire from hell, it was still a living thing waiting to devour her. Despite herself her eyes were drawn to the window. Forked lightning suddenly split the sky from top to bottom and made her scream like the child she once was.

She'd climbed a ladder into the hayloft of a barn and was playing with her favourite doll when she smelt burning. She went to the head of the ladder and looked down and saw fire, writhing across the straw-covered floor like a live snake. Then there were firesnakes everywhere and smoke billowing up from a dragon's nostrils. She tried to climb down the ladder but the snakes and the dragonsmoke drove her back. She was sure she was going to die and started shrieking. Then the floor collapsed, but its fall was cushioned by bales of burning straw. And the firesnakes started dying of suffocation. She ran out through an open doorway straight into her father's arms. He threw his coat over her and rolled her on the ground. That was when she realized her clothes were alight.

It happened long ago, but the thought of it still made her

heart beat like someone knocking at the door. Then she realized someone was knocking at the door.

It was Josef, sopping wet and grinning down at her.

'Christ, I'm glad to see you,' she said.

'I know you don't like storms,' he said, hugging her.

She took him into the kitchen, poured him a mug of coffee and topped up her own. It tasted bitter, even through the sugar, but at least it warmed her.

Josef said there was a message from London that the requested items would be dropped at the field near Dourdain around 0100 hours tomorrow.

'Good,' she said. 'They must have pulled their finger out. Did you contact Nikki?'

'He'll be at the Bar Kazimierz later this morning.'

She glanced towards the window again as sheet lightning lit the kitchen with a flash of brilliance that made her jump and the rain rods glitter.

'Shit and fornication,' she said.

'And Doctor Charvet can't see you till later – '

'I haven't time to see him.'

'Because he has to call at the prison. To see an injured airman.'

She stared at him. Another flash of lightning lit the kitchen, but she didn't even notice it.

'What did you say?'

Yaka had finished breakfast and was sitting in the kitchen over a cup of coffee, staring out of the window at the falling rain. The thunder was gone, the lightning gone. Only the rain was left. In the distance he heard the clanking of a slow train and tried not to think of cattle trucks and the images he would always associate with them.

Someone was knocking on the front door and for a moment he half expected shouts of 'Juden 'raus!'

He got up, went into the narrow passage and opened the front door to another image: black felt hat pulled down, long trench coat, hands thrust deep in pockets.

'Good God,' he said. 'Gestapo.' And pulled her in out of the rain. 'You look ill.'

He took her into the kitchen, made her take her coat off and sit by the fire while he poured her a coffee.

'The wages of sin,' he said. 'Real coffee.'

'Any news of the airman?' she said.

'Raab's worried about his condition, mainly because he's a Luftwaffe prisoner.'

'Anything else?'

'He also thinks your mission must have something to do with the Second Front, though Blech thought it might be something to do with the airman. But Raab said you wouldn't be sent on a special mission to recover a squadron leader.'

'A squadron leader?'

'An instructor at some flying school, according to Raab. Didn't you know?'

'What interests me is how Raab knows.'

'Bernadette says he got the information from a collaborator. Would you like to speak to her yourself? She came back late and is having a lie-in.'

'No, don't disturb her.' She stared out of the window and saw Romaine's face through a shifting curtain of rain. A shrewd, smiling face. Shrewd enough to conceal his true rank with a plausible story. Shrewd enough, perhaps, to fool her. In all sorts of ways . . .

'And there's a price of two million francs on your head,' Yaka was saying. 'Posters are going up with a charcoal sketch of you that Raab thinks is a good likeness.' He stopped, looked at her. 'Did you hear what I said?'

She was still staring out of the window. 'I'm going to need a hideout in the next forty-eight hours.'

Yaka spread his hands. 'The house is yours.'

She turned from the window, shook her head. 'I need a place with a drive-in yard.'

There was a knock at the front door and she got up. 'That could be for me.'

'Wait a minute. Can you give me a phone number or something – in case I need to get in touch with you.'

She hesitated from habit, then gave him her address. In normal operational practice only one or at most two other members of her circuit would know her address. But in a mission that would be over in a few days cut-outs would merely hamper communications. And communications were vital.

Rain was bouncing off the roof of Charvet's car.

'I understand you've been asked to see a British airman at the prison,' she said as she got in.

'I was about to go there when you called,' Charvet said, driving off. 'I thought you must be ill. You look ill.'

'Is he badly hurt?'

'You ought to be in bed. You'll have a breakdown.'

'It's the airman's health I'm interested in.'

'From what they said it sounds like badly bruised ribs. Maybe some torn ligaments. They think he might have some fractures, but they don't know of course because the prison doctor's on leave. And I'm the nearest one around who speaks English. They're in a real panic because he's a Luftwaffe prisoner.'

He braked suddenly, pulled into the kerb. 'Hold on,' he said. 'Where am I supposed to be taking you?'

'The Bar Kazimierz.'

'But that's miles out of my way. I've got sick people to visit.'

She started to get out of the car. He pulled her back, clucking with irritation, and drove off. 'You're in no state to walk around in this weather.'

She stared out of the window at the rain. 'Does the prison hospital have X-ray apparatus?'

'Good heavens, no. It's hardly more than a sick bay. If a prisoner's really ill he's transferred to hospital.'

She went on staring out of the window and he wondered if she'd heard. Then she turned and the intensity of her stare surprised him. 'When you've examined him tell him, if you get the chance, that we're planning to rescue him, and to follow any instructions you may give him.'

'What are you talking about? What instructions?'

'Then tell the prison authorities to keep him in bed and that you'll see him again tomorrow. I need twenty-four hours to set things up.'

'What things?'

'And then, when you go back tomorrow, tell them you

125

think he might have a couple of fractured ribs and you'd like him X-rayed. Okay so far?'

'No, it's *not* okay. Not okay at all. Because I look after the resistance when they're sick or wounded doesn't mean I'm *in* the resistance. It may seem a rather fine point to you – '

'He'd be transferred by ambulance, presumably?'

Charvet nodded.

'And would you go with him?'

'I expect so – in case of language difficulties.'

'Right. Then arrange the transfer for late tomorrow afternoon. I need all the time I can get. But try not to travel in the ambulance with him.'

'Why not?'

'Because I'm going to hijack the fucking thing.' She felt in her pockets. 'Got a cigarette?'

The Bar Kazimierz was empty apart from two old men frozen over a chess game and a couple of whores leaning on the bar, sipping *fines* and waiting for the rain to stop.

Marius was wiping the bar top and only the whores stared when she came in. Marius was an obsessive wiper of bar tops, she remembered. Then he looked up and said: 'What would you like madame?'

She ordered a glass of red. He served her, wiped the immaculate bar top and jerked his head towards a beaded curtain over a doorway. She went through the hanging beads into a small back bar. The only occupant was a short ugly man with light eyes. He was sitting by the window pouring a drink from a bottle of vodka. She went and sat opposite him.

'I was going to say you don't look well,' he said. 'Then I thought: that's no way to greet a lady. So I'll tell you the truth. You look marvellous. But not very well.'

All of a sudden they were laughing. She put her arms round his neck, hugged him and kissed him.

'Old Nikki,' she said. 'Bloody old Nikki.'

'What do you want?' he said.

'Your help.'

'You have that anyway. But I'm down to four men, two guns and no ammo.'

'You know the dropping zone near Dourdain?' she said. 'Meet me there around midnight and you'll have all the stuff you want. I've arranged a drop.' She looked out of the window at a truck parked half on the pavement. 'That yours?'

'I borrowed it. Without the owner's consent.'

'Could you borrow another?'

'I don't see why not.'

'You know where the prison is?'

'I ought to.'

'A British prisoner is being transferred to hospital tomorrow afternoon.'

'Which hospital?'

'Don't know yet. Anyway, I'm going to lift him.'

Nikki smiled and tossed back a small vodka. 'What sort of guard is he likely to have?'

'Nothing a few men and a woman with clarinettes couldn't handle.'

Nikki poured himself another vodka. 'In a firefight the prisoner himself might get killed. Have you thought of that?'

She nodded, slowly. 'I've thought of it.'

But she hadn't. Except in general terms. War means killing. And killing's okay if it's the enemy. Inhibitions are released then. But who is the enemy?

'A good question,' she said aloud. 'But what is the answer?'

'I beg your pardon?' said Nikki.

'Hooray fuck is the answer.'

The square opposite the prison was deserted, which wasn't surprising. The rain was still coming down in stair rods.

'Drive slowly,' she said. 'I want a looksee.'

'What are you trying to find out?'

'I don't know.'

Nikki drove slowly while she stared up at the prison walls and what she could see of the buildings beyond.

'Stop,' she said suddenly. 'Stop!'

He stopped. 'Now what?'

She got out and stood in the rain staring up at a barred

127

window. Within a few seconds she was soaked. But she stood there like a statue. Nikki jumped out and pushed her back in the car.

'What are you playing at?' he said. 'You'll catch your death.'

'I thought I saw someone I knew,' she said. Every time she saw a face at a barred window she thought it was his.

'Where now?'

She pointed to the other side of the square. 'The little grocer's shop.'

Jacques Lacaze was short and thickset and looked like a pirate with his scarred face and the black patch where an eye used to be. But he saw more with the other eye, it was said, than most people saw with two. He was busy with a customer and didn't appear to look up when she came in, but he must have seen her because he called his wife to take over. Then he wiped his hands on his apron, gave Ryfka a gap-toothed smile and took her into the back parlour, embraced her and said:

'You're wet and cold. You need a cognac.'

'Not on an empty stomach.'

'Then try a little black-market Brie that's ripe enough to spread.'

She protested, but he cut a section from a baguette, sliced it longways and on each half spread the Brie thick.

'Eat,' he said.

To save argument and for the sake of politeness she tasted the Brie and the bread, which was still warm from the oven. Both seemed to melt in her mouth.

'I didn't realize I was so hungry,' she said.

'You don't have to apologize,' he said, serving her the same again. Then he poured two glasses of a translucent red wine from an unlabelled bottle.

'The fruit of the Gamay,' he said.

'You're sure it's not the, er, same stuff you sell to the prison guards?'

'No,' he said. 'It's from a different sewer.' And raised his glass. 'Your health.'

'And yours,' she said and drank. It was smooth and light and fruity, and seemed to dance over the palate. Or maybe she was just feeling light-headed.

'Luc reckons you know more about the prison than the prison staff.'

'How is old Luc? Still scraping along?'

She nodded. 'And screwing the ladies at every turn.'

'What's your interest in the prison? The airman?'

'How is he, do you know?'

'They're worried about him. Because Raab's worried about him.'

'Could you give me a rough idea of the layout of the prison?'

'Maybe a little better than rough,' said Lacaze.

He cleared the table, then reversed the tablecloth, which was a kind of patterned oilcloth, and spread it out carefully. On the reverse side was a detailed sketch map of the prison, showing the cell blocks, workshops, exercise yards, administration buildings, guardhouse, reception office and, just behind the prison gates, an area that had been cross-hatched with pencil. Ryfka pointed to it.

'What's this?'

'A yard where the prison van drops new prisoners cr picks up the ones being transferred. And where the occasional official visitor parks.'

She nodded, staring at the sketch map in silence. Then she said: 'I wish I could take a look at that yard.'

'Nothing easier,' said Lacaze. 'I'll be delivering some wine there in a few minutes.'

The van pulled up outside the prison gates and tooted. A wicket in the gates opened and a guard poked his head out, grinned and shouted: 'Ein moment.'

Then the big gates swung back and the van drove in. On the side, in faded lettering, could be seen the legend:

Jacques Lacaze
Epicier
Marchand de Vins

They pulled up in the cobbled yard and Jacques got out and went into reception.

She stayed in the van, huddled in her overcoat, with the collar turned up, listening to the rain drumming its fingers on the roof. Behind her the prison gates started to close and she had to fight down a feeling of panic. Past the administration building she could see the side of a cell block, grim and glistening in the rain. A big solid bare wall pierced high up by a row of mean-looking windows, each obscured by a grid of iron bars. She knew what the cells would look like. Only too well. She wondered which cell he was in, and whether he was hungry or in pain. Then she dragged her eyes away and studied the layout of the yard, the disposition of the sentries, the distance from the guard-house to the gates.

She heard the rear doors of the van being opened. Heard Jacques talking in broken German to two of the guards as they helped him unload the cases of wine. She huddled deeper in her trenchcoat and didn't look round.

A few minutes later the van doors were shut and Jacques climbed in beside her. 'See everything you wanted?'

'Enough.'

Jacques started the engine, tooted the horn and the gates swung back. He drove out, grinning and waving to the guards.

She felt able to breathe again.

After two days at high-level security conferences, including a combined chiefs-of-staff conference, Major General Mossop returned to the office and a mountain of paperwork. 'And Bumf begat Bumf unto the third and fourth generation,' he said, and went straight out to lunch. Some two hours and several brandies later he returned in much better humour and decided that most of the paperwork could be chucked away or shoved into the shredder. Till he came to the message from Ryfka.

He grunted irritably, pressed the intercom switch and told Jean to find Colonel Smith. But Colonel Smith wasn't to be found. 'Then 'e'd better be found,' Mossop said. 'And quick.'

Twenty minutes later he pressed the intercom switch again. ''aven't you found 'im yet?'

'No, sir.'

'Where the bloody 'ell's he got to in the middle of the afternoon?'

'I don't know, sir.'

''ave tha' tried Orchard Court?'

'Yes, sir.'

''is club?'

'Yes, sir.'

''is flat?'

'Everywhere, sir. Except his maiden aunt's in Cheltenham.'

In the silence that followed she imagined she could hear a string of sub-vocalized obscenities.

'Jean, 'e's not got a bit on the side somewhere, 'as 'e, lass?'

'I'm afraid I wouldn't know, sir,' Jean said in the kind of voice that goes with a lifted nose.

'Oh yes tha' bloody would,' said Mossop. 'Tha' knows everything that goes on in this place. 'Specially if it's mucky.'

He switched off the intercom, pushed the rest of the paperwork aside and studied the message from Ryfka. It still didn't make sense. There was a knock at the door and Frank Smith came in.

'Where t'bloody 'ell 'ast tha' been?'

'Shopping. I'm a bachelor, you know. Have to do my own. And don't tell me there's a war on.'

Mossop muttered something, then held up the message.

' "Temporarily lost contact through enemy action." What the 'ell's that supposed to mean?'

Smith shrugged. 'How should I know? Perhaps he's been captured.'

'Then go and bloody find out.'

'How?'

'Fly over there. Speak to 'er on the S-phone.'

131

'Can't,' said Smith. 'I'm a Bigot too, remember. And you should know better than to ask me.'

'You can do it be'ind me back, can't you? Tha' always were an artful sod.'

'And if I get shot down and captured? Like Romaine?'

'Take a bloody suicide pill with you.'

'That would be a bitter pill to swallow.'

Doctor Charvet's surgery was running late, partly because of his visit to the prison, an unscheduled addition to his usual round, but mostly because the patients took up more time than he'd allowed for. They always did and it always surprised him. But old Madame Lemercier was the last. The buzzer that sounded when the waiting room door was opened had remained silent. All he had to do was write out the prescription for the usual placebo for her aches and pains, then see her out and lock the door before any more patients drifted in. If he didn't lock it they'd come in all night with their real or imaginary ills. Since the war though there had been a dramatic decline in imaginary ills. Something he must look into one day, or perhaps even do a paper on.

He quickly wrote out the prescription. 'No one else outside, is there?'

'What?' Madame Lemercier cupped a hand round her ear and smiled with pearly white teeth that didn't quite fit.

'Forget it!' he shouted good-humouredly. He should have remembered she was deaf as a post.

He saw her out and locked the door with a sigh of relief. With a bit of luck the rest of the evening would be his. Then he saw a bedraggled woman dozing on a bench in a corner, a felt hat pulled down over her face, rain dripping from her clothes.

'Madame,' he said, 'the surgery is shut. Unless it's urgent – '

She sat up and pushed the hat to the back of her head.

'You look like a drowned rat,' he said. 'What *have* you been doing?'

'Standing in the rain.'

132

He took her into the surgery and sat her in an armchair. 'Or would you rather lie on the couch?'

'I might fall asleep again. Did you see the airman?'

'If you don't get some rest you'll collapse.'

'Did you see him?'

He got a bottle of armagnac from a cupboard, poured her a stiff one. She drank it down.

'Good medicine,' she said, feeling the colour come back to her cheeks.

He poured her another. 'Take it a bit more slowly.'

She looked out of the window. The rain had stopped but the trees in the street were still dripping. In the hush she could even hear them.

'He must have put up quite a fight, that chap of yours.'

'Is he badly hurt?'

'Extensive bruising to ribs and back. No obvious sign of a fracture. But there could be hairline fractures of one or more ribs. I'll know more when I see him tomorrow.'

'Can he walk?'

Charvet shrugged. 'With help maybe. But I told him to pretend he was in a bad way. Not that it'll take much pretence.'

'Then you managed to tell him something of our plans?'

Charvet nodded. 'I also told the prison authorities to keep him more or less immobile till I've had him X-rayed.'

'When will that be?'

'Late afternoon. I'll let you know.'

She stared at the dripping trees. 'When you see him again, tell him . . .' She hesitated.

'What?'

'I don't know,' she said.

Luc picked her up in the van and drove her back. 'You look rough, baby,' he said, as they swished through wet streets. 'Real rough.'

'Tired, that's all,' she said and leaned against the door pillar and closed her eyes. He tried to speak to her but she didn't answer and he thought she was asleep – till they pulled up outside the flat. Then she suddenly sat up and said: 'Call for me at midnight. If you don't get an answer, use your key. I may be asleep. And bring Josef.'

'Something on?'

'They're dropping Nikki's stuff. And drugs for Charvet.'

She started to get out of the van, then turned to Luc. 'I've recruited Yaka Mnouchkine,' she said. 'I thought you ought to know.'

'What makes you think you can trust him?'

'Instinct.'

'That's not much to go on.'

'It's all I went on when I picked you.'

'Yes, but I'm not . . .' He stopped.

'What? A dirty little Jew?'

'I didn't say that.'

'No. But that's what I heard.'

He was driven there in a Gestapo Citroën after a curt phone call telling him to be ready in five minutes. He was waiting on the doorstep with the big case holding his accordion when the car arrived. Neither of the Gestapo men spoke to him on the journey. He was *dreck*.

At Les Sapins Argentés, knowing his place, he went straight into the kitchen by the back door. Therese was waiting for him, dressed in black as usual. It suited her saturnine looks.

'Have you eaten?'

'I don't want anything, thank you.'

'I saved some of the casserole for you.'

She took a dish and a warm plate out of the oven and put them on the table. Yaka suddenly recovered his appetite.

'What's his mood?'

'Almost mellow. The effect of Tilly, no doubt.'

'And yours?'

'Also mellow,' she said, looking at him. 'For the moment.'

Then Raab could be heard calling from the dining room: 'Where's the Jew?'

Yaka got up. 'Perhaps I'll see you later.'

Their eyes met. She smiled. He turned and went out.

*

134

Yaka sat in a corner of the dining room, his accordion on his knees, meekly awaiting the order to play.

Raab, seated at the head of the long table in full dress uniform of the SD, was drinking a glass of milk. On his right was Solange, on his left Blech. At the other end of the table Therese was pouring coffee. Next to her Grandma Tilly muttered to herself between spoonfuls of her third helping of chocolate mousse.

'Is it the neighbours again, Tilly?' said Raab.

Tilly nodded. 'It's not safe to go to the lavatory.'

'Really?'

'They stand outside and send electric shocks through the walls. And sometimes,' she added with relish, 'through the seat.'

'No,' said Raab, 'not through the seat, surely?'

'Through the seat.'

'Barbarous.' He turned to Blech. 'What do you say?'

Blech, who was watching her eat, said: 'Where does she put it all?'

'She's got hollow legs. Haven't you, Tilly?'

'What?'

'Got hollow legs.'

'Yes,' she said. She looked up at the ceiling. 'I can hear them in the loft.'

'I thought they were outside the lavatory,' said Blech.

'That was this morning. Now they're in the loft.'

'Why should they go up there?' said Raab.

'Because,' said Tilly, spelling it out, 'that's where the electric wires are.'

'You see?' said Raab. 'There's always an explanation. Seek and ye shall find.' He turned to Yaka. 'Play something, Jew.'

Yaka, whose thoughts were elsewhere, responded automatically with an old lullaby. Grandma Tilly started to nod. Then her head dropped forward and she fell asleep like a child.

'Solange,' said Therese, 'I think you'd better take her up to bed.'

11

Dog minus 9

She dreamed of Harry leaning over her, making love to her, and the bombs raining down, shaking the earth, shaking everything . . . She woke up to find Luc leaning over her, shaking her awake. With him were Josef and Michel.

'What's the time?' she said.

'After midnight,' said Josef. 'Charvet phoned a couple of hours ago and said he's arranged for the ambulance to be at the prison soon after five tomorrow afternoon.'

'And there's a message from London,' said Michel. 'An S-phone will be dropped with Nikki's stuff and Woodpecker will be flying over to talk to Linnet.'

'When?'

'Soon after the drop, according to the message.'

The drop had already taken place when they got there and Nikki and his men were picking up the canisters of equipment and their attached parachutes and loading them on a truck.

Ryfka told him she was expecting an S-phone for her to be dropped with the other stuff. It was soon found and taken out of its canister, and the loading went on. She asked Michel to set up the S-phone in the back of Luc's van and test it.

When the loading was finished Nikki passed round a bottle of brandy. It was a cold night and still wet underfoot from the rain. She was glad of a nip.

'What next?' he said.

'A meeting at the Bar Kazimierz. Around noon. Perhaps you can fix it with Marius to let us have the back room. And bring your men.'

'You have something worked out?'

'Nearly,' she said. 'But not quite.' She looked up at the sky, wondering where Woodpecker had got to.

'Can you hear a plane?' said Luc.

'No,' she said. 'And not likely to. It could be flying at twenty thousand feet. The S-phone has a range of fifty miles.'

Then she saw Michel signalling her. The doors at the back of the van were open and she could see the S-phone on the rear platform. She went over and put on the head-phones. And almost immediately recognized Frank Smith's voice.

'Woodpecker calling Linnet, Woodpecker calling Linnet. Come in Linnet. Over.'

'Linnet calling Woodpecker. Receiving you loud and clear. Over.'

'What the hell's going on? We didn't understand your last signal. Over.'

'Don't worry. Contact with Bigot re-established. Over.'

'You mean he's in your hands? Over.'

'He will be. In a few hours. Over.'

'Your orders have been changed. You are to finish the job at the first possible opportunity. Pull the trigger and get out. Transport TBA. Understood? Over.'

'Understood perfectly. But I'm CO on the ground and you must rely on my judgment. Over.'

'Pull the trigger and get out. That's an order. Please confirm. Over.'

'Closing down. Gestapo approaching. Over and out.'

She took off the headphones and handed them to Michel, who was peering anxiously into the darkness. 'Where?' he said. 'Where are the Gestapo?'

'That's the trouble,' she said. 'You never bloody know.'

The house was quiet. Blech, leaning on the table, head in hands, yawned in the hope that Raab would take the hint and give him permission to retire. But Raab, immaculate and upright, moodily sipping milk and staring dreamily into the distance, was oblivious of hints. He was listening to

Yaka playing an old ballad on the accordion, which seemed to bring out its plaintive qualities.

In the kitchen Therese was ironing by the light of an oil lamp and an open fire. It was cosy and she felt relaxed away from Raab. His attitude towards her was subtly proprietorial, as if his rights over her daughter implied similar rights over her. Sometimes she caught him looking at her and it made her uncomfortable. He seemed fascinated by her hair, which she wore swept up and pinned, in a severe style that made her hard-featured face seem even harder and more aloof. But she preferred it should be that way.

He always brought a hamper of food and drink with him. And he had opened accounts in her name at shops in the nearby village, but she spent her own money in the shops, and he must have known this because there were few bills to pay. Any food left over after his visits was given to an elderly widow in the village. Therese had a small war pension, a tiny annuity and the pride of a Spanish grandee.

Tilly, who wasn't mad all the time, had no time for pride. 'That's for the rich. People like us can't afford it.'

'On the contrary,' said Therese, 'it's the only thing we can afford.'

'Another thing you can't afford,' said Tilly, 'is being sweet on the Jew.'

'You talk nonsense.'

Tilly gave her a toothless grin. 'Not all the time.'

'And don't call him the Jew.'

'I don't know his name,' said Tilly. 'But I expect you do.'

Yaka also looked at her sometimes, when Raab's attention was elsewhere. And then the hint of a smile would flicker in her eyes. No more than a hint though, in case Raab noticed.

She stopped ironing and put the flatiron on the hob as the plaintive sounds of the accordion began to drift in from the other room. She moved dreamily in front of the fire, then found herself swaying to the slow music and its underlying melancholy.

The door opened and Raab walked in, jackboots clattering on the flagstone floor. He stopped in front of her, clicked his heels and gave a jerky bow. 'Ah, what a pretty picture by firelight,' he said in a voice as dry as dead leaves.

She picked up the flatiron, spat on it, watched the spit sizzle, then went back to her ironing. Raab stepped closer, till only the ironing board separated them. He reeked of milk, like a grotesque suckling child.

'Why don't you let your hair down?' He leaned towards her and she got a blast of milk-sour breath in her face. 'One day, my dear, I'm going to have it down. And not only your hair.'

She brought the flatiron up so quickly and so close to his face he had to step back to avoid being burnt.

He laughed. Even that sounded like dead leaves. Then he turned and clattered out.

In the dining room Yaka was still playing the ballad when Raab came back.

'Stop that row,' he said. Yaka stopped.

Blech was dozing at the table, unaware of Raab's return. Raab poured himself a glass of milk, sipped it, then poured the rest over Blech's head.

'Wake up, you idle slob.'

Blech sat up, felt the milk trickling down his face. Then he heard the dead laugh. He took out a handkerchief and wiped his face and tried to keep the hatred out of his eyes. By then the milk felt warm and sticky and faintly disgusting.

Yaka looked down, pretending he hadn't seen, knowing Blech would never forgive him for witnessing his humiliation.

Raab spoke: 'I don't want any hitches when that airman's taken to hospital. Or any chances given him to escape. We'll have enough explaining to do to the Luftwaffe – without losing him.'

'If he does have broken ribs, mein Herr, he'll hardly be in a fit condition to escape.'

'That's what we said about Ryfka. She's half dead, we said. Too weak to escape, we said. Tell the prison governor I want him strapped to the stretcher.'

'Anything else, mein Herr?'

'Give the ambulance an escort. A Gestapo car. Perhaps

a motorcycle escort as well ... Whatever happens he mustn't be allowed to escape. And if he tries, tell the escort to kill him.' He smiled. 'Shot while trying to escape. That might even shut the Graf von Kirchen-Scheissbein up.' He broke off and stared at Yaka. 'Who said *you* could listen?'

'I – I wasn't listening, mein Herr.'

'Don't argue with me, you Yiddisher dreck.'

He crossed the room in swift strides, grabbed Yaka by the lapels. 'If I say you're listening, Jew, you're listening.'

'Yes, mein Herr. But I couldn't help it, mein Herr.'

'No,' said Raab, releasing him. 'Not with those big ears. But we can always shorten them.'

He drew his Luger PO8.

Yaka watched him pull back the recoil spring. That would force a cartridge into the chamber, he knew. Then the gun was levelled at the left side of his head.

Another stupid joke, he thought. Trying to scare me. Then he saw the safety catch was off. The report deafened him and he felt a tingling sensation in his ear and blood beginning to trickle down the side of his neck.

'Get out, Jew,' Raab said, raising the Luger again. 'Or I'll put the next one *between* your ears.'

Yaka saw Therese standing white-faced in the kitchen doorway. He limped unsteadily towards her.

It was nearly three before she got to bed and fell into a drugged sleep. A few minutes later, it seemed, she was woken up by the telephone. The sun was shining and it was ten o'clock.

Yawning, she picked up the receiver. It was Charvet to tell her the ambulance would be at the prison at five o'clock. 'And I've been ordered to accompany the prisoner to the hospital.' He paused. '*In* the ambulance.'

'Tough,' she said. 'But you'll be all right. If you hear any sudden noises though, duck.'

'I suppose you think that's funny,' Charvet said and hung up.

She had a quick bath, dressed and breakfasted on toast and coffee in a kitchen now warm with sunlight. Then she lit a Gitane, watched the blue smoke curl upwards and wondered how she was going to hijack an ambulance. And then what? Abandon it and transfer Romaine to another vehicle? And if something went wrong? Maybe she'd need a temporary hideout for the ambulance . . . What she needed now, though, more than anything, was information.

There was a knock at the door. It was Yaka in his shabby clothes. 'I've got information about the airman,' he said.

'You must have heard my prayer,' she said. 'Come in.'

After she'd taken him into the sunlit kitchen and offered him grain coffee, which he politely declined, he said: 'Be careful when you go out. There are Wanted posters up everywhere. With a picture of you. And a two million francs reward.'

'Tell me about the airman.'

'You know he's being transferred to hospital later today?'

She nodded. 'For X-rays.'

'Raab's ordered an escort for the ambulance when it leaves the prison.'

'What sort of escort?'

'A Gestapo car. Perhaps with a motorcycle escort. He wasn't specific. But he's afraid the prisoner might try to escape. Said he must be killed if there were any danger of that. He remembers how you escaped. And he's . . . jumpy, I suppose.'

It was then she noticed the sticking plaster on his ear. Blood was beginning to seep out from under it.

'What happened to your ear?' she said.

For some reason he didn't want to tell her. It now seemed trivial. 'I cut it shaving.' He hesitated. 'You're planning to rescue him, aren't you?'

'Why do you ask?'

'I'd like to help.'

'You are helping.'

'I meant . . . in a more active way.'

She opened her mouth to say no, then remembered the Knight's Cross of the Iron Cross in its shabby case. It reminded her of Yaka himself. Valour in a shabby suit.

*

She walked through the Place des Lices with head lowered and the felt hat pulled well down. The posters were on every hoarding, every bare patch of wall, every *panneau-réclame*. She stopped and looked at one. The likeness frightened her. She walked on, feeling that all eyes were on her, relieved when she reached the Pompes Funèbres without being challenged.

Victor was french-polishing a coffin in the workshop at the back. 'If you're looking for Luc – '

'I'm looking for Victor,' she said.

He stopped work, stared at her. 'No,' he said. 'Victor doesn't want anything to do with you. He just wants to make coffins and bury the dead. Not add to their number.'

'Victor, all I need is a yard where I can hide a vehicle for a couple of hours. Just a yard.'

'Not my yard. Oh, no.'

'If you leave the gates open around five o'clock, say – '

'Didn't you hear what I said?'

'It's only a fallback, Victor. In case.'

'In case of what?'

'In case of need.'

'No,' said Victor. 'No, no, NO!'

'And if I'm in trouble? With no one to turn to?' She hugged him, kissed him. 'Ah, Victor, I knew I could rely on you. Just a couple of hours and I'll be gone.'

'Shit,' said Victor, almost in tears. 'Shit.'

On her way back across the Place des Lices she spotted an SS patrol approaching. She hurried into a side street – no point in taking chances with all those posters about – only to find a couple of gendarmes strolling towards her. She stopped and pretended to look in a shop window full of dusty period costumes and wigs. The place had a desolate air and she wondered if anyone still ran a business there. The answer lay in fancy lettering on the glass panel of the shop door.

Henriette de la Barre
Costumière, Perruquière

142

Then, in the plate glass window, she saw the reflection of one of the posters on a wall across the street. Her own face looking down at her. The footsteps drew nearer. She opened the door, a bell tinkled above her head and she stepped quickly inside, nearly knocking over a figure in an elaborate *robe de bal*, all hoops and crinoline. The face was partly covered by a slim black mask on a silver stick, held like a lorgnette by a dainty white hand. The effect was so vivid it was like gatecrashing a *bal masqué* of the last century.

The footsteps stopped outside, and brought her back to reality. Were the gendarmes just looking in the window? Or looking at her? Or at the poster across the street? She didn't dare turn round to find out.

Then, from somewhere at the back, came a dry cough.

She looked around, trying to locate the source, but the place was dark and gloomy away from the window. As her eyes became adapted she made out a long counter, almost the width of the shop, piled high with costumes, uniforms and wigs. But no sign of life. Then one of the wigs moved. An elaborately coiffured blonde wig. The leathery face beneath it appeared to be lifeless and disembodied, balanced on a pile of old costumes. Only the eyes were alive, shining, coal black, with points of fire. Then the red slash that did for a mouth started to move.

'You are looking for something, madame?' The voice sounded sharp, young.

'I – I don't know. I mean I'm not sure.' She wasn't easily put out but that disembodied face and sharp young voice unsettled her. The coal-black eyes seemed to see through her. 'I'm acting in an amateur group and thought I should get a wig.'

The face moved out from behind the counter and she saw there was the body of a little old woman attached to it.

'Let us go into the back room,' said Madame de la Barre, 'where I keep a range of wigs, ancient and modern.'

It must have been an artist's studio once. The only window was a big northern light that couldn't remember when it had last been cleaned. In the gloom she made out racks of costumes and shelves of wigs. A long table was also piled with wigs.

Madame de la Barre switched on an overhead light and stood her under it, then stared intently at her face as if it were of purely theoretical interest. It was a bit like being in a Gestapo cellar, she thought.

'Take your hat off.'

She took her hat off. The old crone lifted her hair away from her face and carefully pinned it up. If she noticed the scar she didn't react. Then she went to the long table and sorted through the huge pile of wigs till she found a luxuriant chestnut wig. She shook it out, combed it, then started teasing it with a small brush. Ryfka grew restless.

'Keep still,' said the sharp voice.

At last the wig was ready. Madame de la Barre fixed it carefully in place, still teasing and patting it. Then she stepped back, examining her work critically. 'Not bad,' she said. 'For a rush job.' She held a looking glass in front of Ryfka's face. 'Not many people would recognize you now,' she added dryly.

For a moment Ryfka didn't even recognize herself. Even the shape of her face seemed different. And the scar was hidden.

'Marvellous,' she said. 'Marvellous. How much do I owe you, madame?'

'There is no charge.'

'Madame, I have plenty of money with me. It is not even my own money. Besides, I need another wig. A blonde wig.'

'There is no charge.'

'But madame –'

'They executed my son.'

'What for?'

'Sheltering a resister.'

The leathery face was impassive, but the bright black eyes grew suddenly brighter. The little old lady lowered her head, ashamed of showing grief before a stranger. Ryfka took her in her arms and hugged her. They clung to each other in silence.

*

The council of war was going as well as could be expected. As doctors said when they didn't know what else to say. Still, she had worked out a plan. Not a very good plan – there were too many unknowns – but a plan. And flexible in case something went wrong, which it always did. You just hoped it wouldn't be anything critical.

She was standing at a table in the back room of the Bar Kazimierz. Spread out on it was a street map of Rennes, and gathered round her, apart from Nikki and his *maquisards* were Josef, Luc and Yaka, whom she had already introduced to the others as Raab's tailor. It was information from him and Doctor Charvet, she added, that formed the basis of her present plan.

'The ambulance should get to the prison about five,' she went on, 'and park inside, close to the gates. There isn't much parking space so presumably the escort will be waiting outside, in the approach road. Then the airman will be brought out on a stretcher, accompanied by Doctor Charvet, and lifted into the ambulance. Charvet will travel with him.'

She studied the map. 'We could take them on boulevard de l'Alma, just past Ange Blaise. There's a turning on the left – '

'I think we should take them sooner,' said Nikki. 'Soon as they're clear of the jail. Knock out the escort and – '

'Hold it,' she said. 'You're the one who said if there's a firefight we could end up shooting the man we're trying to save. I have a feeling Raab wouldn't mind him being shot. It might avoid awkward explanations to Kirchen-Wehbach.' She turned to Yaka. 'What was it he said?'

'If the prisoner tries to escape, kill him. He has also ordered him to be strapped to the stretcher.'

She turned back to Nikki. 'Still, you have a point about taking them early.'

She frowned in concentration. The scar started twitching. Then Nikki said: 'What *do* you want us to do?'

'Cut the escort off from the ambulance.'

'How?'

'That,' she said, with the scar twitching her smile, 'is what I'm about to tell you.'

*
145

Raab ate alone in his salon at the Hotel Abelard. He always ate frugally, but now, after toying with a slice or two of chicken breast he dabbed his mouth with a napkin and pushed the plate away. He was too preoccupied to eat and poured himself a cup of coffee from a silver pot. He could hear faint splashing sounds from the bathroom. Solange rarely got up before lunch. After a while the splashing stopped.

He finished his coffee and went into the bedroom. Solange was sitting on the bed, naked, waving her hands in small graceful patterns to dry her scarlet nails. He shut the door behind him and stared at her. She stood up and came towards him, a mass of rhythmically moving curves, all in harmony.

After fifteen years of a wife who insisted on one time, one place and one position for sex, and that not too often, she was an Aladdin's cave of sensual delight.

He laughed his rustling laugh. 'Open Sesame,' he said, and reached for her. Somewhere in the salon a phone rang.

Blech knocked and entered. The salon was empty. The bedroom door, he noted, was shut. Behind the Chinese screens the phone was ringing. Blech waited a moment or two, then went through the opening in the screens and answered it.

'No,' he said, 'I'm afraid he's not. I think he's in conference. Can I take a message? . . . Yes, I'll tell him.'

He hung up and went to the window, which overlooked the Jardin du Thabor. The leaves were on the trees, the sun was shining. A girl was talking through the gardens pushing a pram. Blech wished he had a girl of his own. Like Solange. He was tired of whores and brothels. He went back into the salon proper, sat in an armchair and stared at the bedroom door in some frustration, wondering what the pig was doing to her.

When the door suddenly opened and Raab appeared it quite startled him. He stood up and saluted. 'Heil Hitler!'

Raab grunted and went through the screens into the office. Blech followed.

'The prison governor rang, mein Herr, to confirm arrangements for taking the prisoner Romaine to hospital for X-ray. Doctor Charvet will travel with him in the ambulance.'

'And the escort?'

'On standby, mein Herr. The SS are providing a motor-cycle combination with rider and machine gunner. They will be in front. Bringing up the rear will be a Gestapo car with driver and three men, all armed with Schmeissers.'

Raab sat at his desk and waved towards a chair. 'Sit down.'

Blech sat down and Raab got up, still restive, and wandered round the office. Blech wondered if the lunchtime lay had left something to be desired. It pleased him to think so.

'Something's wrong,' said Raab.

'Wrong, mein Herr?'

'Wrong. I can feel it.'

'Wrong in what way, mein Herr?'

'If I knew that, I'd know what to do about it.'

He paced the floor while Blech leaned back, dreaming of Solange.

'If only I had an idea what the bitch was up to,' said Raab.

For a moment Blech wondered which bitch.

'Posters up all over town, double the usual reward, and no one's even seen her. Or no one's saying.'

He stopped pacing and stared at Blech, who felt obliged to comment. 'You don't think she's still interested in the prisoner, mein Herr?'

'I told you, that was little more than a gesture. She happened to hear there was a British airman on the loose and . . .' He shrugged. 'The rest followed.'

'Yes, but . . .' Blech hesitated.

'Go on.'

'Well, if she's over here on some big job, how come she wastes all that time chasing after some airman who's been shot down?'

'She just happened to be around – '

147

'Oh no she didn't . . . I beg your pardon, mein Herr – '

'Never mind the apologies, say what you mean.'

'Where did the airman come down? North-west of Le Mans. And where did *she* first surface?'

'Coincidence,' said Raab.

'Then she goes round asking questions, trying to trace his movements. Then she takes the train to Rennes, kills an SS driver, heads for the farm at Talensac. That's a lot of coincidence, mein Herr. And a lot of trouble.'

'Maybe she was going to Rennes anyway, and when she heard the airman was at Talensac . . .' Raab stopped. Blech's words were making sense. 'Why didn't you mention this before?'

'I didn't think of it before, mein Herr.'

Raab went to the window, contemplated the view, then turned abruptly. 'It still doesn't answer the crucial question: why mount a special operation to recover a squadron leader?'

'Perhaps he has special skills they need.'

'Then why risk him on some piddling raid in the first place? It makes no sense.'

'I'm not saying it makes sense, mein Herr. I'm just saying . . .' Blech shrugged. 'Maybe . . . *Maybe* she's still planning to rescue him. For reasons we don't know. Have you heard anything from avenue Foche or the Hauptamt?'

Raab shook his head, went back to his desk and put his feet up and stared into space. Suddenly he crashed his feet to the floor and pointed his finger at Blech like a gun.

'You take charge of the escort. Travel in the Gestapo car and keep in radio contact with me. Understood?'

'Yes, of course,' said Blech, trying not to look startled. 'Keep in contact with you. And, er, where will you be, mein Herr?'

Raab gave his rustling laugh. 'Right behind you. With a ninety-millimetre cannon.'

The ambulance driver and the stretcher-bearer were given their instructions by the hospital's medical superintendent, who had a habit of addressing inferiors like a priest intoning

148

Holy Writ. The ambulance driver, a veteran of two world wars, couldn't pay proper attention because his piles were playing up. They always did if he had to stand in one position listening to long speeches.

'Remember,' the superintendent intoned, 'that you have been entrusted with an assignment of the utmost importance. And we expect you to apply yourselves to it with the utmost conscience, not to mention care.' He paused to let his words sink in. 'After you have picked up the prisoner an SS motorcycle escort will lead the way back to the hospital. And a Gestapo car will be following close behind. These security precautions may seem elaborate for the transport of one sick prisoner, but they have been laid down by no less a person than Standartenfuehrer Raab. And ours is not to reason why ... Remember, the reputation of this great hospital and, in a way, of la belle France herself, will be in your hands. For a brief but not, we hope, inglorious hour.'

The ambulance men nodded dumbly, climbed into their vehicle, which, like themselves, was old and a bit clapped out, and drove off.

'Now what the fuck was all that about?' said the driver in a bemused voice. He was still talking when he took the first corner and saw a blonde girl pushing a pram step blindly in front of the ambulance. He stood on the brakes. The blonde screamed, fainted. The pram rolled into the gutter and overturned.

'Jesus God,' said the driver. 'It's all we need.' He jumped out of the ambulance and went to the girl, who was lying very still. As he bent over her she sat up and pointed a gun at his belly.

The stretcher-bearer, who had jumped out of the near side, also found himself looking down the barrel of a gun, held by a grim-faced man in a shabby suit.

12

At a quarter to five an SS motorcycle combination and a
Gestapo Citroën pulled up in the approach to the prison.
Blech got out of the Citroën, crossed to the prison gates
and rang the bell. He was expected and a wicket let into
the gates opened promptly. A prison guard took him to
the reception office where he completed paperwork for the
release of a prisoner into Gestapo custody. Then he went
back to the car, leaned against the nearside wing and lit a
cigarette. It was hot in the afternoon sun.

A couple of minutes later an armoured car lumbered
round the square and pulled in behind the Citroën. Raab
got out and was joined by Blech.

'Everything in order?'

'We're just waiting for the ambulance, mein Herr.'

At two minutes past five an ambulance appeared on the
far side of the square, then pulled up.

'What are they stopping for?' said Blech. 'They can't be
lost.'

The ambulance moved off again, slowly.

'And now they're going the wrong way round,' said Raab.
'Woman driver, you can bet.'

'Ryfka was a woman driver.'

'She was something else. An original.'

'Highly original,' said Blech. 'The cow nearly killed me.
With your armoured car.'

'I still think they'll recognize me,' said Yaka.

'They'll be on the offside when I pass them,' she said.
'That's why I'm going the longer way round. They won't
even see you.'

'They will when I get out.'

'They'll be thirty or forty metres away. Not that anyone'd
recognize you in that uniform. And that hat.'

The gates were already opening as she turned into the short approach road. She put her foot down, shot past the escort and into the prison yard, then did a fishtail turn quickly and expertly so the ambulance was facing the exit. She switched off, pleased with the way the ambulance handled. A good old girl. With a bit of poke under her bonnet, what's more.

'Not bad,' said Blech. 'And it *is* a woman driver, mein Herr.'

They had both seen the shoulder-length blonde hair under the peaked cap as the ambulance swung into the yard.

'Well,' said Raab, 'they're not all bad drivers. As we have reason to know.'

In the driving cab of the ambulance Yaka said: 'What happens if they do recognize me?'

'I'll cover your retreat,' she said dryly.

'It's just that I'm a little nervous.'

'Me too,' she said. 'A little shit-scared, in fact.'

Raab and Blech saw a man in a baggy uniform and a peaked cap that rested on his ears, get out of the ambulance and limp round to open the doors at the back.

'They must be hard up for stretcher-bearers,' said Raab. 'And uniforms.'

'We've taken most of their able-bodied men for forced labour, mein Herr.'

'You don't say, mein Herr.'

Two uniformed prison guards appeared carrying a man on a stretcher. They were escorted by four other guards and two men in civilian clothes, one of whom Raab recognized as the prison governor. He assumed that the other, a small fussy man with a black bag, was the doctor.

'Why don't we put a couple of our own men in the ambulance?' said Blech.

'Because it might inhibit me if I have to blow it to bits,' said Raab. 'Let's take a closer look.' He started towards the prison yard.

'You really think she'll try to rescue him?'

'That was your idea, Blech.'

Yaka, standing by the ambulance doors with his back to them, glanced over his shoulder and froze.

In the driving cab Ryfka cocked a Sten gun and put the change lever on automatic. She drew a bead on the approaching Raab, immaculate in the uniform of an SS Standartenfuehrer. At his throat was the Iron Cross, Second Class. For torturing prisoners, presumably. He pulled off his heavy black leather gauntlets and memories flashed before her, like rapid cuts in a film, of herself strung up naked in a Gestapo cellar and being whipped by those gauntlets till the blood ran. Her finger tightened on the trigger and she imagined him flung back in a bloody heap as the bullets tore his chest to scarlet ribbons.

Then one of the crew of the armoured car got out and called to him. 'Herr Standartenfuehrer! Herr Standartenfuehrer! Radio message.'

Raab turned back and Blech followed him. Her hands, still clutching the Sten, were clammy with sweat. But steady.

She saw Raab get into the armoured car, then heard someone climbing into the ambulance. She turned to look through the opening in the bulkhead and saw Charvet, fussing and worrying and giving orders. Then she saw the stretcher being lifted in. All she could see of the man on it was a head of untidy fair hair. It gave her an odd feeling. He muttered something to Yaka, but she couldn't catch what it was.

Then the doors shut with a metallic bang. She dragged her eyes away to study her line of escape. The armoured car, the Gestapo car and the motorcycle combination were lined up to her right, in the prison approach. Then there was a ninety-degree left-hand turn into the street. Take them by surprise . . . That's always worth nine out of ten, the instructors used to say. Yaka climbed in beside her and she started the engine and prayed the old girl wouldn't let her down.

'How is he?' she said.

Yaka shrugged. 'Poorly.'

'What was it he said to you?'

152

'It made no sense. Something about a piece of cake.'

Raab got out of the armoured car and called out to Blech: 'Stop the ambulance – he's an air commodore!'

Blech didn't immediately grasp the full meaning of Raab's words, but turned towards the ambulance and drew his gun.

Ryfka floored the accelerator, then dropped the clutch. The ambulance rocketed out of the yard straight at Raab and Blech with a roar of maximum revs and a Sten gun poking out of the nearside window.

Raab and Blech flung themselves to one side as the ambulance screeched past and a hail of bullets whipped up the loose gravel around them, then ricocheted off the armoured car with a dying whine.

She took the ninety-degree turn sideways, then straightened the old girl up with an armful of opposite lock, rocking her so much it was a wonder she didn't turn over. She glanced in the mirror and saw the motorcycle combination had taken off in pursuit.

'I had him,' said Yaka. 'I had him in my sights.'

'The barrel always rides up on full automatic,' she said. 'Reload and get that motorbike. A short burst and keep it low.' She could see the machine gunner lining up on them.

'I had him. And I missed.'

The machine gun stuttered, but the aim was off target, disturbed by a burst from Yaka. A row of windows shattered with a sound like Chinese wind bells gone crazy. Then the machine gun opened up again and this time the old ambulance shuddered as bullets thudded into her. Ryfka winced in sympathy.

Yaka was leaning out for another burst, taking careful aim. And taking too long. She was about to yell at him when the Sten gun spoke, briefly and to the point. In the mirror she saw the motorbike combination go suddenly out of control and career into a fruit and vegetable stall at the side of the road, overturning everything. Terrible mess.

She leaned against the bulkhead. 'All right back there?'

'Fine.' Charvet's voice, calm as a summer's day. 'A few more ventilation holes, that's all.'

She'd wondered why the resistance had picked this nervous little doctor. Now she knew. When the chips were down he was something else.

'And the squadron leader?'

'As well as can be expected.'

'Hold tight, I'm turning left,' she said. 'Might be rough.'

In the mirror the Gestapo Citroën was growing bigger. A man leaned out of the nearside, another out of the offside. Both had Schmeissers.

Raab was on the radio-telephone to Blech. 'Go for the rear tyres. Over.'

'Jawohl, mein Herr. Shall I put out an ambulance call for the injured men? Over.'

'And a call for roadblocks. I want the whole area cordoned off. And get those Schmeissers into action – or move over and I'll blast her with the cannon. Achtung! She's going left.'

Ryfka heard the Schmeissers open up, felt the old girl shudder again. Then she was into the left-hander, much too fast and running wide. She pulled the wheel hard over to provoke a rear-end slide, then hit the accelerator to fight the oversteer with power understeer in the hope of getting a four-wheel drift. All she got was a spin. As she came out of it a stationary truck seemed to be coming straight at her. Somehow she managed to miss it, backing off the loud pedal, waiting for the tyres to generate some grip and the steering more feel and hoping to Christ the old girl would stay on her feet. Miraculously, she did.

But where the fuck was Nikki?

Then she saw the big truck swing across the road behind her, and block it. The sweat of relief ran down her flanks.

The Citroën, followed by the armoured car, went into the left-hander fast but pulled up faster, just short of the big truck blocking the road. Blech jumped out and started yelling at the driver to get the truck out of the way. Then the Stens opened up – from the roof of the truck, from under the truck, from the driving cab, from everywhere. Blech raised his Schmeisser, but suddenly spun and fell into the gutter. Wounded. In fact, dying, he was sure.

The three other Gestapo men jumped out of the Citroën and started firing, but were cut down in seconds.

Then the armoured car put a 90mm shell into the petrol tank of the truck and the whole lot went up in a swirl of smoke and flame.

Blech, covered with debris from the truck, watched the armoured car nudge the Citroën aside, then smash through the debris of the truck and disappear up the street. He crawled across the pavement, leaving a trail of blood that frightened him to death, then got to his feet and staggered into a café.

'Gestapo,' he said to a woman cowering behind the bar. 'Have you got a phone?'

She looked at him in fear and dislike and pointed to a phone at the end of the bar. His one idea was to hurry the ambulance service up. He'd already put out a call on the R/T, but now it was urgent. He could feel the coldness of death on him. Even the woman must have sensed he was dying, and poured him a cognac without being asked. He drank it down and began to feel less cold. And realized that the dying might take a little longer.

She couldn't shake the armoured car off. The ambulance had the edge in speed and was nippier through the bends, but the armoured car was always there, in her mirror. Twice the gunner loosed off a round with the 90mm cannon, but Yaka disturbed his aim by peppering the gun turret with his Sten.

In the end she managed to shake it off by going the wrong way up a one-way street without actually hitting anything, despite some alarming near-misses. Luck was with her. But not with the armoured car. Behind her she heard the crash of metal on metal, followed by the sound of shattering glass.

'It's gone straight through a window full of lingerie,' said Yaka. 'Be funny if it came out in French knickers.'

But she was no longer listening. Straight ahead was an SS roadblock. She turned down a side street, then into a tree-lined boulevard, then into another street. And almost into another roadblock.

She reversed on to the pavement, went back down the street and then followed a sign that said: *Le Vieux Rennes*. That was where Victor had his workshop and yard.

After the armoured car had extricated itself from the lingerie, Raab ordered the driver to roam the streets at random in the hope of sighting the ambulance again.

'They were heading in the general direction of the Old Quarter,' he said. 'If we do the same we might get lucky.'

And they did. They were approaching a crossroads when an ambulance shot across in front of them from right to left. Raab got a glimpse of a scarred face and blonde hair.

'After them!' he snapped. But the driver was already going into the turn. As they came out of it they found themselves facing a steep hill. Near the top, accelerating hard, was the ambulance. Any moment it would be over the brow and out of sight.

'Got the range?' said Raab.

'Seventy-five,' said the gunner coolly. 'Elevation twenty-three.'

Raab's voice was flat and hard. 'Fire!'

The gunner fired.

The 90mm shell smashed through the rear doors of the ambulance, which swerved out of control into a street lamp. The armoured car drew up alongside it and Raab got out, followed by two uniformed SS men with Schmeissers.

A bullet-headed Frenchman got out of one side of the wrecked driving cab, a tow-headed youth out of the other. The youth had a badly scarred face and wore an old uniform jacket of the French air force. He coughed into a handkerchief. Bullethead had two rows of medal ribbons stitched over the left breast of his jacket. He went straight up to Raab.

'You murdering fuckpig,' he said.

The SS men cocked their Schmeissers and stepped between Raab and Bullethead. Raab waved them back.

'There was no one in the ambulance, I take it?' he said.

156

'Of course not,' said Bullethead. 'We were answering a call from *you* bastards. Like every other ambulance.'

'We made a mistake,' said Raab. 'I'll radio for a car to take you back.'

'We'll walk,' said Bullethead. He put his arm round the youth's shoulder and they trudged off.

Raab turned to the SS men. 'Get back in the car,' he said, and followed them in.

'Where to, Herr Standartenfuehrer?' said the driver.

'I don't know,' said Raab. 'All cats are grey by night.'

Ryfka was thinking along similar lines. She pulled up at a crossroads, unable to decide which way to go. Trouble could lie anywhere.

'What are we actually looking for?' said Yaka.

'A hiding place,' she said. 'I'd arranged for one in the Old Quarter, but the area's blocked off. I should've looked for an alternative place. Out of town.'

Yaka hesitated, then said: 'I know a place.'

'Where?'

'Out of town.'

'Can we hide the ambulance there?'

Yaka shook his head. 'That wouldn't be possible.'

'Then it's no good.'

She let the clutch in, drove off.

'Where are we going now?'

'Out of town,' she said. 'To look for an old barn or some woods where we can dump the ambulance.'

'Couldn't we . . .' Again he hesitated.

'What?'

'Just dump it in a ditch?'

'Brilliant,' she said. 'That's brilliant.'

'No,' said Yaka slowly, searching for exactitude, 'not brilliant. But not bad. Listen – '

'Shit,' she said. 'another roadblock.' And fishtailed the ambulance and turned back.

Raab went back to the Hotel Abelard, outwardly calm, and looked for Solange. He found her soaking herself in the bath, legs crossed, feet resting on the rim at one end. He stood by her feet, looking down at her. His face was expressionless and she couldn't see his eyes behind the smoked glasses, but sensed his mood was bad.

He smiled, bent down and began stroking her feet. Then, still smiling, he gripped her ankles and eased her legs apart. She smiled back, hoping it was just one of his strange games.

He contemplated her for what seemed an eternity, then suddenly, swiftly stepped back and jerked her legs upwards till she was almost standing on her head under the water. She struggled and tried to kick but his grip never slackened. Then she started swallowing mouthfuls of warm soapy water and choking, drowning...

Raab, an expert in water torture, let go of her, pulled the plug out of the bath and left her gasping, retching and half fainting.

He went into the elegant salon, took two small white tablets with a little mineral water and went down to an office on the floor below, refreshed and ready for work.

This, his official office, was part of an administrative complex that included a communications room with a switchboard, telex and radio-telephone and a combined map room and conference room.

The first thing he saw was a message on his desk to the effect that Blech had been taken to hospital with a gunshot wound that turned out to be superficial. Of the other Gestapo men, one was dead, one dying, the third badly wounded.

He would have to send a report of the incident to avenue Foch, with three copies (or was it four?) to the Reichssicherheitshauptamt in Berlin... He must get a result before then. A success to justify the mayhem. He must catch Ryfka *and* the air commodore...

An orderly knocked and entered from the communications room. 'Ambulance sighted heading north on the N12, mein Herr, between Thorigne and Liffré, where roadblocks have been set up.'

Raab nodded and got up to study the wall map. Thorigne

was five or six kilometres out of Rennes and Liffré a few kilometres farther on. He knew Liffre well. That was the junction with the road leading to Les Sapins Argentés.

He dismissed the orderly and went back to the map to decide the placing of roadblocks.

There was a knock on the door and Blech entered in his black SS uniform with a black silk sling for his wounded arm.

'Ah,' said Raab, 'the wounded hero back in uniform and reporting for duty with an empty sleeve and matching sling. Still, it's not as bad as the Russian Front, I imagine.'

'I was also wounded on the Russian Front, mein Herr.'

'Yes, I know,' said Raab. 'I read the report in your personal file. But this time, at least, you didn't shoot yourself in the foot.'

'It was someone else who shot me in the foot, mein Herr.'

'And then you were posted to Einsatzgruppe D, behind the lines in Eastern Galicia. Where you were supposed to shoot Jews. Easy enough, I'd have thought, and a lot less painful than being shot in the foot. But you couldn't even manage that, it seems.'

'I joined the SS to be a soldier, mein Herr, not an executioner.'

'Killing Jews is everyone's duty.'

Another knock and the orderly entered and saluted. 'The ambulance has been found abandoned, Herr Standartenfuehrer, near the village of Launay, not far from – '

'Launay? That's only a few kilometres from Les Sapins. Any indication why it was abandoned?'

'It seems to have taken a bend too fast, mein Herr,' said the orderly. 'And ended up in a ditch.'

'Anybody in it? The ambulance, I mean.'

'Only the doctor, mein Herr. On the floor. Trussed up like a chicken.'

'Anything else?'

'I don't think so, mein Herr. Oh, yes. A blonde wig. Also on the floor.'

A brief silence, then Raab got up. 'They can't have got far. I want the whole area cordoned off. We'll search every house, every barn, every byre. And hold the doctor. I want to question him.'

He turned to Blech. 'Get the armoured car. We'll take a look at the ambulance – tell them not to move it. And that doctor must know something. And get tracker dogs down there.' He laughed his dry laugh. 'Take quite a dog to catch that bitch.'

She supported him on one side, Yaka on the other, which worked quite well since he was taller than either of them. But the going was rough over the fields. And it was a hot day.

'How much farther?' she said.

'Two or three kilometres,' said Yaka.

'That's what you said three kilometres ago.'

'Distances can be deceptive.'

She looked up at Romaine. 'You all right?'

He nodded. His face was flushed, almost hectic, his breathing laboured, any movement obviously painful. His ribs were heavily strapped. She could feel the strapping through his clothes. He must have taken a hell of a kicking. But his face wasn't badly marked, just a black eye and some bruising down one side. It was still a shock though when she climbed into the back of the ambulance and got her first good look at him. He had looked ill then, his face pale apart from that consumptive flush. Now he looked even worse. He must have felt her glance because he turned and looked down at her. She had an odd feeling whenever their eyes met. Was he really a stranger? Or was it some sort of pretence? When she looked in his eyes she couldn't believe he was a stranger.

He seemed to be leaning most of his weight on her. Not that she minded. It was easy to be a beast of burden, something simple and unthinking for once. An *instrumentum mutum*. A state akin to innocence or virginity. And about as long lasting.

They crossed a field and came to a stream. 'Let's follow it,' she said.

'It will take us out of our way,' said Yaka.

160

'It will take the dogs out of their way, too.'

'I never thought of that.'

'You can bet Raab has.'

They stepped into the stream, but it was too narrow for three to go abreast.

'You go ahead,' she said to Yaka. 'You know the way.'

Now his whole weight seemed to be on her. But she hardly noticed; strength flowed through her like an electric charge. Twice he stumbled and she caught him before he fell. But progress was slow. At first the coldness of the water was a relief from the heat, but soon it began to bite. She could hear the rasp of his breathing, sense his pain. Suddenly, as they were wading through a field bordered by open woodland, he stopped.

'I can't feel my feet,' he said, sounding like a small boy.

'It's the cold,' she said. 'We'll get out. In just a minute.'

There were cattle in the field and she was looking for their drinking place, which would have been trampled into a wet muddy morass. The wetness and the heavy smell of cattle would throw tracker dogs off the scent. Like as not, they'd pick up the wrong scent and follow it straight to the farmyard.

She soon found the place where the bank had been trampled into a gently sloping morass, and they climbed out. With Yaka supporting him on the other side they reached the woodland and made better progress. At the far edge of the woodland, near a fallen elm, they stopped again. Before them lay another field, a cornfield, bordered by a hedgerow and a road. Beyond the road, more fields, then a stand of silver birches, shimmering in the heat.

Yaka pointed. 'The house is behind the birch trees.'

'Looks bloody miles away,' she said.

'Stay here a minute while I make sure everything's all right.'

'Supposing she says no,' said Ryfka.

'She won't say no,' said Yaka.

Ryfka was suddenly full of doubts. 'It's crazy. Why should she?'

161

'It's our only chance,' said Yaka and started off across the field, walking quickly. Then he broke into a run.

She turned and saw Romaine sitting on the fallen elm, his head in his hands.

She went and sat beside him. 'Are you all right?'

'Tired,' he said.

She put her arm round him. Then, faint and faraway, she heard the deep-throated menace of the dogs. She got to her feet.

He looked up at her. 'Give me a gun and leave me.'

'Come on.'

'I'll see they don't take me alive.'

She held out her hands. He grasped them, but didn't move. The touch of his hands – warm, dry, alive – was like a direct current. She felt she couldn't let go. Then she heard the deep-throated menace again and pulled strongly against him and brought him to his feet. He swayed and she quickly slipped her arm round him.

'It's not far now,' she said. 'Just beyond the trees.'

They left the shelter of the wood and started to cross the field. It was hard going over the rough, tussocky ground and his weight seemed to grow with every step. She was also beginning to tire, but the thought of being caught in the open by the dogs fired up her strength. They struggled on. Then he stopped, flanks heaving like a winded horse.

'Don't give up now,' she said.

He shook his head, too breathless to speak.

'Lean on me,' she said.

Again he shook his head.

'*Lean* on me, you bastard.'

The ambulance was lying on its side in a ditch, like a dead sheep torn by bullets. Raab walked round it as far as he could, nearly slipping into the ditch at one point, but saved by Blech with well-concealed reluctance.

'And nobody killed or even injured,' Raab said.

'Don't the English say it's better to be born lucky than rich?'

'Now she's due for some bad luck,' said Raab. He looked around. 'Where's the doctor?'

Blech pointed to one of three Gestapo cars lined up behind an SS troop carrier at the side of the road. 'In there, mein Herr.'

'Fetch him.'

Blech fetched him. Raab tried questioning him, but got nowhere. The little doctor was too nervous and shocked to be coherent. And too concerned about the correct form of address. He knew that Standartenfuehrer was the SS equivalent of a full colonel but wasn't sure whether to address him as *mon colonel*, since they were speaking French, or simply *mein Herr*, which might, in the circumstances, be more judicious.

'But you did realize it was la Balafrée?'

'Well, yes, mon colonel. I mean, no, mon colonel. I mean not at first, mein Herr. You see, I was tied up in the back of the ambulance and she was wearing this blonde wig. It was only when she took it off and threw it on the floor that I realized who she was. My God, I said to myself, it's – '

'Who tied you up?'

'The man, mon colonel.'

'What man?'

'The one who was with her, mon colonel.'

'Can you describe him?'

'I'm not sure. My impressions were vague.'

'Try,' Raab said patiently.

'Certainly, mein Herr.'

'And stop calling me mein Herr. Just answer the questions.'

'Yes, mon colonel. Well, he was dressed like an ambulance man. With a peaked cap that was too big for him.'

'Good,' said Raab. 'Fine. And his face? Fresh complexion? Sallow complexion?'

'Medium complexion, mon colonel.'

'Medium,' said Raab dryly. 'A great help. Any distinguishing marks? Outstanding features?'

'His ears. They were outstanding, mon colonel. He had, as we say in the profession, jug ears.'

163

'So we look for a man with jug ears.'

'Ah, a moment, I've just thought. Maybe it was the hat pressing *down* on them that made them stand out. If you see what I mean, mon colonel.'

Raab's face was impassive, his voice calm. 'And how was the prisoner?'

'The prisoner? In what way, mein Herr? I mean, mon colonel.'

'Physically. Could he walk? Could he run?'

'Run? No. Walk? Yes, I should think so. With help, perhaps.'

'How far would he get?'

'Difficult to say.'

'Then guess.'

Charvet lifted his shoulders. Once the questions took a medical turn his answers became more confident, if non-committal.

'I only had time for a brief examination, mon colonel. There was extensive bruising around the ribs. Almost certainly some torn muscles. Probably of the external inter-costals, possibly the internal as well. Even the accessory muscles – '

'How far could he get? That's all I want to know.'

'Who can say, mon colonel? Courage and will power cannot be measured against . . .' Another lift of the shoulders. 'The standard metre in Paris.'

'I understand that,' Raab said, taking off his black leather gauntlets. 'I am asking you to guess.'

'Well . . .' Charvet began.

Raab whipped the heavy gauntlets across his face, first one way, then the other. The little doctor staggered. Raab whipped his face again. And again. The little doctor fell. Blood was running down his face and into his mouth, tasting salt. He got to his feet.

'Guess,' said Raab politely.

'N-not far,' said Charvet.

Raab drew his Luger. 'How far?'

Charvet stared at him in silence, his tongue tentatively searching his cut mouth, which had started to swell. Raab whipped the gun across his face. Again the little doctor went down. This time he got to his feet with some difficulty.

'I asked you a question,' said Raab.

'I was trying to answer.'

'Then answer.'

Another deliberate silence, then: 'A kilometre perhaps.'

Raab cocked the gun. 'What does perhaps mean?'

'Perhaps two kilometres,' said Charvet steadily. 'Perhaps four.'

Raab turned to Blech. 'Get him out of my sight. Before I kill him.'

He went over to the ambulance. The SS man guarding it came smartly to attention. The rear doors were open and he stared inside. On the floor was a long blonde wig. He picked it up, combed it with his fingers, absently. 'Anything else found?'

'Only some empty Sten gun magazines, Herr Standarten-fuehrer,' said the SS man. 'And two hairpins.'

Blech joined him. 'Radio message from the dog patrol, mein Herr. They've picked up a scent.'

'Of what? Chickenshit? You'll never catch her with dogs. Our best hope is the prisoner. He'll be slowing her down all the time. He'll need rest and shelter . . . And then we'll have them.' Raab smiled tightly. 'Trapped.'

Looking back she wondered how they'd made it. Over rough fields, through shitty farmyards and filthy wet ditches till at last they came to the stand of silver birches that she was beginning to think was a mirage, always just beyond reach. The last part of the journey was hell. Harry – she tried to think of him as Romaine, to keep an emotional distance between them, but his name kept coming up Harry – was getting progressively weaker, his breathing more laboured. And now, for the first time, she really began to feel the weight of him. She was glad when Yaka came back to give her a hand.

'Everything okay?'

'Fine,' he said.

'You're sure?'

'It's the one place they'll never find us.'

'But can we trust her? I mean, why the hell should she stick her neck out for us? We could be walking into a terrible trap.'

'You have to trust people.'

'Sure,' she said. 'Famous last words.'

'See the path on the right, between the silver birches? It leads to the back of the house.'

'I can't see any path.'

'Follow me.'

Harry, she thought, as they stumbled along the narrow path that wound through the birch trees, Harry will be the death of me. Of us all. Unless I do something about it.

Then they were out of the trees and there it was, the back elevation of the old house, spread out before them: long, sprawling, angular. Its overhanging eaves seemed to frown at her, like an old man trying to look severe and fooling no one. Or perhaps she was just assigning magical properties to it in the relief at finding a haven. Well, the illusions of animism were harmless enough, if childish. *Lacrimae rerum* and all that. Or perhaps she was just tired and imagining things.

They took Harry straight up to the loft, which was warm and fairly comfortable. In fact, sheer luxury after the discomforts of the journey. The floor had been boarded and covered in coconut matting, and there was a flat narrow ceiling between the roof trusses with long sloping sides in line with the pitch of the roof. The sloping sides were broken by two dormer windows, one overlooking the front of the house, the other the back. The loft had obviously been converted into a room for servants or perhaps a nursery – there was a broken cot in one corner. And plenty of junk everywhere, including an old mattress on the floor that looked as if it had come from a double bed. There was even a cracked and speckled mirror on a broken washstand.

It was easy enough to get him on to the mattress, he practically fell on it, then closed his eyes.

'Marvellous,' he murmured, and was asleep. But his breathing was still uneven, his face flushed.

166

She heard a noise and went to the dormer window over-looking the front and saw a cobbled courtyard entered by a long straight drive bordered by yet more silver birches.

She spoke over her shoulder to Yaka. 'What was it you said about this being the one place they'd never find us?'

Rumbling down the drive was Raab's armoured car, squat and ugly against the silver birches, now catching highlights from a dying sun. Behind it came three black Citroëns.

13

The armoured car pulled up in the courtyard, the three black Citroëns fanning out in line abreast behind it. Raab and Blech got out of the armoured car, Gestapo men out of the Citroëns.

'Split them into armed squads,' Raab told Blech, 'and search every barn, shed or outbuilding in the fields and paddocks behind the house. You know what the prisoner and the woman look like. As for the other man, we never saw his face, but he was about my height, wouldn't you say? And limps. But he'll be armed, remember. And so will the woman. Report to me in the house.'

Blech saluted and moved smartly off, very soldierly in his black uniform with one arm in a black sling. Raab gave one of his tight smiles, then crossed the courtyard to the house. The front door opened and Therese came out on to the covered porch.

'I wasn't expecting you,' she said.

'Had any callers?' said Raab. 'Especially strangers, asking for food or shelter?'

Therese shook her head. 'Just the postman, with a letter from my cousin in La Roche-sur-Yon.'

'Nothing unusual then?'

'Only your arrival.' She nodded towards the Gestapo cars. 'Why the army?'

He jerked his head. 'I'll tell you inside.'

'Would you like some coffee?' she said as they went in. 'I've just made some.'

Over brioches and coffee at the refectory table in the big farmhouse kitchen Raab told her of the hijacking of the ambulance and the rescue of the prisoner.

'And where are they now?'

'Here.'

She raised her eyebrows. 'Here?'

He gestured casually. 'Within a radius of three or four kilometres, I expect.'

'That's quite an area.'

'We've got an even bigger area cordoned off by a battalion of SS troops and armoured vehicles. And I'm calling in more. Plus the local milice. We'll seach every house and outhouse, comb every wood with dogs, look under every hedge, every blade of grass. It's just a matter of time. Meanwhile, not a mouse will move in or out of this area without my knowledge.'

'Never mind a woman,' said Therese with the ghost of a smile.

'Exactly,' said Raab.

He sounded more confident that he felt. Ryfka was still at large. La Balafrée. A living legend of resistance – and a living contradiction of Nazi dogma that Jews were subhuman. *Untermenschen. Dreck.* Fit only for extermination. He'd seen them stumble to their deaths with glazed eyes in the camps in Poland: old men, women, children, already half dead from hunger and maltreatment. But he'd also been a subaltern with General Stroop at the Warsaw ghetto and seen Jews fight to the death in cellars and sewers and burning buildings that after three weeks of continuous battle became their funeral pyres. The memory of their courage stuck in his throat like a fishbone. It seemed to him a mockery that it should have taken the Germans longer to conquer the Warsaw ghetto than to conquer all France.

At the moment, though, there was only one Jewish problem for Raab. And his whole future could depend on its solution. A problem called Ryfka.

The signal from the Reichssicherheitshauptampt in Berlin, relayed through SS headquarters in avenue Foche, said there were two Romaines on the RAF list. An Air Commodore Harold Julian Romaine and a Pilot Officer John Edward Romaine, missing believed killed in action. But no Squadron Leader Romaine. Avenue Foche presumed Standartenfuehrer Raab's inquiry was about Pilot Officer John Edward Romaine, since an air commodore would be non-operational, and that the earlier reference to a squadron leader was a mistake. Would Standartenfuehrer Raab please confirm? Standartenfuehrer Raab was only too pleased to confirm the mistake, due to an unfortunate transmission error.

A lucky escape. If avenue Foche, never mind the Reichssicherheitshauptampt, found out he'd used an air commodore, unwittingly or not, as bait to capture a minor resistance leader – and then lost both – he, Otto Raab, would be for the high jump. But they were not going to find out. The only one likely to shop him, inadvertently or deliberately, was Blech. And Blech could be fixed.

It still puzzled him why an air commodore should go on an operational flight. But one thing was certain. If Ryfka's mission was to recover this Romaine then he must be vital to Allied plans for the Second Front. Which meant he must *know* about the Second Front.

He may have murmured something under his breath at that point because Therese said: 'I beg your pardon?'

'Another coffee,' Raab said, brusquely.

She watched them from the rear dormer window searching the barn nearest the house. Four men armed with Schmeissers went into the barn. Four others, similarly armed, covered every entrance and exit. Blech stood a little way off, watching the operation and smoking a cigarette.

The four men who'd gone into the barn came out dragging an old white-haired tramp in a tattered military jacket. They had the air of a conjuror producing a rabbit from a hat. Blech ground his cigarette under his heel, gestured angrily and swore at them. At least, that was what it sounded like. They let the old tramp go and he scurried back into the barn.

Then she heard Yaka say: 'I think he's delirious.'

She went over and knelt on the mattress. He was asleep, but muttering unintelligibly, his face still pale, despite the flush. She leaned closer, trying to make out what he was saying.

'I know,' he said. 'I know. She doesn't think I know.'

'What do you know?' she said softly. 'Tell me what you know.'

'Ah,' he said. 'I know she has a lover. I've known for a time. Oh, yes . . . John. Where's John?' Tears rolled down his cheeks. 'And Elizabeth? Under the rubble?'

Then he turned over and slept without words.

Raab was still in the kitchen when Blech came in to report that the search was complete and nothing found, apart from an old tramp.

'Sit down, Blech,' said Raab. 'And have some coffee.'

Blech sat down, a little wary. Raab had a naturally cold voice. When he tried to be friendly it rustled like dead leaves. Blech preferred it cold.

Therese poured Blech a coffee. Raab laced it with cognac, then said to her: 'Did you know you had a tramp in one of the barns?'

She nodded. 'He does odd jobs – chops wood, keeps the garden tidy and so on – in return for food and shelter.'

'Where's Tilly?'

'In the sitting room, putting a hem on some new curtains.'

'Why don't you join her? I have business to discuss.'

He watched her as she crossed to the door. She had a good figure. Long legs. Should strip well. He put more cognac in Blech's coffee. Drink had addled better brains than his.

'You were right about Ryfka's mission,' he said. 'It *was* to rescue the airman. He's a senior officer, it seems. An air commodore.'

'Then why pretend to be a squadron leader?'

'There's an explanation for that,' said Raab smoothly. 'According to René le Court, he got a bang on the head when he landed. And suffered lapses of memory as a consequence. Not that it matters now. He'll soon be back in our hands. And so will Ryfka.' He smiled his tight smile. 'And that won't do us any harm with avenue Foche or even the Reichssicherheitshauptamt. Any harm at all.'

'Could mean another promotion for you, mein Herr.'

'I wasn't thinking of myself.'

171

'No?' said Blech. 'I mean, I'm sure you weren't.'

'You've been a great help in this business.'

'I have?' said Blech, wondering if he'd heard right.

'And when that truck blocked our path you were the first out of the car – to face the bullets. And the first to be wounded, what's more.'

'But that was . . . well, I mean, if I'd known – '

Raab held up an admonitory hand. 'Allow me to be the judge.'

'Of course, mein Herr. Of course.'

'Drink your coffee.'

In his confusion Blech swallowed too much laced coffee and spluttered as the cognac hit him.

'I have decided to recommend you,' said Raab, 'for a decoration and promotion.'

'You what?' said Blech in a daze, wondering where the catch was.

'And my recommendations go through on a rubber stamp. Without question.'

'Well, thank you, mein Herr,' said Blech, and hiccupped.

She sat on the mattress dabbing his forehead with a small handkerchief. He was sweating a little and still pale, though his breathing was less laboured. She leaned closer to listen, and suddenly his eyes were open, looking into hers. She went on automatically dabbing his face.

Then he sniffed. 'Is that cologne on the handkerchief?'

'Please keep your voice down,' she said. 'This is Standartenfuehrer Raab's country house. And he's here.' She pointed downwards.

'Raab's house?'

'At least it's unlikely to be searched.'

'But how did you – '

'Not now,' she said. 'Explanations later. How are you feeling?'

'Weak,' he said.

She got up and went over to Yaka, who was at the window overlooking the front of the house.

'Looks as if they've finished searching the grounds,' he said. 'They're going back to their cars.'

'As soon as Raab clears off,' she said, 'I'll phone Luc and get him to come out in the van and pick you up.'

She turned and was in time to see Harry Romaine trying to get to his feet. She went quickly towards him but before she could get there he lost his balance and fell heavily back on the mattress.

'What are you trying to do?' she said. 'Get us all killed?'

She drew her Walther P38, pushed down the safety catch and crossed to the door. She opened it carefully and listened, but heard nothing. A short flight of stairs led down to the landing where the bedrooms were. She crept down and hid herself in the shadows at the head of the main flight of stairs. If Raab or anyone else came up to investigate he'd be a dead man. After that, though, all the options looked bad.

Therese heard the thump and looked up. She was in the sitting room with Tilly, sewing tapes on the new curtains.

'I wonder what that was?' she said, more to herself than Tilly.

'Those people up in the loft, of course,' said Tilly. 'Who do you think?'

'What people up in the loft?' It was Raab's voice. Therese turned and saw him standing in the doorway.

'The ones who send electric shocks through the ceilings, I expect,' she said dryly.

'It's getting worse,' said Tilly. 'It's getting to the point where you can't go to the lavatory. Even that beautiful lavatory with the chain you built for us. I must admit the Prussians are years ahead of us in lavatories, if not in culture. But really, colonel, you ought to speak to them.'

'I will, Tilly.'

'You're always saying that, colonel. But you never do.'

'I'll do it now. Straight away. At once. All right?'

Tilly nodded. 'As long as you remember to take your boots off.'

'My boots?'

173

Tilly sighed and looked up to heaven. 'Otherwise they'll hear you coming – and hide.' She spoke slowly, as if to a child. 'They can make themselves so small they'll slip into a crack in the plaster.'

'Next time I come,' said Raab, 'I'll bring tennis shoes. And creep up there and surprise them.' He turned to Therese. 'Did you hear a noise?'

She saw the cat asleep under the table and out of Raab's sight. As long as it stayed there.

'May have been the cat after a mouse in the loft. She always goes up there if the door's not shut.'

'It wasn't the cat,' said Tilly. 'It was those people.'

'Of course it was,' said Raab. He laughed his dry laugh and went out into the hall, calling for Blech.

Therese saw them to the front door.

'The great thing about Tilly,' said Raab, 'is that she keeps me sane.'

Another dry laugh, then he and Blech marched across the courtyard to the armoured car, jackboots ringing on the cobbles.

The *Herrenvolk*. She closed the door and leaned against it, suddenly weak. She was still leaning against it when Ryfka came down the stairs.

'Are you all right?'

Therese nodded. 'Had a bit of a fright, that's all. Raab got curious about a noise and I managed to fob him off with a story about the cat.'

Ryfka explained about the fall and apologized. 'I can't tell you how grateful I am.'

Therese shrugged it off. 'You're a friend of Yaka's.'

Victor was french-polishing a coffin when Luc walked in. Victor ignored him. Luc was always bad news.

'Hi, Victor. How's tricks?'

'Whatever you want,' said Victor, 'the answer's no.'

He polished the coffin even more assiduously.

'Old Victor, always beavering away. No wonder you're rich.'

'What do you want?'

'Me? I don't want anything.'

'You mean you just looked in to pass the time of day?'

'Just had Ryfka on the blower. She asked after you.'

'I don't want anything to do with her either.'

'Ah, don't be like that. She's very fond of you, Victor.'

'She's in trouble, isn't she? After hijacking that prisoner from under Raab's nose. She wants something, doesn't she?'

'A little advice, Victor, that's all.'

'The only advice I can give is about funerals.'

'Funny you should say that, Victor, because that's just what she does want.'

Victor stopped work, cocked his head to one side. 'Then how come she rings you, instead of me?'

Luc spread his hands. 'Because, Victor, old friend, she doesn't want to talk about it on an open line. Too risky. She wants me to drive you out there to talk to her.'

'Drive me out where? She's in hiding, surrounded by roadblocks and SS men. Haven't you heard the news?'

'Of course I have, old son. But what's a few roadblocks? All you need is an excuse. I got thousands of excuses. So have you. Business contacts all over the place. It'll be a cinch.'

Victor banged his fist on the coffin. 'Get one thing clear – '

'Careful,' said Luc, 'you'll wake the dead.'

'I am not, repeat not, going anywhere with you. To see anyone. Least of all Ryfka.'

'That's final?'

'Final.' Victor was beginning to shake, though Luc wasn't sure whether it was anger or nerves.

He sighed and shrugged, accepting the inevitable. Then he lit a cigarette.

It was getting dark and the blackout curtains were already drawn when Luc's old van pulled into the courtyard. Ryfka was already at the front door and watched Luc get out. He spoke to someone in the driving cab, but apparently got no answer, shrugged and started towards the house. Then

175

Victor got out, reluctance in every line of his angular figure. Luc waited for him and they crossed to the house together.

'I want you to know,' Victor said to Ryfka, 'that I am here under protest.'

'Of course you are,' said Ryfka, giving him a hug and a kiss.

'And in a purely consultative capacity, what's more.'

'Come and have a bite to eat. You never eat properly.'

Therese had prepared a meal in the kitchen and they all sat down at the long refectory table to eat by the light of oil lamps and the warmth of a log fire. Therese sat at one end with Yaka, Ryfka at the other with Luc and Victor. Tilly, tired out by the excitements and traffic of the day, had gone to bed. Romaine, still running a temperature, didn't want to eat and had gone back to sleep. Before she left him Rifka pulled the blackout curtains across the dormer windows and lit an oil lamp provided earlier by Therese.

'Well,' said Victor, 'what's so important about funerals that you have to drag me all the way out here?'

'Let's have something to eat,' said Ryfka.

'And a drop of wine,' said Luc.

'Don't care much for wine,' said Victor.

'You might care for this one,' said Ryfka. 'From the Chalonnais. Light, delicate.'

'And a bouquet like spring flowers,' said Luc.

Ryfka poured a little into Victor's glass. 'Try it.'

Victor wrinkled his nose and tried it.

'Well,' he said, 'it's not bad, I suppose.'

She poured more wine into his glass, then poured for the others and finally for herself. Then she raised her glass. 'A toast,' she said. 'To Madame Therese, who gave us sanctuary – with no thought for her own safety.'

Everyone raised his glass. Therese felt herself blushing and lowered her head. Yaka, with a boldness that surprised both of them, reached across the table and squeezed her hand. It was the first time he had touched her and it thrilled him like an embrace.

The wine, the food and the warmth of the kitchen relaxed everyone. Even Victor lost his air of mourning, and smiled.

Ryfka and Luc between them saw that his glass was never empty.

Ryfka excused herself and went up to the loft. She opened the door quietly and crept in. He was still asleep, or seemed to be. She couldn't see much of his face because it was in the shadows thrown by the oil lamp. She lowered herself carefully on to the mattress so as not to disturb him, and put a hand on his forehead. It felt hot, but he was no longer sweating.

Then she realized his eyes were open and looking at her. She withdrew her hand.

'Leave it there,' he said. 'It's cool.'

'I have to go.'

'Go to hell,' he said and turned over.

'As we moved the body,' said Victor, 'it groaned. A dead man groaning. It made my hair stand straight up. Of course, it was only the air being expelled from his lungs. But I was a young apprentice and didn't know that.'

'Amazing,' said Luc. He turned to Ryfka. 'Isn't that an amazing thing?'

'Amazing,' said Ryfka and decanted a little more of the Chalonnais into Victor's glass.

'Steady on,' said Victor. 'I'm feeling a bit zigzag.'

They were alone in the kitchen. As soon as Ryfka came back Therese had diplomatically excused herself, saying she must finish the new curtains. Ryfka suggested Yaka might like to keep her company. Yaka was only too pleased.

The wine was relaxing Victor. Ryfka topped up his glass. She needed him relaxed.

'Any trouble getting through the roadblocks?' she said to Luc.

'Not really. They asked a lot of questions and pissed around searching the van, then waved us through.'

Ryfka stared dreamily into the distance. 'Do you think they'd wave a funeral through?'

Luc shrugged. 'They might. On the other hand, they might prise the coffin lid open and take a look. You know what the bastards are like.'

'I'll tell you one funeral they'll wave through,' said Victor. 'The Truchet funeral.'

'Truchet?' said Ryfka.

'Raab's little friend. I told you about him. Jean-Paul Truchet.'

'Ah yes, the mayor.'

'The collaborator. The real mayor refused to collaborate. So Raab appointed his favourite stool pigeon. Name of Truchet.'

'Anyway, the funeral will be in Rennes, presumably. So it won't need to go through roadblocks.'

'Wrong,' said Victor. 'Truchet was born in the sticks. Some little village between here and Fougères. And that's where he'll be buried. I should know. I was going to do the funeral.'

'It's all coming back. And now it's Achille Leblanc who's doing the funeral.'

'Taking the bread out of my mouth,' said Victor. 'Bastard.'

'That's tough, man,' said Luc. He turned to Ryfka. 'Isn't that tough?'

'When's the funeral?' she said.

'What's today,' said Victor. 'Saturday? Or Sunday?'

'It's the day of the funeral we want,' said Luc.

'Tuesday,' said Victor. 'That's it . . . Or maybe Monday. I'll find out the details and let you know.' He drank some wine too fast and started coughing. Ryfka thumped him on the back till he recovered, then refilled his glass.

'Tell you this,' said Victor. 'I'll get even with the bastard. If it kills me.'

Ryfka raised her glass. 'Down with Achille Leblanc.'

They all clinked glasses, the men echoing her words.

Then they drank. Victor drained his glass, Ryfka refilled it. 'Did you really mean it about getting even with him?'

'Mean it?' said Victor. 'Give me the chance. Just give me the bloody chance.'

Ryfka laid a hand on his arm and spoke softly. 'Maybe I'll do that, Victor.'

'Whaddya mean?' he said, suddenly suspicious, fixing her with eyes that didn't quite focus.

'Maybe you'll get to do the Truchet funeral after all.'

'Yeah?' said Victor. 'And maybe you're mad. Mad as a March hare. Maybe I'm mad too. Or soon will be.' He turned to Luc. 'She's mad.' He sighed like a blowing whale, leant across the table, put his head in his arms and fell asleep.

'You'd better take him home,' said Ryfka.

'You know what?' said Luc. 'Soon as he sobers up he'll back down. He's not man enough for the job.'

'No? Let me tell you something. He's more of a man than you think. And certainly more of man than *he* thinks.'

'Ah, you like him, you're soft on him.'

Ryfka lit a Gauloise and blew out a stream of blue smoke, mostly in Luc's face. 'Good job someone's soft on him.'

Raab was in his proper office, standing in front of an enormous wall map of Rennes and the surrounding countryside. Beside him was Blech. Before him were the assembled chiefs of the local SS, Gestapo and milice, including the chief of the Rennes police, Anatole Loubain.

On the map an area of about ten square kilometres, between Liffré and Dourdain, was cordoned off by little black flags attached to pins, indicating the position of the roadblocks.

Raab had given a brief report of the events of the day and the setting up of roadblocks. The area confined within them would be divided into sectors to be thoroughly searched, one at a time, so that the noose around Ryfka and the hijacked prisoner would gradually tighten. 'Till she's forced to make a break for it,' he added. 'And then we'll take them. Alive if possible. Especially our prisoner.' He hesitated, not wanting to give too much away. 'He could have vital information. Any questions?'

Loubain stood up. 'What sort of information, mein Herr?'

Raab shrugged. 'He's a senior officer, an air commodore, which in army terms is equivalent to a brigadier. He might well have information of value to our high command.'

'About the Second Front?'

'Who knows?' It wasn't a subject Raab wanted to pursue. 'Any other questions?'

Someone asked what had happened to the original ambulance driver and stretcher-bearer. He explained that they were bundled into a waiting van by two men they had never seen before and their uniform jackets and caps removed. Then they were driven to an unoccupied house on the southern outskirts of the city. Raab gestured towards the wall map. 'And locked in a cellar. A couple of hours later they were released.'

'Any descriptions of their assailants, mein Herr?'

'Only the vaguest. Apart from the description of a woman with yellow hair. But we know who she is. The man who assisted her was said to be of medium height and to have, I quote, "something of a Jewish look". Well, that could apply to half the population.' There was a ripple of laughter. 'The chances are this man is a local man, and will be able to pass through roadblocks as part of the legitimate traffic. Not that communications will be a problem for her. The real problem will be to get herself and the prisoner out of the area before we find her. The obvious way would be to radio SOE headquarters for a night pick-up by Hudson or Lysander.'

He pointed to the cordoned-off area on the map. 'Anyone familiar with the area? I'd like to know if there are any fields inside the cordon big enough to take a landing strip.'

Again Loubain stood up. 'I was born there. It's mostly small farms, though some of the larger ones might have grazing land of a suitable size. But size is only one of the requirements. A Lysander needs a field of at least six hundred metres from hedge to hedge. And that's the plane they'll use if the pick-up doesn't involve more than two or three people.'

'I know the land has to be level and firm,' said Raab, 'and the landing strip free of ruts and other obstacles. Any other requirements?'

'Well, there should be no tall trees in the funnel

approaching the landing strip from either end. Small trees don't matter if their tops are below a given angle.'

Raab stared at Loubain in silence. He had never quite trusted the man. Probably because he was French and therefore not of Aryan or even Nordic stock. The Latins, like the Slavs, were inferior. Still, he obviously knew about landing fields.

'Would you do a survey of the bigger farms for me? At first light tomorrow?'

'With pleasure.'

'And if you find any fields you think might serve as landing strips, have them ploughed up. Immediately. Understood?'

'Perfectly, mein Herr.'

'You'll have written authority for the action, of course.'

Loubain made a brief bow of humble acknowledgement, as befitted one of inferior race.

Luc and Yaka helped Victor into the back of the van, where he stretched out full length and fell asleep. Before they drove off Ryfka gave Luc a written message for Michel. 'For immediate transmission, tell him.'

Then she went back to the kitchen to help Therese with the washing up. It was nice to do a few domestic chores again and chat with another woman. For three years she'd worked almost exclusively with men, trained with them, fought with them. Even learned to think like them. But she hoped she was still feminine. The thought of being mannish appalled her.

The flow of small talk dried up with the dishes. Then Therese spoke about Yaka. 'They'll kill him, won't they? Or deport him. And the girl.'

Ryfka shook her head. 'I'm making arrangements to have them flown out. To England.'

'You can arrange that?' Therese sounded incredulous.

'It's been done before. We don't forget those who help us.' She looked at Therese. 'You can always join them.'

'I couldn't leave Tilly and Solange.'

'Bring them too. We'll cope.'

'Five people? In one of those little planes? I saw one that crashed. It looked tiny.'

Ryfka smiled. 'Must have been a Lysander. We'd use a Hudson for a big pick-up. With the rear gun turret removed it can take eight or ten passengers. And luggage.'

Therese was silent. Then she said: 'I wonder if she'd go. Solange, I mean. I think she may love that creature. He's the only one who's ever really taken notice of her.' She jerked her head upwards. 'You like him, don't you?'

'Who?'

'The man,' said Therese. The man. It seemed an odd way to refer to him.

'I'd better get back to him,' said Ryfka. 'He's not well. A fever, I think.'

'Do you want to move him down to one of the bedrooms? It would be more comfortable.'

Ryfka shook her head. 'If Raab came back suddenly, it could be awkward.'

'At least we can give him proper bedclothes.'

She went out into the hall, Ryfka following, and stopped by a big old-fashioned tallboy. She pulled open a drawer, took out some neatly folded sheets and blankets and a coverlet and gave them to Ryfka.

Then she opened another drawer and took out a pair of pyjamas. 'These belonged to my elder son,' she said. 'They were too big for him anyway.' Suddenly she buried her face in them.

'Keep them,' said Ryfka. 'Please.'

Therese shook her head. 'Nothing lasts. Not even grief.'

The man, as Therese called him, was awake when she got back and said he felt better, though he still looked pale. And still didn't want to eat.

'The only thing I want is a bath,' he said.

She showed him the bathroom on the floor below, then made up the mattress into a bed. She lay down and tried to work out future plans, but was too tired to think straight any more.

When he came back in his striped pyjamas with his clothes over his arm and his face shiny he looked like a schoolboy in the light of the oil lamp. She wanted to ask if he'd washed behind his ears.

He got into bed and she went down and had a bath herself. When she got back he was fast asleep. She turned out the lamp and pulled back the curtains, letting some moonlight in, then lay down beside him. It was a warm night though and difficult to sleep with her clothes on, despite her tiredness. Also his presence was a reminder of that night in the past. Memory had a tendency to put a romantic gloss on the past, like moonlight on the present. Perhaps it wasn't even the same man. She deliberately nurtured the doubt in the hope that it would make it easier to kill him when the time came. As come it must.

She looked up at the white ceiling, which seemed to sparkle in a shifting blue twilight, and saw his face swimming there, changing shape, deceptive as ever ... Then, suddenly, she was asleep.

Something woke her. A noise, a movement ... She sat up. He was murmuring, turning restlessly in his sleep. She touched his shoulder. The pyjama jacket felt wet. He was sweating.

She got up, drew the blackout curtains and lit the oil lamp, then knelt on the mattress beside him.

'Harry,' she said. And shook him.

His eyes came open, but didn't seem to focus. 'Who are you?' he said.

'Don't you know?'

'Where's Elizabeth?' He tried to sit up, mumbled something and fell back.

'Harry,' she said. '*Harry*.' But he was unconcious: she wasn't even sure he was breathing. She put her ear to his chest, listened to his heart. Irregular, she thought, but strong. At least he was alive and kicking. And sweating like a pig.

'And John,' he said. 'My son, my son ...'

Maybe the fever was coming out, as her mother used to say. If only she could remember Mother's expert advice (Mother had been a nurse) ... Sponge him down. *With tepid water, not cold.*

She flew down to the kitchen. Tepid, not cold. Tepid, not cold. The kettle was on the hob, the fire banked down. She poured some water into a bowl. It was too warm. She added a little cold. That was better. Tepid, not cold. She went back to the loft, stopping only at the bathroom to get a sponge and a couple of towels.

He was still out, murmuring and sweating. She pulled back the bedclothes and gradually eased his pyjama jacket off. Quite a job since he was half asleep. Then she saw the strapping round his ribs. Three bands of something like Elastoplast. Easy enough to pull off. But not to put back.

'Shit,' she said.

'I beg your pardon?' he said, opening his eyes.

'You do know me then?'

'Why the hell shouldn't I?'

'Ah, you're feeling better.'

'I'm feeling bloody awful,' he said. 'And bloody hot.'

'You've got a fever. I'll sponge you down. Maybe we should leave the strapping on though.'

'Don't see why. It's beginning to itch. That little doctor didn't think anything was broken. Said he'd only put the strapping on to make it look bad. All part of the act, he said.'

She pulled the Elastoplast off carefully, a little at a time. His right side, from his armpit to the bottom of his rib cage, seemed to be one livid bruise. The left side was almost as bad. She sponged him down gently, especially over the bruised areas, then asked him to turn over. The bruises on his back weren't quite so bad. But bad enough.

That'll teach him to play the gallant knight.

When she'd finished sponging him she helped him into his pyjama jacket and remade the bed. She turned out the lamp and pulled the curtains back to let what was left of the moonlight in. The moon itself was veiled in thin cloud and reminded her of Raab's bloodless face. She turned away, kicked off her shoes.

The Man was sleeping . . .

Finally, she lay down beside him, but again couldn't sleep. It was too dam' warm. And he was too bloody restless.

Because he was ill, no doubt. But every time he shifted or turned in his sleep he dragged the covers. Just when she was about to drop off. It was uncanny. No wonder she couldn't sleep ...

In the end she couldn't stand it any longer and got up and took her clothes off; then got between the sheets.

Immediately she felt comfortable. And he stopped shifting and turning and lay with his back towards her. After a time she began to feel cold and inched her back towards him. His back was nice and warm. She relaxed and soon dropped off.

She dreamed she was back in England, lying in a hammock under the old apple tree in the garden of Aunt Lottie's cottage. It was a hot summer's day and she drowsily watched a big butterfly hovering over her, a Red Admiral. Slowly it moved down, cooling her with its wings, and settled on her breast. That was when she realized with a shock that she was stark naked. What on earth had possessed her to take her clothes off? What if Aunt Lottie, or oh my God the rural dean, wandered into the garden? She must get up, put her clothes on. But she couldn't move. Her limbs would no longer obey her brain. As if a spell had been cast over her. By that bloody Red Admiral. Now it was fluttering down her belly; its wings caressing her, like fingertips made of feathers ... My God, any moment now it would be at first base!

Then she woke up. Her back was still towards him, but his arms were round her, his hands everywhere, moving over her, stroking her, caressing her, lightly as a butterfly. As if trying not to wake her. Oh boy, was he going to get a surprise ... First she'd pretend she was still asleep, all innocent. And then, just when he thought he was in control, sneaky bastard, she'd show him, she'd ... she'd ... An oddly exciting but at the same time soothing sensation began to spread through her limbs, relaxing her like a warm wind blowing from the south ... And then before she realized what was happening, desire swept over her like a flash flood and she was in his arms, all pretence gone.

14

Dog minus 8

The signal was picked up by the SOE signals station in the Chilterns at 3 a.m., decoded by the cipher staff and telexed to SOE in Baker Street.

Frank Smith, who had a bed put up in his office when the operation began, was woken by a pretty Welsh WAAF known as Blodwen (her real name was said to be unpronounceable), and given the telex. He rubbed the sleep out of his eyes and read the message. Then he rang Mossop at his Kensington home, a mansion flat on the fifth floor of a rambling Edwardian folly with turreted towers that always made Frank Smith want to laugh. It gave him a schoolboy pleasure to wake Mossop up in the middle of the night. But Mossop was a heavy sleeper and Frank Smith had to change the phone to the other ear while it rang and rang and rang.

Good God, he thought, the old ram hasn't got a bird up there, surely? At his age? Anyone over fifty was past it. And if he wasn't he jolly well ought to be. Sexual activity in the old was obscene. And old started at fifty. It used to start at forty, but had to be adjusted upwards when he himself reached thirty. Now thirty-two, he still felt a safe distance from the dread day when failing powers would force him to hang up his boots.

''Ullo?' growled a voice at the other end of the line with a suddenness that made him jump. ''Ullo?'

Major General Albert Mossop was awake. Red-eyed and ropey, if Frank Smith knew anything.

'Smith here. Our Bigot's been recovered. Message just in from Ryfka.'

'Read it, if it's short.'

'It is. She was told to keep signals short in case the Boche direction finders – '

'Don't waffle, son, *read* it.'

'Bollocks,' said Frank Smith *sotto voce*.

'Speak up, son,' said Mossop. 'Can't hear nowt if tha' mutters.'

'T-O-R: 0–two hundred and eighteen, bluff check present, true check present – '

'Fuck the initials, son, and all that guff, what does she say?'

Frank Smith took a deep breath. 'Message begins: "BIGOT RECOVERED STOP NOW IN SAFE HOUSE STOP ROADBLOCKS ALL AROUND STOP PLAN TO CRASH OUT MONDAY STOP REQUEST LYSANDER PICK-UP LES COLOMBES TUESDAY 0–TWO HUNDRED HOURS STOP OR THERE-ABOUTS STOP COULD DO WITH ERROL FLYNN STOP" Message ends.'

'What the 'ell does crash out mean?' said Mossop.

'Perhaps what it says.'

'And 'oo's Errol Flynn?'

'Paddy Flynn. The mad Irishman of One-six-one Squadron.'

'What's so special about 'im, apart from 'is being mad?'

'That doesn't make him special, the whole squadron's mad. But she's had a soft spot for him ever since he picked her up when she was in trouble and flashing the wrong code letter.'

'You mean 'e *landed* when 'e was getting the wrong letter?'

'He thought she might've forgotten the right one.'

'But 'e could've been walking straight into a Gestapo reception committee.'

'He was. They were right on her heels. But that's Flynn. Where angels fear to tread.'

Mossop muttered something rude and said: 'All right, set it up. Give her what she asks for. Including Flynn.'

Frank Smith hung up and Blodwen, whose name had been given a graphic extension by the office males, appeared with coffee and brandy.

'Brandy,' he said. 'No coffee. It ruins the taste.'

187

'I used to know Paddy Flynn,' Blodwen said dreamily. 'Smashing bloke.'

'Does he still stand on his head in public bars?'

'Dunno. I haven't seen him for some time. But he's a smashing bloke.'

'Ring up Tangmere and find out if he's still around, will you?'

'It'll be a pleasure,' said Blodwen, still dreamy. 'A real pleasure.'

She woke up feeling refreshed, stretched luxuriously and yawned. Sunlight was filling the loft, sparrows were chirping and twittering on the roof . . . Then she realized he'd disappeared. She sat up, remembering the other time he'd disappeared in the dawn and never come back.

Then she noticed the door was open . . . and heard faint splashy sounds filtering up the stairs, followed by a baritone voice singing off key, *I don't want to set the world on fire*. He was singing in the bath. Like her dad. He couldn't sing either.

She got up, pulled on some slacks and went to the dormer window overlooking the meadows at the back and opened it. The feeling of the sun on her bare shoulders and breasts, and the breeze gently lifting her hair, was marvellous. She thought of the night before and smiled. As she turned away from the window she caught sight of her upper body in the cracked and speckled mirror of the washstand. In the morning sunlight the scars looked hideous, like the ritual scars of some savage tribe.

Then she realized he was standing in the doorway, staring at her. She grabbed her slip and held it up in front of her.

'Sorry,' he said. 'Didn't mean to stare.'

'It's all right,' she said dryly, 'I'm not shy. But the view doesn't rate any stars.'

He shut the door and went towards her. 'Really,' he said. 'What are you trying to hide?'

It wasn't easy for her to drop the slip, but she did.

He studied her naked torso. 'They have a pattern,' he said. 'Like a kind of decoration.'

'Decoration?'

'For valour.'

'That's sentimental shit,' she said.

'Is it?' he said.

They breakfasted in the kitchen alone and mostly in silence. He had recovered his appetite, eating hungrily from a platter of cold cuts, but seemed to have lost his voice. He followed the cold cuts with bread and goat cheese. She nibbled a roll, drank coffee and watched him.

She was dying for a cigarette, but waited till he had finished eating. Then she poured him more coffee and lit up.

'Why did you pretend you didn't know me?'

For a moment she thought he was going to keep up the pretence.

'I didn't want to . . .' He shrugged. 'Inhibit you.'

'In what way?'

'Any way.' He reached over and took her cigarette. 'May I?' He dragged on it, grimaced. 'It's like dried manure.' He gave it back. 'Ever heard of Slapton Sands?'

She shook her head, wondering what was coming.

'It's a beach in south Devon,' he said. 'Long, wide and sandy, backed by a line of low hills. Just like one of the American invasion beaches. So the Americans decided to hold a dress rehearsal there. Exercise Tiger. The first full rehearsal of the actual assault formation to be used on D-Day. Complete with secret weapons like rocket boats and amphibious tanks. And eight tank landing ships to carry the US Fourth Infantry Division and the First Amphibian Engineer Brigade. On the night of 27 April they sailed out of Plymouth Sound into Lyme Bay. And disaster.' He let out a long breath. 'I went with them.'

'I thought you said it was an all-American show.'

'It was. We provided the escort. Big deal. One corvette, in case of trouble. And, boy, was there trouble.'

He stared past her out of the window towards a sunlit meadow full of buttercups. But what he was seeing was the night sky, the faint track of a quarter moon glittering across dark water and the black shapes of the 500–ton landing

189

ships in line astern. And darkness all around. A darkness suddenly stitched with tracer fire. Then explosions, flames ... A gun crew blown straight over the boat davits ... A landing ship rolling over and going down like a stricken animal ... men screaming in agony ...

'Ten miles off Slapton Sands we ran into a squadron of German motor torpedo boats, E-boats, working out of Cherbourg. In less than fifteen minutes there were six hundred American dead, Christ knows how many burned and wounded, two landing ships sunk and one crippled. And their only protection? One British corvette. With me on board as observer. Some protection.'

He took a sip of coffee, then pushed the cup away. It was half cold and tasteless.

'When we got back to Plymouth we found out that some of the E-boats had been seen cruising around among the survivors, scanning the waters with searchlights. It was thought that prisoners might have been picked up – perhaps even a Bigot or two.' He broke off. 'You know about Bigots, I suppose?'

She nodded.

'At dawn an American general from SHAEF intelligence and a colonel from SHAEF security arrived and checked a list of Bigots against the survivors, many of whom were still soaked in oil. All Bigots were accounted for. But among the missing were a number of men who had some knowledge of the D-Day operations. And that was enough for the general to issue strict orders that every missing man had to be accounted for, the identity of every corpse checked. Divers and frogmen were sent down to search the wrecks and bring up the identity discs of all the dead. I thought that was going a bit far. And said so. And you know what the general said? Shook me at the time ...'

He stared out of the window again. She wondered what he was seeing this time.

'He said nobody who knows about our D-Day plans must be allowed to fall into German hands alive.'

He smiled wryly. 'So I felt pretty sure a similar sort of fail-safe clause must have been included in your orders.'

After a brief silence she said: 'I still don't see why any of this should make you pretend you didn't know me.'

'You had your orders,' he said. 'I didn't want to take advantage of a ... brief relationship. Which you might've forgotten anyway. So I pretended it didn't exist.'

'And pretended to be hostile. All part of the act?'

She waited, but he didn't reply. 'If you thought my orders included putting a bullet in you,' she said, 'why come to my rescue?'

Another shrug. 'I couldn't stand by and see you hurt.'

She stubbed out her Gitane. 'Well, well,' she said, 'and there was I thinking the age of chivalry was dead.'

She got up and went round the table to him. He swung round to face her, and they stared into each other's eyes.

'Come on,' she said in an odd, throaty voice.

'No,' he said.

'You going moral on me – after what you did last night?'

'That was ... I couldn't help myself.'

'But you can now?'

'Listen. When this is over – '

'Bollocks, we could both be dead.'

Anger was making the scar twitch, pulling her mouth into a sneer. She could have killed him on the spot.

The sound of an armoured car rumbling over the cobbles of the courtyard jerked her back to reality.

'Come on,' she said and grabbed his hand.

By the time the rumbling had stopped they were back in the loft. She crept to the window overlooking the front and was in time to see Raab and Blech get off the armoured car, now flanked by Gestapo Citroëns, and cross the courtyard towards the house. Raab stopped almost below her and turned to Blech. The words floated up on the morning air.

'Well, we've done our part – searched every house in our sector.'

'Not every house, mein Herr.'

'We've missed one?'

'This one, mein Herr. We haven't searched this one.'

'Search my own house?'

'For the record, mein Herr. Just for the record.'

191

Raab seemed about to say something, then evidently changed his mind and went into the house. Blech followed.

The sun was shining, the air was soft, but suddenly she felt cold. Almost clammy. She turned to Romaine, who was just behind her.

'You heard that?'

He nodded. 'They're going to search the house.'

She went to the mattress, took the P38 from under the pillow, pulled the slide back.

'What are you going to do?'

'If they try to come in here, stop 'em.'

She went to the door, opened it a crack. Enough for a view of the landing below and the short staircase leading up to the loft. In fact, she hadn't thought out exactly what she was going to do. But if Raab and Blech came up here they wouldn't get out alive. No one would. No one.

Therese met them at the front entrance and led them into the kitchen.

'Coffee?' she said, calmly enough to cool anyone's suspicions. 'Or a glass of wine? There's a reasonable Beaujolais or a very acceptable white Macon.'

'A glass of mineral water,' said Raab shortly. Then he remembered that Blech was to be humoured. 'What would you like, Blech?'

'Oh, a glass of Beaujolais for me.'

Therese served them. She sensed Raab was in a bad mood and guessed it had something to do with Ryfka.

Raab nodded towards Blech. 'He thinks we ought to search the house,' said Raab.

'This house?' said Therese, desperately trying to think of some way of deflecting the search.

'Only for the record,' Blech mumbled, slurping the Beaujolais. 'Only for the record.'

'Whatever that means,' said Raab.

He clearly didn't take the search of his own house seriously. Therese smiled at him. Perhaps . . .

He took off his smoked glasses and smiled back, white

eyelashes blinking over pale eyes, reminding her of an insect unused to the light of day.

'We have nothing to hide,' she said. Again she smiled at Raab. 'When the lieutenant has finished his wine perhaps he would like to inspect the downstairs rooms while the colonel and I . . .' She shrugged delicately. 'Inspect the bedrooms. If you approve, colonel.'

'Fine,' said Raab. 'Fine.' Her oblique approach – if that was what it was – excited him. She had an aloofness that was in itself sexual. He patted Blech on the shoulder. 'Don't hurry yourself, Blech. Have some more wine.'

Therese refilled his glass, then left the carafe of Beaujolais on the table in front of him. Blech, slightly bemused, thanked her.

Then she turned to Raab, but he was already at the door, holding it open for her.

Ryfka was still at the door of the loft, peering down at the landing. She could hear footsteps, voices, a moderato male rumble mixing with the lighter tones of a woman. Both getting nearer. She drew the P38 from her waistband, pushed down the safety catch, checked the floating pin. Then she saw Therese come up on to the landing, followed by Raab.

She watched as Therese opened the door to one of the bedrooms.

'See for yourself, colonel.'

Raab went in, reappeared a few seconds later.

'Nothing,' he said.

'What were you expecting?' said Therese, and opened the bathroom door.

Raab poked his head inside, grunted and withdrew it. He looked at the short flight of stairs leading to the loft. Ryfka froze. She felt he was looking straight at her.

'What about the loft?' he said.

'Afterwards.'

'After what, my dear?'

'I don't want you in my bedroom covered in dust and

193

cobwebs,' she said and unpinned her hair and shook it loose. It flowed down over her shoulders like a dark river.

He had never seen her with her hair down. She gave him a small cold smile, turned and went along the landing. He stood staring at her back, as if in a trance. Then he went after her. And the landing was empty.

Ryfka let her breath out slowly, afraid that even a sigh might be heard. And stayed by the door, gun in hand.

After half an hour or so Raab reappeared on the landing and went downstairs, buttoning up his uniform. A few minutes later Therese appeared in a dressing gown, her clothes over her arm, and went into the bathroom.

From below came the sound of the armoured car rumbling across the courtyard.

Ryfka remained by the door.

'Relax,' said Romaine, 'they're going.'

She looked over her shoulder. He was lying on the mattress, hands behind his head. The Man. He smiled at her. 'What are you doing?'

'Waiting,' she said and returned to her vigil.

Therese came out of the bathroom in a long black dress, her hair swept up and carefully pinned. Outwardly immaculate, almost regal. Ryfka went quickly down to meet her, wanting to say something, but unable to think of anything adequate. It was always the same when her emotions were involved. The real words drowned and only banalities came to the surface. 'You look terrific,' she said. 'You *are* terrific.'

'No choice,' Therese said dryly.

Ryfka squeezed her arm in gratitude.

'Careful,' said Therese with a grimace. 'I'm bruised enough already.'

Then the phone rang.

'It could be Luc,' said Ryfka.

They went down into the hall. Therese answered the phone, then handed it to Ryfka.

It was Luc.

'The funeral arrangements are in hand. But Victor wants to see you.'

'Not worried, is he?'

'I'm the one that's worried, baby, he's on fire. Or maybe he's still high after all that booze.'

'Come off it, that's not possible.'

'Metaphorically high, if you know what I mean. Anyway you can't trust jerks that don't drink. They're either alcoholics manqués or crypto-alcoholics. That's why they're so goddam' nervous. They're *born* two drinks under par. Then one sniff of a barmaid's apron and they're high as a kite. And he's still up there, if you know what I mean.'

'Let's meet.'

'Where?'

'Not here. We've had one nasty surprise. And get hold of Nikki. Oh yes, and a map. And mark it for me. If you know what I mean.'

'You still haven't told me where, baby.'

'I'm thinking. Baby.'

And she was. Even after she put the phone down she stood there in the hall thinking, trying to work out a plan, trying to foresee the unforeseeable. From the kitchen she heard the clatter of pots and pans as Therese prepared lunch. The sounds of normality.

She went into the kitchen and said she wouldn't be in for lunch. Therese was stirring a ragout in a big iron pot and adding herbs, spices and chopped onions.

'If you don't get something warm into your stomach,' said Therese, 'you'll end up anaemic.'

It reminded her of her mother. *If you don't eat your crusts your hair won't curl.*

Therese ladled some of the ragout into a bowl and handed it to her.

She was going to say she hadn't time and wasn't hungry, then got a whiff of the ragout and found she was. It had slices of sausage and grated cheese in it, apart from onion and spices and God knows what. It made her taste buds tingle and warmed her right through.

He was asleep. She'd gone up to the loft to tell him she was going out for a while, but he was stretched out on the bed. In the land of Nod. Maybe he needed the rest. He still looked pale. But peaceful.

She looked down at his untroubled face and for a moment hated him – the cause of all the trouble. She ought to shoot him and be done with it. But not in a fit of pique.

Therese was in the kitchen, ironing sheets with a steady rhythm she found soothing.

Watching her, Ryfka began to calm down herself.

'The old tramp,' she said, gesturing towards the back of the house. 'Is he to be trusted?'

'He's not old,' said Therese. 'He just looks old. He has a metal plate in his head.'

'From the war?'

'He has a uniform jacket full of medal ribbons. Of course, he could have taken it from a dead body, though it seems to fit well enough. He can't remember where he got it. In fact, he can't remember anything about the war.'

'You haven't answered the question.'

Therese shrugged. 'I trust him.' As Ryfka turned to go she added: 'He's nervous and a bit strange. Has visions.'

'Religious visions?'

'Just visions. Anyway, he's harmless. Please don't frighten him.'

Ryfka, who had no intention of going near him, left by the outside kitchen door and took the path that wound through scrub and silver birches to the lane at the back of the house, where she had arranged to meet Luc.

As she rounded some rhododendron bushes a man stepped out, blocking the path. She recognized the thinning white hair and tattered military jacket. The tramp. Up close she could see he wasn't old, no more than forty-five or so. It was the prematurely white hair that made him look old. He smiled timidly.

'Are you the one they call Scarface?'

'Why do you say that?' She had dressed her hair carefully to hide the scar.

'Oh, I can't see it,' he said. 'But I know it's there. On the left side.'

196

It gave her an eerie feeling and she casually slipped her hand in her coat pocket and felt for the gun.

'Please,' he said. 'You don't have to defend yourself. I wouldn't harm you.'

The feeling grew even more eerie. Then he lowered his head and rubbed his eyes with the heels of his hands, like a child. When he looked at her again there were tears in his eyes.

'You've had terrible experiences,' he said. 'Terrible.'

'Excuse me,' she said, 'I'm late.'

He still blocked the path. 'Listen to me,' he said. 'Underground passages are dangerous.'

'What do you mean?'

'I don't know,' he said pitifully. 'Things don't always make sense.'

'Excuse me,' she said again and moved past him.

'You'll survive,' he called after her. 'At least, I think you will. But the man . . .'

She stopped cold. The Man again. 'What man?'

'Someone close to you.'

'What about him?'

'The future's dark for him.' He shook his head. 'Very dark.'

She hurried away. She could do without that kind of thing.

The van was parked in the lane, near the silver birches. Luc was leaning against it, smoking a cigarette.

'Hi, baby,' he said.

They got in.

Nikki and Victor were squatting in the back.

'Where can we talk?' she said to Nikki. This was his stamping ground, close to the Forêt de Chevré, where he knew every blade of grass.

'I've got a place,' he said. 'A farmhouse. It's already been searched.'

'There's nothing to stop them searching it again.'

'We'll get warning if they do,' said Nikki. 'I've got men posted round about.'

She nodded. 'Good. We've already had one visit from Raab this morning.'

'Listen,' said Victor. 'I've got an idea about the funeral.'

'Save it till we get to the farmhouse.'

As they drove out of the lane into the road leading to the front of the house they had to pull over to let an armoured car and two Citroëns race by in a cloud of dust.

'What do you know,' said Luc. 'Raab himself, going back to his country house for a bit of lunch or something.'

'Let's hope it's not for a bit of something,' said Ryfka.

15

Therese brought the suitcase down to the hall. Tilly, dressed in her best black bombazine and a high-crowned black hat, watched with beady eyes.

'You're trying to fob me off on Josephine, aren't you?'

'Cousin Josephine said she'd like to have you there for a few days, that's all.'

'My arse,' said Tilly.

'I beg your pardon?'

'That's what your father used to say if you tried to sweet talk him.' She sighed. 'Such a witty man, always the bon mot.' She looked at Therese sideways. 'Are you having a liaison with the Prussian officer?'

She meant Raab, of course. Part of her mind was fixed in the period of the Franco-Prussian war, which she regarded as the death both of the Second Empire and the age of elegance. From 1870 till the Great War everything had been in slow decline. 'And after the Great War,' she was fond of saying, 'there was the so-called jazz age. Booze, boredom and barbarism. The age of the Common Man. In other words, the second rate.' The present war had gone completely over her head. She either ignored it or confused it with the Franco-Prussian war, which she remembered vividly. She was sixteen at the time and in love with a handsome hussar who was killed with the army of the Loire at Orleans, trying to stem the German tide. She went into deep mourning, in which she looked both elegant and fetching, and everyone said she'd soon get over it. But everyone was wrong. His death put a permanent shadow over her young mind.

She looked Therese up and down. 'Of course, women of conquered territories always sleep with the conquerors. Survival, I suppose. Or masochism.' She sniffed tearfully.

'You know I hate Josephine, but you want to be rid of me, don't you? So you can have a free hand with the Prussian.'

In her lucid intervals Tilly had a good mind. But it was not possible to make real contact with her. She always seemed one remove from reality. Therese sighed, her thoughts broken by the unmistakable sound of an armoured car pulling up outside, Then the front door opened and the Prussian came in, carrying a black hide briefcase. He was followed by Blech.

'Hallo,' he said to Tilly. 'Going somewhere?'

Curiously, she was one of the few people he felt relaxed with.

'She's going to my cousin's at Dourdain for a few days,' said Therese. 'I was about to take her.'

'One of our cars can run her there. Blech will see to it.'

Blech picked up the suitcase and took Tilly's arm.

Tilly shook him off, turned to Raab. 'She's the youngest of six. I had her when I was supposed to be past child-bearing. She is precious to me. Treat her with respect.'

'Don't I always?' said Raab.

'My arse,' said Tilly and swept out. Blech followed, keeping a straight face.

Once it had been a famous stud in fifty acres of prime paddock and pasture, now shrunk to a few overgrown fields and an echoing house with empty stables. And once Charles Legrand had been a famous name in the bloodstock world. But he sold off all the stock and most of the land when his wife ran off with the head groom. It left him soured and without direction in life.

Then came the war, and his only son, and only consolation apart from animals, was killed in the French rearguard action at Dunkirk. He listened to the BBC broadcasts, full of stories of the little ships and British bravery but lacking any reference to the gallantry of the French rearguard action, which played a major part in saving the British Expeditionary Force. That soured him even more. He went on living in the house, cared for by the only remaining servant, a peasant girl from the Midi called Sylvie, whom

200

he had taken in when she lost her home and job after giving birth to an illegitimate son. Legrand even adopted the son. He kept a few old horses and a couple of dogs because he felt more at home with animals than humans, though he slept with Sylvie occasionally. Then, one sunny morning when the fields were alive with the promise of spring, he went into the stables and hanged himself from a roof beam. The house and what was left of his fortune were inherited by Sylvie, the only one who'd stuck by him, rain or shine.

The house, which looked dilapidated, mostly through lack of paint, was called l'Abri.

'Didn't give Legrand much shelter, did it?' Ryfka said as Luc pulled up by the front porch. As she and the others got out a couple of barking dogs ran from the back of the house. Nikki spoke to them and they shut up, fawning and wagging their tails.

The place made her feel uneasy. 'You're sure you can trust this Sylvie?'

'She lets us use it as a hideout when the SS do a sweep of the local forests.'

'And the son?'

'He's twenty now. And with us.'

The front door was opened by a woman of about forty. She had an ordinary, unremarkable face, but friendly.

'Nikki,' she said. 'Come in, and bring your friends.'

Inside it was light and airy and well furnished, and Ryfka began to relax. Sylvie took them into a big kitchen overlooking a paddock and stables at the back. The table was laden with food: baguettes, cheeses, liver pâtés, a joint of smoked ham and jugs of red wine. On the stove was a pot of coffee.

'I'll leave you to help yourselves, if you'll excuse me,' said Sylvie, smiling.

It was the same wherever you went: food and shelter. For the stranger. *Pour la Résistance.* Of course there weren't the shortages in the country there were in the towns, where a *marché noir officiel* operated. But whatever they had they shared.

After the ragout she wasn't hungry and drank a cup of

coffee while the men ate. Then she studied the map Luc had spread out at one end of the table. It was a large-scale map with the roadblocks neatly inked in.

'Where do we break out?' she said.

'There's a roadblock at Saint Aubin-du-Cormier,' said Victor. 'About ten kilometres further on is the village where Truchet is to be buried. La Chapelle something or other. If we time it properly we should go through the roadblock without trouble. They'll be expecting a funeral cortège.'

'And I'll be waiting with the van on the other side,' said Luc. 'Simple. Like all the best plans.'

'Maybe too simple. Raab always keeps something up his sleeve.'

'Like what, baby?'

'Like I don't know, baby,' she said in a flash of irritation. 'I can't *see* up his fucking sleeve.'

Victor, surfacing from dreams of funerary splendour, broke the tension. 'We really ought to have horses,' he said. 'Black horses. With big black plumes. For a proper funeral, that is. But then it's not a proper funeral, is it? And horses are impractical anyway. Still, we'll have proper undertakers' mutes. In tall hats . . . And lots of flowers. I'll take your breath away with flowers.' He turned to Nikki. 'Four men, you said?' Nikki nodded. 'About the same height?'

'No.'

'Pity,' said Victor. 'Never mind, it'll be a lovely funeral.'

'Can we take a look at the Saint Aubin roadblock?' Ryfka said. 'Without being seen ourselves?'

The hill rose smoothly out of the land with scattered woodland at the top, where Luc parked the van. They got out and Nikki led the way to a vantage point with a view over some pretty countryside and three ugly roadblocks.

'The middle one,' Nikki said, handing Ryfka a pair of field glasses. 'With the one-ton half-track across the road and an armoured car forming a chicane behind it. Then a little Kuebelwagen and a Gestapo Citroën backing them up. Plus a dozen or so SS men, bristling with guns.'

She checked it through the field glasses. 'Formidable,' she said. 'I'd hate to try and crash through that one.'

'And there might be another one a few kilometres on. He's starting to put in secondary roadblocks here and there.'

'Couldn't we avoid all roadblocks by going through the fields on foot?'

'Sure,' said Nikki. 'But sooner or later you'll have to go back to the roads. Or you won't even get to Fougères. Never mind beyond. Anyway, they've got spotter planes up.'

His last words were nearly drowned by the noise of a low-flying aircraft. As they moved back into the shelter of the trees a little Fiesler-Storch flew over. He grinned. 'Bastard must've heard me.'

Raab hardly looked at Therese, nor she at him when she served lunch. She simply put the food and drink on the table, then withdrew. Neither spoke and it was obvious there was constraint between them.

Blech was dying to hear about Raab's search of the bedrooms, but didn't dare ask, though he was sure that whatever got searched it wasn't bedrooms. If only he could think of a nice innocent-sounding question. But he couldn't. Besides, he knew better than to attempt light conversation when his master was in a mood.

Raab finished the meal and his glass of mineral water in silence, then rang for Therese. When she came he pointed to his empty glass. She refilled it.

'Anything else?'

He looked at her as if considering the question, then shook his head. She left.

He really has got the hump, Blech thought, and decided to keep his head down.

Raab sipped the mineral water. 'Someone's hiding her.'

Blech kept his head down and made affirmative noises that were barely audible. And meant to be.

'A price of two million francs on her head. A fortune. And yet they still hide her. The most venal people in the world refusing to be bought.'

He shook his head, not understanding, and took another

sip of mineral water. His pale face looked paler. All that water can't be good for you, Blech thought. Dilutes the blood.

'Well, if we can't buy them,' Raab said in his rustling voice, 'we'll have to frighten them.' He stood up, leaned on the table and stared down at Blech.

'Lidice,' he said. 'Remember Lidice? We'll give them a simple choice: Ryfka – or another Lidice.'

'Perhaps,' said Blech, 'they've never heard of Lidice.'

'Then we'll have to spell it out.'

Blech, who had seen much, felt himself going cold.

'Now,' said Raab, 'I want you to get a hundred posters printed, soon as possible, and have one put up in every café in the area, every . . .'

He stopped, looked towards the door as if he had heard something. Then he put a finger to his lips, tiptoed to the door – and whipped it open. Standing there was Therese, with a tray of coffee.

'Thank you very much,' she said and walked gracefully in. She put the tray on the table, got a bottle of cognac and two glasses from a sideboard and arranged them next to the coffee. She always put out two glasses. For some reason Raab was shy of giving the appearance of a teetotaller.

'If there's anything else you need,' she said in her cool voice, 'please let me know.' And walked gracefully out.

Raab watched her go, his face impassive.

After a good lunch at his club and several brandies, Mossop felt distinctly heavy. He took a taxi to Baker Street and went straight to his office, telling his secretary he wasn't to be disturbed. The afternoon sun was dazzling and he closed the venetian blinds. Then he sat in his swivel chair, put his feet on the desk and settled down for a well-earned rest. Well earned after listening to some of the bloody old bores at the club, who ought to be shot with a humane killer, like old horses.

The thought amused him and he was drifting gently into sleep with a smile on his face when he heard the door open and shut again with unnecessary loudness. Then Frank

Smith's voice, hearty and detestable: 'Having a post-pran-dial zizz, are we?'

He removed his feet from the desk, straightened his uniform and said with dignity: 'What do you want, you bastard?'

'Signal from Ryfka.'

He put it on the desk.

'Anything new?'

'Confirming details of the pick-up at Les Colombes. But if she can't make it Tuesday 0–two hundred hours, she suggests the same time, same place Wednesday.'

'She's expecting trouble?'

'After she gets back she wants to return with a Hudson to pick up some people who helped her.'

Mossop grunted. 'If she gets back. Why's she mucking about? Why don't she get on wi' t'bloody job and get out?'

'Maybe . . .' Smith hesitated. 'Maybe she's trying to bring him out alive.'

'But didn't tha' tell 'er over the S-phone – '

'We were interrupted by the Gestapo. Maybe she didn't . . . hear properly or something.'

'Bollocks,' said Mossop. 'Ah say, she's not gone and fallen for t'boogger, 'as she?'

'She fell for Gerard, but she still shot him.'

'Different circs. Why not ask 'er wireless op – the one that don't like working for a lass – to give us an unofficial report, like?'

Smith pulled a wry face. 'I already have.'

'Tha' sneaky boogger,' said Mossop delightedly. 'What did tha' get from 'im?'

'A flea in the ear. Seems she saved his bacon at some Gestapo checkpoint, and now he thinks the sun shines out of her you-know-what.'

Mossop clicked his tongue in irritation. 'That smooth bloody major's on t'blower every bloody day from Downing Street, politely chewin' me balls off. Did tha' get in touch with that pilot she asked for?'

'Flynn?' Smith shook his head. 'He's on leave, God knows where. Racketing round the West End probably.'

'It's beginning to sound like Operation Cock-Up.'

'Wait a minute – the Waaf in the war room might know. She went out with him once.'

'Which Waaf?'

'The Welsh one. Blodwen.'

'Oh aye,' said Mossop, brightening. 'The one they call Blodwen Big Tits.'

As they crossed the courtyard to the armoured car Raab was aware that Therese was watching him through the sitting room window. She had hated him when she had no reason to. Now he had given her a reason. The thought pleased him. He never minded being hated as long as he was feared. Like the Romans. *Oderint dum metuant.*

Blech's voice broke in from what seemed a long way off.

'I was wondering, mein Herr . . .'

'What?'

'By the time we've had all those notices printed and distributed . . . she could have gone. Escaped.'

Raab stopped by the armoured car. 'That's a chance we have to take.'

'And if the Graf von Kirchen-Wehbach gets hold of a copy?'

'So?'

Blech shrugged. 'He's a friend of Goering's, isn't he? And you'd be handing him something that could be used in evidence, as it were. But if, for instance, you let Loubain handle things for you – '

'Loubain?'

'And let *him* warn the local people – since he's local himself. Then the rumour will spread like wildfire. And if Kirchen-Wehbach picks it up . . .' Another shrug. 'It's just a rumour. We simply deny it. But the effect could be even more terrifying. After all, rumours never lose in the telling.'

Raab considered the implications. 'Now that, Blech, is an intelligent idea.' For once the compliment was genuine. 'One drawback though. I'd never take Loubain completely into my confidence. And he knows it. He'd be suspicious. However . . .'

The smoked lenses were pointing straight at Blech. 'If *you* told him, Blech, he'd believe it. You'd be a natural, as they say, for the part of the Good German. No?'

He smiled, and for once Blech had the feeling the smile might have reached his eyes, though he couldn't see them through the smoked glasses.

'Why,' Raab went on, 'we might even pick Loubain's own village as the target.'

The smile broadened, and this time Blech was sure it reached his eyes.

It was warm and sunny and Loubain sat in the shade of a tree, smoking a cigarette and watching a farmer plough a field that might by a considerable stretch of imagination be regarded as suitable for a landing strip. Since the farmer was being paid to plough land he was going to plough anyway it must, Loubain thought, be giving him some satisfaction. It showed in the way he handled the horses, especially on the turn. He probably felt he had to put on a bit of a show for the money. It gave Loubain some satisfaction too, since the farmer was his second cousin once removed.

Above all, and for the first time since the German occupation, he felt relatively free. He had at last persuaded his wife to move south with the two children and join his sister, who was married to a farmer in Lot-et-Garonne.

A Gestapo Citroën pulled up on a road that ran along one side of the field. Blech got out and started to make his way round the edge of the field towards the entrance gate. Loubain got on well enough with Blech, even found him *sympathique* compared to some of the other SS bastards. But he was, of course, the enemy. Loubain stood up and ground the cigarette under his heel.

Blech, who had a casual, easy-going manner as a rule, greeted him with constraint and avoided his eyes. Instead, he looked at the man ploughing. A peaceful, almost idyllic scene, which might be replaced by a scene of mass murder.

'Something wrong?' said Loubain.

'Ever heard of Lidice?'

'A village in Czechoslovakia, isn't it?'

'Was,' said Blech. 'Was.'

'Ah yes. Didn't the SS destroy it, following the assassination of Heydrich?'

'They shot all the men, rounded up the women and children and locked them in the church. Then they set fire to it. Any who managed to get out were gunned down. Finally, the whole place was razed to the ground.'

A sudden hush descended on the countryside, Loubain thought. Even the sun felt cold.

Blech turned and faced him. 'If Ryfka isn't surrendered to us in twenty-four hours that's what Raab threatens to do here. Destroy a whole village.'

'Which village?'

'He'll pick one at random. Maybe yours. The idea seemed to amuse him.'

'You said he threatens to do it. Would he really carry it out?'

'He wanted to stick warning notices up all over the place, but I talked him out of it. And suggested *you* should spread the warning. By word of mouth.'

'Why did you do that?'

'First, the printed notices would commit him. At least, he'd feel committed – and unable to change his mind. Second, it's more efficient, it saves time. Third, *she'll* get to hear of it as soon as anyone. And won't want to put the community in danger, she's not the type. She'll make her move – perhaps before she's ready.'

'The first two points are intelligent,' said Loubain. 'The third's a guess. How do you know how she'll behave?'

'I joined Raab's staff just after he captured her,' said Blech. 'I'd come straight from the Eastern Front, where we fought men. And was supposed to watch a woman being tortured. Only it turned out I didn't have the stomach for it. Or the guts, as Raab put it. "Not that it matters," he said. "I'll soon break her." But he didn't. He made her scream – Christ, he made her scream. But he didn't break her.' He stared at the farmer, still peacefully ploughing, but

208

that wasn't what he was seeing. 'She wasn't bad-looking, in a semitic sort of way. Till he put those scars all over her.'

'What you're saying,' Loubain said gently, 'proves she's brave. It doesn't really indicate how she'll react to the present situation.'

'She's also – what's the word? Honourable. Yeah, that's the word.'

Therese was stuffing the sheets from her bed into the washtub. Pity memory couldn't be washed as clean as sheets.

She heard the door open and looked up. Raab was standing in the doorway, briefcase in hand. 'Tell Blech I've gone back to the Abelard.'

She nodded and he turned to go, then apparently changed his mind and came right into the kitchen. The pallor of his face was emphasized by the black uniform. The pale eyes were hidden as usual behind blue glasses. The last time she had seen him without his glasses was something she wanted to forget.

She went on working.

'Ah,' he said. 'Clean sheets. I like fastidious women.'

He glanced out of the window. 'And there's the tramp. Interesting fellow, according to Blech.' He turned and looked at Therese. 'How long has he been here?'

She shrugged. 'Since before you bought the place. The last people took him in.'

'You never mentioned his presence to me.'

'I didn't think you'd be interested.'

Raab gave her a tight smile. 'I wouldn't mind a little chat with him.'

As he went out through the back door she said: 'Don't frighten him.'

'Who? Me?' said Raab.

The bitch still disliked him, but it didn't bother him. Repulsion and attraction were merely the reverse and obverse sides of the same coin. And like many women, even the proud ones, she felt in need of a little humiliation from time to time. Remarkable figure for a middle-aged woman, though. Big, firm-fleshed, smooth as a peach. And warm to the touch. An image of her sprang to mind, kneeling naked before him, head bent, long hair flowing down over her shoulders, like a devout figure from a pieta.

Suche-moi, chérie, ou je t'étrangle.

Lost in memories he tripped on a fallen branch and fell flat on his face in the lush meadow. He lay there winded, then rolled over and sat up – to find a white-haired man in an old French army jacket standing beside him. The tramp.

'Are you all right, monsieur?'

He got up, straightened his uniform. 'A bit shaken, that's all.' He grimaced. 'I was dreaming – and not looking where I was going.'

The tramp picked up the briefcase and handed it to him, then indicated the barn near by. 'Would you like to rest a while, monsieur? It's quite comfortable.'

To Raab's surprise it was. A corner of the barn had been partitioned off with some old cupboards, a dilapidated screen and a broken sideboard. The enclosed floor space was covered with bits of odd carpet. There was even a truckle bed, a worn armchair and an ancient iron stove.

The tramp sat on the bed, Raab in the armchair, which was also comfortable. Raab looked around.

'Where did you get all the stuff?'

'From the people who lived here before, mostly. Though Madame Therese gave me some things too. She's been very kind.'

'She's a very kind woman,' said Raab.

Then he noticed that one wall of the barn was hung with pencil drawings. Mostly landscapes, but also some maps.

'Are they local maps?'

'Yes, monsieur.'

Raab got up and went to examine them. At the edge of one map was a small hatched area near the entrance to a wood. Next to it were the words: Old Mine. He pointed to it. 'What sort of mine was this?'

'I don't know, monsieur. Perhaps a tin mine. It hasn't been worked for years.'

'Are there other exits and entrances?'

'Oh yes, monsieur. But they're off the map.'

Raab went back to the armchair. 'You must know the area pretty well.'

'Oh yes, monsieur. I do.'

Raab put his hands together and made a steeple of his fingers, trying to look magisterial. In fact, he looked like a louche priest.

'Have you ever heard of La Balafrée?'

'I-I don't think so, monsieur. I . . . have trouble with my memory.'

'Perhaps this will refresh it.'

Raab opened the briefcase, took out a rolled-up poster, unfurled it in one movement and held it up. It was the poster of Ryfka. Dark, resolute, scarred.

The tramp flinched.

'You know her?' It was more a statement than a question.

'No, monsieur. I mean, I don't think so. You see, my memory . . .'

'Is troubled,' said Raab, his voice rustling. 'Yes, of course. Perhaps it needs an aide-memoire.'

The tramp was becoming more and more agitated. 'I cannot always remember. Please believe me, monsieur. I was wounded. At least, I think I was . . . I mean, I have a metal plate in my head . . .'

Raab stood up, smiling. 'Let's have a look at that old mine, shall we?'

'It's a long walk, monsieur.'

'We're going by car.'

The tramp started to shake.

'What's the matter.'

'I have a presentiment, monsieur . . . of doom.'

A few minutes later he was sitting in the back of a Citroën between two Gestapo men. Raab was in front with the driver. A tear rolled down the tramp's cheek. He knew what he was going to do. He would show them the entrance to the old mine, which was close to open woodland. Then, while they were looking at it, he would run silently into the woods, through the tall trees, the copper beech, the silver

211

birch and others, all friends, beckoning him to shelter. And he would run to them, silent as a ghost . . .

He ran swiftly, easily, lightly through the woods, but not silently. The dead leaves stirred and susurrated underfoot, murmuring encouragement. Twigs snapped and cracked as he ran, then intermingled with other, sharper cracking sounds that rent the air like gunshots.

But he went on running, happily, surrounded by friends waving him on. And then, as he leapt gracefully over a fallen log, he seemed to tumble, like an acrobat doing a roll in slow motion, head over heels . . . Then he was lying on his back, looking up at a delicate tracery of leaves and branches that seemed far above him, as if etched by God's finger on the sky. As he watched it the tracery gradually became blurred and dim . . . The day was ending. *Sweet day, so cool, so calm, so bright . . . The dew shall weep thy fall tonight; For thou must die.*

And then night fell.

16

With Nikki as guide she started to survey other roadblocks
in the area, looking for weaknesses. But each one was a
miniature strongpoint, with either an armoured car or troop
carrier, and armed SS men. Plus the usual spiked mats.

It was a warm day and progress was slow, much of it on
foot and some of it belly-to-earth, to reach vantage points
without being seen by the SS manning the *barrages* as the
French called them. And the presence of SS patrols, liable
to pop up anywhere in their search of houses, farms and
outbuildings, was a constant threat. After half a dozen roadblocks she decided to call it a day.

'It's too dangerous,' she said. 'Sooner or later we'll run
into a patrol.'

'Anyway, what's the point?' said Luc, who had just
crawled through a smelly ditch. 'You're not thinking of
crashing through a goddam barrage, are you?'

'I'm trying to look at every option,' she said and turned
to Victor. 'Did you check the time the funeral's due?'

'It should reach the roadblock at Liffré around half-past
four.'

'Then you must be through that roadblock by four. We
need half an hour's start. We'll be waiting further on, in a
little side road on the edge of the forest. You know it?'

'I'll find it.'

'Nikki will be with you. He knows it.'

Then Luc said: 'What time do you want me to come
over?'

'We'll have a final briefing around nine. To give Nikki
time to get back to Rennes and pick up Victor. Leave your
van in the lane at the back.'

'What if Raab shows up?'

'Forget about Raab. He'll be out looking for me, not

thinking about social calls. Anyway, one of Nikki's men will be posted in the drive as lookout.'

Therese was worried. She'd seen the tramp leave with Raab two hours ago. She hadn't seen him come back, though that wasn't significant in itself. He could have slipped back without her noticing. He had a chameleon quality of merging with his background. She'd been down to the barn once to see if he was there, and was wondering whether to go again. She was fussing, of course, like a hen over a lost chick. Or a woman over lost sons maybe. Lupin, as she called him, was like a lost child himself, an orphan of war, who might not survive without help. And helping him also helped to fill some of the empty spaces war had left in her own life.

She went down to the barn and found it empty. Served her right for fussing over nothing. She looked around. The place had a crazy kind of harmony, odd bits of furniture and odd bits of carpet seeming to reflect elements of Lupin's personality, like shards of a broken mirror. Lupin. He couldn't remember his own name so she'd given him a new one, though she'd no idea why she picked Lupin. Perhaps because of the Arsène Lupin novels. Or because the massed lupins outside the kitchen window were in bloom at the time . . .

She heard a noise and swung round.

Raab was standing in the doorway, briefcase in hand, blocking the light.

'What have you done with him?'

Raab spread his hands. 'What do you mean?'

It irritated her that since the bedroom incident he presumed to *tutoyer* her. She always took care to *vousvoyer* him back. With icy politeness.

'You took him away in a Gestapo car.'

'I simply asked him to show me a place he had pointed out on the map. But when we got there he ran off into some woods. We fired a few shots in the air to attract his attention – and tried to call him back, but . . .' Again he spread his hands.

'You must have frightened him.'

'Why should I do that, my dear?'

'You tell me. Mein Herr.'

'You may call me Otto. My dear.'

She couldn't see his eyes because of the smoked glasses, but his pale lips curved in what she supposed was a smile. Then he crossed to the wall where the drawings hung.

'This was the map,' he said, pulling it off the wall and putting it carefully in his briefcase.

'He wouldn't have run away,' she said, 'unless he thought there was danger.'

'Who knows what goes on in that deranged head, my dear? He'll be back. Sooner or later.'

He turned and went out of the barn. She followed him in silence to the house. A few minutes later he left. She listened to the armoured car rumbling out of the courtyard into the drive. The sounds grew fainter and fainter. Then there was silence, and she felt she could breathe again.

When Ryfka returned dusk was already falling, softening the outlines of everything. She went in the back way, following the path through the birch trees and hoping the tramp would step silently out of the shadows to surprise her. She tried to remember something he'd said. About darkness and a man who was close to her . . . But she could only remember that it frightened her. She'd not had time to stop and question him then.

And now he didn't seem to be around. He wasn't even in the barn, which had a cold deserted air. She checked to see if any Gestapo cars were parked at the front, but the courtyard was empty. And silent too, apart from a rustle of dead leaves vexed by the wind.

She found Therese in the kitchen preparing a coarse pâté. Something cooking in the oven smelled delicious and the feelings of tension she'd had all day began to give way to hunger. She opened her mouth to ask for a report on Raab's visit, but found herself saying: 'What's for dinner?'

Therese told her, adding: 'You're not eating enough.' Then she described how she'd overheard Raab's plan for another Lidice. 'But it sounded as if Blech was trying to head him off.'

'Don't worry. We'll be out of here by tomorrow afternoon.' She glanced up at the ceiling. 'How's the man?'

'I've been up there twice with a cup of coffee, but he was sleeping. I thought it better not to disturb him.'

The Man. That was how she usually thought of him now. It helped to keep a distance between them. A distance he had recently re-established.

She went up to the loft. He was lying on the mattress in the dark, still asleep it seemed. Then he said: 'Hallo.'

'How are you feeling?' she said.

'Hungry.'

'Dinner will be ready soon.'

She went to the window and looked out over the paddock at the barn. It looked more like an old burial mound in the thickening dusk. Above it the stars were beginning to come out. She didn't hear him get up, but suddenly he was beside her. His closeness disturbed her and she moved away.

'Are you fit to travel?'

'Fit as I'll ever be.'

'We're leaving tomorrow.'

'Where for?'

She hesitated, then decided to tell him. There was no point in withholding the information. And if there was any danger of his falling into German hands she'd deal with it when it arose.

'Les Colombes, codename for an airstrip north of Fougères. I'll give you details and map co-ordinates later.'

'But you're coming with me, aren't you?'

'We might get separated,' she said dryly.

The moment she sat down to dinner her hunger disappeared. She could think of nothing but the plans for tomorrow. She kept going over them in her mind, searching for weaknesses, trying to think of other contingency plans for 'what if' situations that might never arise. Not that you could allow for everything. There was always the unknown.

216

And that included the Man. What did she really know of him, apart from a few facts out of his personal file?

He ate like a horse, complimented Therese on her cooking in execrable French, delivered with English aplomb, and drank several glasses of a young and aromatic red wine.

'I say, this is good stuff, isn't it?' he said to Ryfka.

Most of the time she was silent, picking at her food and pretending not to watch him. He had good features, well-set eyes, nice teeth which glinted in the lamplight when he smiled. Altogether, not bad-looking in an open English sort of way. A nine millimetre bullet through the back of the head would soon alter that though.

Then she realized he was smiling at her.

'Penny for them,' he said.

Raab dined alone on grilled fish in his salon at the Abelard. Solange had taken to her bed with an unspecified ailment, probably the vapours. She couldn't have known what had happened with Therese, but she could detect a false note like a singer with perfect pitch. Anyway, he preferred dining alone. Solange had her uses, but being a table companion wasn't one of them.

He poured himself a coffee and took it through into the office where a map was already spread out on the desk. He sat down, hunching over the map to study the inked-in roadblocks for the umpteenth time. The whole area was crawling with SS and Gestapo, house searches were still going on and yet . . . It was like trying to track down one of those will-o'the-wisp lights that flickered over marshes at night and disappeared when you drew near. If only he had a clue to her movements . . .

Then he realized that he had. He was simply overlooking the obvious. He sat up and rang for Blech, who arrived within a couple of minutes, slightly breathless. Raab told him to pour himself a coffee and sit down. His mood struck Blech as almost benign.

'Thank you, mein Herr,' said Blech. He sat on the edge of the chair. Raab in benign mood worried him. He was usually benign before interrogations.

'You spoke to Loubain?'

'As instructed, mein Herr.'

'And his reaction?'

'He's not one to show his feelings, but I think he was shaken. He thought the threat excessive.'

'It was meant to be. A threat that succeeds is always more effective than its execution.'

'You think the people who are hiding her will really betray her?'

'She'll betray herself. That's the cleverness of our idea of spreading the rumour. It will force her hand.'

Our idea? Blech thought. Do me a favour . . .

'She'll never jeopardize the people who are hiding her, she's got too much, what's the word . . .'

'Honour, mein Herr?'

'Honour. Too much honour. The rumour will reach her tonight. Perhaps already has. And tomorrow she'll make her break. Whether she's ready or not.' He gave a tight little smile. 'And we'll be waiting for her. We'll set up secondary roadblocks.'

'By tomorrow, mein Herr?'

'We've got the men and the vehicles. It's simply a question of deciding where to deploy them.' He looked at the map. 'Shouldn't take more than two or three hours. We'll see to it personally, you and I.' A tight smile. 'Do you more good than a night in the brothel.'

'Yes, mein Herr,' Blech said without enthusiasm.

'Meanwhile,' said Raab, raising his coffee cup, 'to honour.'

Blech raised his own cup. 'To honour.'

'That American,' said Raab, 'the one who wrote that book about bullfighting – '

'Hemingway?'

'Didn't he say that nothing can kill a man quicker than too much honour?' The tight smile again. 'Perhaps it can kill a woman too.'

Flynn was proving hard to find, though Blodwen obviously knew his haunts. They started soon after opening time at a pub in Cork Street, but the bar was deserted apart from a hotel porter and half a dozen whores gathered for an early evening drink and a chat before going back on the beat.

'A chat?' said Frank Smith, intrigued. 'About sex?'

'About black market food prices and where to buy clothing coupons,' she said, surprised at his naïvety. 'Only enthusiastic amateurs talk shop.'

She finished her drink. 'Come on, Frank bach, let's try the French House in Soho.'

But he wasn't there either. Or at the Marquis of Granby or the Fitzroy or anywhere else they looked.

It was beginning to look like a wasted evening. When he'd picked her up at her Bayswater bedsitter she was wearing a smart two-piece suit, her only remaining pair of silk stockings that hadn't got holes in and her best silk blouse, which was on the tight side. All her blouses were on the tight side, but that was hardly their fault.

Frank Smith, who was in uniform, said: 'Where does he usually stay when he's in town?'

'The Regent Palace, but I phoned earlier and they hadn't seen him in ages. Shacked up with some popsie, I expect.'

Frank Smith cleared his throat. 'Were you, er, friends with him long?'

'About six months. Lovely bloody time we had. Music all the way, boyo.' She sighed. 'Then he met this other popsie – and, well, the music had to stop some time, I s'pose. But I was real bloody sad, I can tell you.' Another sigh. 'He still wears my silk stockings though.'

'Your silk stockings?' He tried not to sound incredulous.

'Round his neck. To keep him warm when he's night flying. Says he wishes my legs were in 'em sometimes . . . Ah, there's romantic for you. Eh, bach?'

Frank Smith felt he'd had enough. 'Have you any real idea where he's likely to be?'

She shook her head slowly. 'He could be anywhere there's a bit of life.'

'Then we'll call it a day,' he said. 'Drink up and I'll see you home.'

'Wait a minute,' said Blodwen. 'There is a place . . . a

little boite near Victoria . . . What's it called? The Bag o' Nails – or something.'

The place was packed out, hot and smoky. You couldn't move for people or see for fug. And somewhere a three-piece combo of piano, drums and double bass was thumping out something, perhaps even music. It was certainly loud.

'Christ,' said Frank Smith, 'you'd never find anyone in this place unless you fell over him.'

'Look!' she said excitedly, 'there he is, standing on his bloody head! On a bloody bar stool, I bet!'

He looked in the direction she was pointing and saw two legs waving above the crowd like a pair of drunken antlers.

'Well, if he can do that he must be sober.'

'No, bach,' said Blodwen. 'He can only do it when he's pissed as a newt.'

By the time Frank Smith got through the crowd Flynn was more or less the right way up and leaning against the wall where it made a convenient angle with the bar. He looked at Frank Smith with eyes that didn't quite focus, then held out his hand.

'Colonel Smith, I presume,' he said solemnly. 'And Blodwen the beautiful. Nosta cariad.'

Smith leaned close and spoke into his ear. 'Can you pick up a Joe for us tomorrow night?'

To the pilots of 161 Squadron agents were known collectively as Joes.

'Sorry, old boy, on leave till Friday. How's about Saturday?'

'It's an emergency,' said Smith. 'Top priority.'

By then Flynn was sliding down the wall in slow motion. Smith waited till he hit the floor, then leaned down. 'Listen,' he said, 'it's Ryfka. She specially asked for you.'

Flynn was sitting against the wall, eyes closed. Then his head fell forward.

'What do you know?' Smith sighed. 'The bastard's passed out.'

After dinner Therese had excused herself and gone early to bed. Harry Romaine sat at the table with Ryfka, drinking coffee and wondering whether to finish the wine. He wasn't used to the stuff and was already feeling sleepy. Yet he needed something to desensitize him to the tension he could feel building up around Ryfka like a field of force. She seemed to be in a world of her own. Attempts at conversation were met with silence or curtness.

She was sitting with her head in her hands, staring down at the rumpled tablecloth. What he could see of her face was half in lamplight, half in shadow, the dark side broken by the pale slash of the scar, which seemed faintly luminescent, though that may have been a trick of the light. An angular face with heavy-lidded eyes, which looked sleepy when she was sexually aroused ... *Passion-dimmed eyes and long heavy hair.* Some people thought her ugly. He thought her beautiful and the scars exotic, but then he was looking with different eyes.

He finished the wine and felt even sleepier.

'I'm going to bed,' he said and got up.

She glanced up at him and he saw a tear roll down her cheek. He was surprised – she wasn't the type for tears. He said goodnight and went up to bed.

He would have been more surprised still if he'd known the tears were for him.

She phoned Luc at home, then Nikki at the Bar Kazimierz, then switched the downstairs lights off before going up to the loft. But she was feeling too restless to go to bed. She needed some air. She let herself quietly out of the kitchen into the garden. The moment she was in the night air she felt better. There was enough moon and starlight to see by and a breeze to lift her hair.

But after wandering around the big paddock for a while she got cold. And went back.

She didn't draw the curtains and light the lamp because she didn't want to wake him. Let sleeping dogs lie. And there was plenty of moonlight to undress by. But when she was down to her slip she hesitated. Then she wrapped a blanket round herself and lay on the edge of the mattress.

She felt wide awake and lonely. Five minutes later she was sound asleep.

She awoke at dawn feeling cold. He seemed to be still asleep and she got up and dressed as quietly as she could. Then she realized he was awake and watching her.

'Who's Elizabeth?' she said.

He sat up, looped his arms round his knees. 'My wife.'

'I thought there must be a wife tucked away somewhere.'

'She was killed in an air raid.'

'Oh.'

'Her lover was killed with her. They were found together in the rubble.'

'Was it a shock? About the lover?'

'A divorce had been arranged. Nice and civilized. No hard feelings. Well, not many.'

She started brushing her hair – her long heavy hair – standing in front of the cracked and speckled mirror of the broken washstand.

'Ah. You had someone too?'

He hesitated. 'Not when the divorce was arranged.'

'But later.'

'Later, there was this girl I met on a train . . . in an air raid.' He lay back and stared up at the ceiling.

She stopped brushing her hair.

'No,' she said. 'I don't believe it. You're making it up.'

'That's why I didn't come back that night,' he said. 'She was killed in the same air raid. Along with the poor bloody lover. The raid was on London. But some planes got driven off course by ack-ack fire. And hit that railway line instead . . .'

She started brushing her hair again, with unnecessary vigour, watching him in the mirror all the time.

'Why did you do it?' she said.

'Do what?'

'You know what . . . Going on that raid.'

She stopped brushing her hair and started pinning it up, holding a supply of hairpins in her mouth. It was an elaborate business.

He sat up and clasped his hands round his knees. 'It

222

wasn't a conscious decision,' he said. 'I just ... did it on the spur of the moment.'

She took the hairpins out of her mouth, looked at him in the mirror. 'Are you telling me you pulled rank to make some poor bloody aircrew setting off on a raid take you along for the ride? On the spur of the moment? Just because you were bored or something?'

She saw that he was no longer looking at her, but staring out of the window at the grey sky. She went on pinning up her hair. He was silent so long she thought perhaps he hadn't been listening. And when he did speak his manner was abstracted, as if his mind was on other things.

'Caesar knew about morale,' he said.

'Who?' she said, wondering if she'd misheard.

'After he'd given the signal for battle, by spreading his scarlet cloak on the ground, he always sent his horse back behind the lines. And the horses of all the other officers too. So if the battle were lost, they were all lost, officers and men alike. It was a risk no other general ever took. And looked at rationally, it does seem an unnecessary, even stupid risk ... But by God it lifted the morale of the poor sods up at the sharp end. Who didn't have any horses anyway. Made them feel he was one of them ...'

'Is there a point to all this?' she said.

'I don't know,' he said. 'But he never lost a battle.'

'Maybe he was lucky. Now, we're leaving today and there's a lot to do ...' He was still staring out of the window. 'Are you listening to me?'

Again he took his time answering, and seemed to be speaking more to himself than to her.

'We'd taken a bashing and morale was low among aircrew. Especially Bunny Meadows's crew. They were a new lot apart from the bomb-aimer and flight engineer. Some months previously he'd brought a kite back from Duesseldorf full of holes and dead and wounded. Been raked from stem to stern by a Messerschmit and a Fokke Wulfe. His navigator was killed so he had to set course by the moon and the Pole star. Nobody knows how he managed to land it since he was wounded himself and half fainting from loss of blood. Couldn't see the runway lights because blood was getting in his eyes. Couldn't even manage the control column by himself. Had to be propped up by the bomb-aimer and flight engineer, who was also wounded. But land it he did. Then the undercart collapsed. But at least it didn't catch fire ... He was given leave and sick leave, of course, but he was anxious to get back to the squadron – and get airborne. Maybe he came back too soon. Maybe the new crew took more licking into shape than he'd bargained for. Or maybe they'd just done too many ops.'

He stopped, looked at her. 'Whatever it was, the tension was building up. You could feel it. So was resentment, which is part of the tension. Resentment of authority. Of me. Of anyone who sends them up into the skies – while he stays behind himself. You may be part of the same squadron, but you're not part of *them*. And you can't be because you've never been up with them. Never been there when the shit hits the fan. They think you don't know what it's really like. No matter how many gongs you won in some war long ago ...

'Of course, you have your tensions too. When you go into your office night after night and sit by the window in the dark, waiting for them to come back. Counting them in ... C for Charlie, F for Freddie, D for Dog ... You get to know the beat of every engine ...

'And one day you can't take any more and you stroll down to the locker room where Bunny Meadows and his crew are collecting their gear and say casually: "Got room for another bod tonight, Skipper? I could do with a change of scene." And Bunny grins. And the crew grin. And then everyone's grinning. And you can feel the tension starting to melt like snow in the sun ...' He shrugged. 'That's what I mean by the spur of the moment. It's not something you plan. It just ... happens.'

She was silent a long time. Then she said: 'I accept that but ...' She hesitated, then went and knelt on the mattress beside him. 'You must have known you were a Bigot. And what that implied. You must have known that SHAEF and Air Ministry had both issued strict instructions – '

'SHAEF, Air Ministry . . . Who cares about a bunch of strangers up in London? Miles away from base, from the squadron – your real home, your real family. Where your real loyalty lies. And what the hell? All you're doing is taking a quick flip across the Channel with the boys. No one will know. And anyway, *nothing's going to happen*. You tell yourself.'

She took a deep breath. 'I know what you mean,' she said slowly. 'Christ, I know.' And flung her arms round him and kissed him. 'There. That's on the spur of the moment too.'

They hugged each other like children. Friends again. Then she heard the sound of a wood-burning *gazo* chugging up the drive. She broke away and went to the window in time to see a battered old truck pull up in the courtyard. Nikki and a lean, dark villainous-looking man in a high-crowned hat got out.

Probably a Basque from the foothills of the Pyrenees, she thought as she turned away from the window.

'I hope you really are feeling fit,' she said. 'It could be a hell of a day. With a rough night to follow.'

Then, from the direction of the courtyard, came the sound of sobbing.

She froze. 'Therese!'

17

Dog minus 7

The body lay in the back of the truck under a ragged tarpaulin. Only the face was showing, dead eyes staring at the sky. Lupin's face.

Therese was standing by the truck, still sobbing, but quietly now. Next to her was Nikki. The villainous-looking Basque was leaning against the side of the truck, hat tipped over his eyes, apparently having a nap.

Ryfka lifted a corner of the tarpaulin and saw a gunshot wound in the chest. An exit wound from the size of it. She let the tarpaulin drop and turned to Nikki. 'Where did you find him?'

'In a ditch. Before dawn. At least, Spanghero did.' He jerked a thumb at the Basque. 'They used to go poaching together.'

'He seems pretty relaxed about it.'

'Just tired,' said Nikki. 'Never goes to bed. Well, not for sleeping purposes.'

'Poor Lupin,' said Therese. She wiped her eyes. 'He was gentle. Wouldn't hurt a fly.' She blew her nose. 'And so timid.'

'Who'd want to shoot him?' said Ryfka.

'Raab took him away in a car yesterday. And returned alone. With a yarn about Lupin offering to show him some place in the countryside. But when they got there, he said, Lupin ran off into the woods. And that was the last they saw of him. He said.'

'But you don't believe him.'

'Lupin wouldn't run away unless he were frightened.'

'You saw the gunshot wound?'

Therese nodded. She seemed suddenly to have aged. 'Leaving him in a ditch to die like a dog.' She sniffed, turned to Ryfka. 'Let me help you. Let me do something, anything.'

'You've done enough already.'

'I want to do more.'

Ryfka patted her shoulder. 'We'll see,' she said, but intending it more as a conciliatory gesture than an offer.

Therese brightened. 'I'll get some breakfast,' she said and went briskly into the house.

Ryfka turned to Nikki again. 'You said you were out before dawn?'

'Out half the night. Spanghero spotted two or three new barrages – on the way home from some girl he'd been shagging. And had the sense to knock me up and tell me. So we went out and did a recce. Only stopped when it got light enough to make it too tricky. Then we found the body and came on here.' He pulled a folded map from his pocket. 'I've marked the new ones we saw, but others were still going up.'

'Fuck,' she said absently, staring into the distance. 'Means we'll have to do another recce.' She took the map and spread it out on the bonnet of the truck. 'Wonder why he hasn't put one here,' she said. 'It's the main road to Fougères.' She shrugged. 'Perhaps he hasn't got round to it yet.'

'What are we going to do with the body?'

'Send it back to Raab,' she said. 'That's what we ought to do. Meanwhile, let's put it in the barn.' She looked at the dead body. 'He's in no hurry, poor bastard.'

Over breakfast she tried to study the map again, but she was too distracted. She ate little. Therese ate nothing, which was no surprise. When she wasn't serving the men she stood by the stove drinking coffee, but keeping an eye on them in case they lacked anything. Nikki ate heartily, so did Harry. Spanghero fell asleep at the table, like a small boy over his porridge. No doubt it had been a hard night, one way and another.

She looked across at Harry, now feeling close to him again. He'd spoken a language she understood. The larger loyalties were fine in their abstract way, but when the chips were down it was the men you fought with, lived with, sweated with who were the ones that counted. And the ones who counted on you. It was for them, not England, home and beauty that you kept your mouth shut – even when screaming your head off, naked in a Gestapo cellar. For the first time she felt a closeness to him that was something more than sexual. She knew that in his place she would have done the same thing.

As if he sensed something he looked up and smiled at her. She smiled back. For Harry, England and St George . . . But mostly for Harry.

Nikki, who had finished eating, said: 'At all the major roadblocks there are Kuebelwagen equipped with wireless sets, so presumably they're in radio contact with one another.'

She nodded. 'And with a command vehicle. Raab's armoured car, no doubt. Did you spot it during the recce?'

'Twice,' said Nikki. 'And if we do run into trouble at a roadblock, I suppose we have to shoot our way out.'

She nodded. 'And head for the nearest woods. Though God knows if we'd ever get through.'

Then a harsh voice said in an *accent du midi:* 'I'll get you through.' It was Spanghero. Awake and fixing her with eyes like burnt holes in a blanket. 'I know tracks that only foxes know.' He drew in his breath. 'And Lupin used to know.'

'What about Lupin?' said Therese. 'He always said he didn't want to be buried in a wooden box in some mouldy churchyard, but out on a hillside. In the wild green earth, he said.' She bit her lip. 'He told me he hadn't long to live, but I thought he was romancing.'

Spanghero stood up, leaned across the table and put a long grimy finger on the map in front of Ryfka. 'There. On the hill that's shaped like a woman's breast. With a stand of trees at the tip like a nipple. Full of wild flowers. That's where he said he'd like to lie.'

Ryfka looked at the map. On the other side of the hill that the grimy finger was pointing at lay the main road to Fougères.

'And why not?' she said softly. 'Why not?'

*

228

Raab and Blech got back to the Hotel Abelard soon after sunrise. Blech could hardly keep his eyes open. The sensible thing would have been to sleep at Les Sapins Argentés instead of schlepping all the way back to Rennes. But when he'd suggested it Raab nearly bit his head off.

'My office at ten,' Raab said as they went up in the lift. 'And don't be late.'

Blech looked at his watch. Nearly half-past five. That meant little more than four hours' sleep. He stifled a yawn. By the time the lift had risen to the second floor he'd dozed off.

Raab shook him. 'This is where you came in.'

Blech staggered out of the lift like a drunk.

Raab went up to his own suite. He opened the door quietly, as he always did. The salon was in darkness. He drew back the heavy curtains and let the early sunlight in. The sky was blue and clear, apart from a few fleecy clouds riding high. A fine day was in prospect. But not for some, if he could help it.

He decided it wasn't worth going to bed for an hour or so and rang for coffee. Then he settled back in an armchair. He was beginning to feel confident. He had set a trap for Ryfka. And with a bit of luck she'd walk right into it. A thin smile cut his face and was still there when an orderly brought the coffee.

They buried him in a shallow grave at the tip of the hill that was shaped like a woman's breast. From the woods there she had a clear view of the road to Fougères and an old water mill, which could be a good landmark.

'I wonder why he hasn't put an extra barrage to the north of Saint Aubin. If he waits much longer we'll be through there and away.'

She was standing in the wild flowers with Nikki and Spanghero after a quick recce of the northern roadblocks because north was the way she'd be heading.

Her watch said it was nearly nine. 'Let's go,' she said. 'Don't want to keep Luc waiting.'

They climbed down the hill to Nikki's truck and in a few

uneventful minutes were back at Les Sapins Argentés. Luc was in the kitchen drinking coffee with Therese and Harry.

She spread her map out on the table. All the roadblocks were plainly marked.

'Now,' she said, 'Victor and Nikki should come through the roadblock at Liffré around four. No earlier or it'll look suspicious. And not more than, say, ten minutes later or you'll be cutting down our start. I'm counting on twenty minutes to half an hour's start before the real funeral appears – and the balloon goes up. Once you're through the roadblock, after a kilometre or so, you'll come to the Forêt de Liffré. Off to the right there's the little side road I mentioned before.' She pointed to it on the map. 'Where we'll be waiting. Then . . .' She looked at Harry. 'We load up the corpse and proceed, with due dignity, to the road-block north of Saint Aubin-du-Cormier. Okay?'

'Why that roadlock?' said Luc. 'I mean, any particular reason?'

'Because it means we only have to go through one road-block instead of two. Look at the map.'

'Of course,' said Luc. 'Smart.'

'Let's hope so,' she said. 'And you'll be waiting for us a couple of kilometres further on.'

'Near the old water mill,' said Luc, nodding.

'Then we split up. The funeral cortège will disappear into an outbuilding at the stud farm. And the rest of us, including the revived corpse, will head for the landing field north of Fougères. Anything else?'

'Yes,' said Therese. 'What about me? Can't I do something?'

Ryfka thought about it. 'Do you have funeral clothes?'

Therese nodded. 'I've been to a lot of funerals.'

'Any that would fit me?'

'They might be on the big side.'

'Enough for slacks and a sweater underneath?'

'Maybe.'

'We'll go into it a bit later,' said Ryfka. 'Anyone see any weaknesses in the plan?'

A brief silence. Then Nikki said: 'Do *you* see any?'

'The timing,' she said. 'If the other funeral's early. Or you and Victor get delayed . . . You can't allow for everything. But if there is a weakness, Raab will find it.'

At five to ten Raab went down to his office. To his surprise Blech was already there, sitting in an armchair, arms folded, head bent as if in thought. In fact, he was asleep. He'd known that if he went to bed he'd never wake up in time for the meeting. So he went straight to Raab's office and slept in an armchair instead. Raab shook him awake.

'Well,' he said, 'at least you're on time.'

Blech yawned his apologies.

Raab told him to ring for coffee, then went to the wall map and marked in the new roadblocks. By the time he'd finished the others had arrived. They included von Heideck, commander of the SS troops manning the roadblocks, the heads of the local milice and the Gestapo and, of course, Loubain.

Raab pointed out the new roadblocks and explained, for those who didn't already know, the objective of his Lidice threat: to force Ryfka to break cover.

'The new roadblocks, as you will see, are to the north. This is because, according to an SOE agent we managed to turn, there's a landing field somewhere to the north of Fougères. He was going to find out the exact location for us, but unfortunately we lost contact with him. He may have been recalled or executed by his own people. Ryfka will know of this landing field and may be intending to use it. It would make sense if she's heading north.'

He paused. 'And I intend making it easy for her.'

Barely suppressed murmurs of surprise drew one of his tight smiles. 'Easy to go the way I want her to go, that is.' He turned to the map, pointed to the cordon of roadblocks. 'Note the secondary roadblocks on the northern side. Except at Saint Aubin-du-Cormier. The weak link.' Another pause to let it sink in. 'She'll have the help of some local resistance group, as always. And she'll know where the weak link is. Let us also hope she doesn't realize it's a deliberate mistake. I'll be waiting for her north of the Saint Aubin roadblock.

With two armoured cars and a truckload of SS. A mobile barrage ready to move at a moment's notice. And in radio contact with the others.'

Another pause. 'She might still fool us. She knows every trick in the book and a few besides. Any questions?'

'Supposing she ignores the roadblocks,' said von Heideck, 'and heads across country?'

'We have a contingency plan for that. But she's unlikely to do it unless it's forced on her. Progress would be slow and difficult, especially with our Fieseler Storch overhead. Which is armed with a light machine gun, remember. Anything else?'

'Yes,' said von Heideck. 'You have at your disposal a battalion of my SS, plus Gestapo and local milice. Why such a massive operation to catch one British agent and a squadron leader? Especially when my troops are supposed to be on standby for the Second Front.'

Raab went over to the window and stared unseeingly at the blue sky and the fleecy clouds as if he hadn't heard the question. When he turned towards the others his eyes still seemed to focus beyond them.

'This information,' he said, 'must not, repeat not, go outside this room.' He took a deep breath. 'I have reason to believe that the so-called squadron leader is in fact an air commodore. With detailed knowledge of the Second Front.'

There were general murmurs of surprise. Only Loubain remained impassive. But the colour drained slowly from his face, leaving it as dead as a waxen mask, apart from the eyes, which were half closed.

The SS sergeant at the Liffré roadblock was the first to spot it as it rounded a bend about half a kilometre away and advanced slowly towards them. The sergeant had a black patch over one eye and a bad limp. He was a veteran of the First World War, the Spanish Civil War and the Russian Front. He left an eye in Spain and part of his left leg at Stalingrad. He was supposed to have been invalided out, but kicked up such a fuss that he was finally transferred to an SS unit deployed mainly on police duties. He was a godsend to young officers.

'Funeral approaching, mein Herr,' he said to the young officer commanding the roadblock.

The officer raised his field glasses. 'Magnificent flowers,' he said.

The motorized hearse slowed to a walking pace as it got nearer, and four undertaker's mutes, in frock coats and tall hats, got off to walk beside the hearse, two on either side.

Directly ahead of them they saw a light armoured car and a spiked mat across the road. Behind that an SS truck positioned on the other side of the road to form a chicane. And behind the truck a tiny Kuebelwagen with a wireless set and operator. Within the chicane area were half a dozen SS men with Schmeisser submachine guns slung from their shoulders and grenades from their belts. The driver of the truck was leaning over the steering wheel, head cradled in his arms, having a nap.

And there'd be a couple of men in the armoured car, making, say, a dozen in all, thought Nikki, who was one of the undertaker's mutes. Another, walking just ahead of him, was the villainous-looking Spanghero.

They were almost at the roadblock when Nikki realized that an inch or two of Sten gun was visible below the hem of Spanghero's coat. He reached forward and quickly pushed it up.

Spanghero half turned. 'What the hell – '

'Your slip was showing,' said Nikki.

The cortège, made up of a hearse followed by two Citroëns, halted before the roadblock. The officer and the sergeant walked slowly past the three vehicles, inspecting them. In the first Citroën was a chauffeur and two passengers, one a heavily veiled woman in black. In the second, apart from the chauffeur, were three men who looked like local farmers.

To the young officer everything seemed in order. But he'd learned from experience to consult the sergeant. 'All right, sergeant?'

'I was expecting a bigger funeral.'

'You mean more cars, more mourners?'

'He was supposed to be a big shot, wasn't he? Deputy mayor or something?'

'Maybe there'll be other cars following on.'

'And those undertaker's mutes look like a bunch of hooligans to me.'

The young officer smiled. 'You have a suspicious mind, sergeant. Let them through. And salute. Respect for the dead and all that.'

The sergeant turned and barked brief orders to the SS men. The spiked mat was pulled aside. The sergeant signalled the cortège through. He and the young officer saluted as it went slowly by, the sergeant staring through narrowed eyes at the undertaker's mutes.

Then the SS men lined up, snapped to attention and saluted.

Then the cortège was through.

Nikki let out a long breath, leaned forward and muttered to Spanghero: 'Didn't like the look of that fucking sergeant, did you?'

About fifty metres down the side road at the edge of the Forêt de Liffré, Ryfka was sitting with Harry Romaine in Luc's van. She was in black: black hat, black dress, black gloves and a black veil long enough to cover her face when it was down. At the moment it was up. She was staring fixedly through the windscreen at Luc, who was at the corner of the main road, the N12, watching for the funeral cortège. Harry, dressed in slacks, his RAF sweater and an old jacket Therese had given him, was watching Ryfka. Her tension was almost palpable.

'Come on,' she was saying. 'Come *on*.'

'You're nervous,' he said.

She turned and looked at him. 'Of course I'm nervous. Bloody nervous.'

He pointed through the windscreen. 'I think Luc's trying to tell you something.'

Luc was waving vigorously.

'At bloody last,' she said, lowering her veil. She got out of the van. Harry followed.

As they reached Luc the funeral cortège was already pulling up. Nikki jumped off the hearse, grinning.

'All okay, Nikki?'

The grin widened. 'You bet. How do you say – a slice of cake?'

'Piece of cake.' She turned to Luc. 'You know where to wait for us?'

'Near the old water mill on the other side of the Saint Aubin roadblock.'

'Change of plan. Don't just wait there, do a recce of the road ahead for a few kilometres. You've got field glasses with you?'

'But there aren't any roadblocks after Saint Aubin – so what's the point?'

'I don't know. Maybe we're having it too cushy. I don't know.'

'And if you get to the old mill before me – '

'We'll wait for you.'

'But – '

'Do it Luc. Just do it.'

Luc gave one of those exaggerated French shrugs, got in the van and drove off.

She turned to Harry. 'Get in the coffin,' she said.

Raab had put Blech in charge at Saint Aubin, with instructions to keep in half-hourly radio contact with Raab's command vehicle and report all traffic movements through the roadblock. So far traffic had been light, mainly local farmers with their carts and waggons and hay wains. And recently an old wood-burning van.

It was a warm sunny day and he was beginning to feel sleepy. Then he saw the funeral cortège approaching slowly with the undertaker's mutes on either side of the hearse. He sat up. Ah yes, the Truchet funeral he'd been told to expect. He liked funeral processions. Stately. Solemn. A reminder of the inescapable. And of the psalms his poor troubled mother used to intone as if they were an incan-

235

tation. *The days of man are but as grass: for he flourisheth as a flower of the field. For as soon as the wind goeth over it, it is gone . . .*

Mutti, he sighed to himself, and climbed out of the armoured car to inspect the cortège, which had come to a halt. His inspection was cursory, except for the hearse. Like the young officer at Liffré he was greatly taken with the massed flowers rioting over the coffin.

He glanced at the two following Citroëns, at the stiff-faced mourners and veiled women inside, then signalled to the sergeant to let the cortège through.

The spiked mat was pulled aside and the cortège continued its stately progression past the saluting SS. Blech told his wireless operator to send a message to Raab that the Truchet funeral was on its way.

Ryfka, through the rear window of the last Citroën, watched the roadblock getting magically smaller.

'Christ,' she said. 'I think we've made it.'

Luc had taken a side road that led to a hill that looked as if would give a good view of the main road. And it did. The top of the hill was more or less flat, with sloping fields on either side where sheep were grazing. He parked the old *gazo* at the entrance to a field, leaned on the gate and surveyed a section of the main road that ran through some woods almost directly below. The road was empty apart from a horse and cart making slow progress towards the woods.

'Looking for something?' The voice at his elbow made him jump. He hadn't heard anyone approach. Next to him was an old man in ragged clothes leaning on a shepherd's staff and smoking a cherrywood pipe.

'Bird-watching,' said Luc, never at a loss.

'Rare sort of hobby that be,' said the shepherd. He pointed to a couple of small birds wheeling in the sky. 'What d'ye reckon they be?'

Luc put the glasses on them. 'Swallows?'

'Swifts,' said the shepherd. 'Never mind, maybe you're interested in the big predators. Like eagles.'

Luc wondered if the old boy was soft in the head. But the eyes looking at him out of a wrinkled, leathery face were sharp and steady.

'Ever seen a German eagle?' The shepherd took the pipe from his mouth, waved it towards the road below. 'Put your glasses on old Duvivier.'

'Who?'

'The farmer driving that horse and cart. Another fifty metres and he'll reach the woods down below. See what happens.'

Luc watched through the glasses as the horse and cart reached the woods. From the trees on either side of the road Raab's command vehicle, followed by another armoured car and an SS truck, shot out to block the way ahead.

'I don't know what kind of bird the Boche are looking for,' the old shepherd said, knocking out his pipe on the gate. 'But I hope she flies free.'

'I could have hugged the old bastard,' Luc said, reporting to Ryfka some minutes later. The funeral cortège had pulled up near the old water mill, to wait for him as agreed.

Ryfka, Luc, Nikki and Spanghero were gathered round a map spread out on the bonnet of the hearse. Luc had just marked the wood where Raab had hidden his forces.

'We're trapped,' said Ryfka.

'No,' said Spanghero. 'I'll lead you out.'

'We can't just abandon the funeral,' she said.

'I thought you arranged to hide it at some stud farm,' said Luc.

'The difficulty,' she said slowly, 'is that between us and the stud farm there's Raab and his armoured cars and a truckload of SS men . . .'

She stared at the rolling Normandy countryside, which had suddenly become a prison. With no way out . . . Almost opposite was the hill shaped like a woman's breast. At the top she could see the wild flowers waving in the wind. Waving farewell for Lupin perhaps.

She turned away abruptly and said to the others: 'I've got

an idea. If there's time . . . Once they get news of the other funeral they'll be bloody suspicious.'

She stopped, lost in thought. The others waited patiently for her to go on. A Fieseler Storch flew low overhead and they all ducked.

The wireless operator in the command vehicle said: 'Message from pilot of Fieseler Storch, mein Herr. Funeral sighted two kilometres north of Saint Aubin-du-Cormier roadblock. Either stopped or broken down.'

Raab nodded, took the headset from the operator. 'Standartenfuehrer Raab here,' he said. 'Funerals have only two speeds, dead slow or stop.' He smiled thinly at his little joke and glanced round for approbation.

Loubain, who was with him in the vehicle, smiled obediently.

Fifteen minutes later he got another wireless message, from Blech this time, to the effect that the Liffré roadblock had told him they'd sighted a second funeral. And was this expected?

Again Raab took the headset. 'Blech, what is this shit about a second funeral? Over.'

'The Liffré sergeant, who's nobody's fool, says it looks like a real big funeral with five or six carloads of mourners following the hearse. And that it must be the Truchet funeral, which he'll be able to confirm shortly. He felt there was something odd about the other funeral, but it was just a gut feeling. And his officer ordered him to let it through. Over.'

'What did *you* make of it? You let it through too. Over.'

'Well, I thought it didn't seem much of a funeral for a big shot, but that's all. Over.'

Raab was silent for a moment. Then he said: 'I'll take a look at it. Over and out.'

He gave the headset back to the operator. 'Get in touch with the pilot of the Fieseler Storch and ask him if the funeral is on the move again and its approximate position.'

Then he turned to the map table to study a large-scale survey map showing local features and buildings, down to individual farms and smallholdings. He marked something with a cross and said to Loubain: 'Know this place?'

Loubain nodded. 'My father worked there till it closed. But that was long before the war. Very few local people know of its existence now, never mind Ryfka.'

'One of her resistance chums might know. Anyway, I can't take the chance. It's about the one place where she could get through, if she's trying to avoid the roads. Now what I want you to do . . .'

The wireless operator cut in. 'Report from the pilot, mein Herr. Funeral moving this way on the N12, presently about a kilometre from our position. He also reports four people heading north-east across country towards some woods.'

'Tell him to try and keep track of the people,' said Raab and turned back to Loubain. 'It could be them. They're heading in the right direction. On the other hand they could still be with that funeral – wouldn't put it past her to try and smuggle someone out in a coffin . . .'

He pointed to the spot he'd marked on the map. 'Take a truck and half a dozen SS men, including a wireless operator and a signaller. And an MG 42. Leave the truck here, where the road stops, and do the rest on foot – it's not far. There's an old road that goes all the way, but it was never more than a track and is now impassable except to a half-track or a tank. Now, when you get there, put the signaller on the hillside about here . . .'

He went on giving precise instructions for several minutes and then said: 'Of course, they may not go this way at all, or even be aware of it. But if they do, you'll be alerted by the signaller. Then radio me immediately. Is that clear?'

'Absolutely, mein Herr.'

'And remember that the airman must be taken alive.'

'Of course, mein Herr.'

Raab paused deliberately and studied Loubain. 'I know you're intelligent and efficient, and I think you're reliable. That's why I'm giving you the job. But if you mess it up I'll have you shot. If you're lucky.'

Loubain bowed impassively.

*

239

The funeral halted at the roadblock. The hearse was now escorted by only one undertaker's mute on either side. Behind it were the two Citroëns.

A dozen heavily armed SS men were waiting for it. At a signal from Raab an SS sergeant ordered everyone out of the cortège and lined them up with their backs to the vehicles. Among them was a heavily veiled woman of about the same height and build as Ryfka. Raab resisted the temptation to walk up to her and tear the veil off. Victory was always pleasanter if savoured. Besides, why hurry? There was no escaping the guns of the SS.

Then, pointing to the hearse and lowering his voice, he told the sergeant to find out, *aber Taktvoll natuerlich*, whether the coffin lid was actually screwed down.

The sergeant clambered on to the hearse and floundered among the massed flowers like a whale in shallow water. Then he got down and reported that the lid was, in fact, unsecured.

Six SS men were detailed to take the coffin from the hearse and lower it to the ground. Then, at Raab's order, two of them took off the lid.

Staring up at him out of a bloodless face were the dead eyes of Lupin.

Raab strode over to the woman, ripped her veil off. Another shock. It was Therese.

'Can't I even bury him in peace?' she said calmly.

18

As soon as the cortège had moved on she got into the back of Luc's van and took off the hat, the mourning veil and the long black dress and rolled down the legs of the slacks she'd been wearing underneath. Then she got out and said to Spanghero: 'Now where?'

But Spanghero, who could hear things that only dogs and bats can hear, was squinting at the bright sky.

'I hear something,' he said.

It was two or three seconds before anyone else heard the approaching plane. Then they quickly got in the van, she and Luc in the driving cab, Spanghero, Nikki and Harry Romaine in the back.

'Fieseler Storch,' she said. 'And the bastard's looking for us.'

The sound of the plane faded.

'You know the Bois de Rumignon?' Spanghero said to Luc.

'Wait a minute,' she said. 'That'll put us behind the roadblocks again.'

'We're already behind them,' said Nikki. 'We were working on the assumption that the N12 was clear north of the Saint Aubin roadblock. And it isn't.'

'Shit,' she said. 'Raab set a trap and I walked into it.'

'And now,' said Spanghero, 'we will walk out of it.'

He had an animal confidence she liked. 'Let's go,' she said.

A few minutes later the van pulled off the narrow road that cuts through the Bois de Rumignon, stopping under some trees. They all got out except Luc. She wondered if this was a signal that he'd had enough. He had an instinct about future prospects, like early warning radar. And future prospects were decidedly grim. She took the mourning

241

clothes out of the van, rolled them into a bundle and shoved them under the nearest bush.

'Thanks, Luc,' she said. 'Be seeing you.'

'Hold it. It's twenty-five kilometres across rough country to that landing field. If you ever make it on foot. And then you'll miss the bloody plane.'

'They'll be shoving up new roadblocks all over the place,' she said. 'We won't stand a chance on the roads.'

Luc ignored her, looked at Spanghero. 'Where do you want me to meet you?'

'Got a map?' said Spanghero.

Luc produced a map, spread it on the steering wheel. Spanghero leaned in the driving cab, pointed with a grimy finger. 'Here. Road junction with the N12.'

'What time?'

Spanghero shrugged. 'Couple of hours. Maybe more. Depends what trouble we run into.'

'I'll be there,' said Luc. 'Ciao.' And drove off.

Luc, black marketeer and womanizer, whose simple philosophy rested on the proposition: *What's in it for me?* must have known there was nothing in it for him. Except a bullet. She watched him out of sight, then said: 'Let's go.'

They made their way to the eastern edge of the forest, which bordered farmland, and listened for the plane. At least, Spanghero did.

'It's over there somewhere.' He pointed into the sky. 'Getting fainter, then louder, then fainter again. Circling.'

He pointed across the farmland to some woods. 'The next stop. Most of the way we can use ditches and hedges for cover. The last bit is across open fields. We might have to run for it.'

The first part of the journey was easy but slow because of the need to use the available cover. When they reached the open fields he said: 'Take it at a steady jogtrot – unless something goes wrong.'

Something went wrong when they had less than three hundred metres to go. 'Run!' Spanghero shouted. 'Run!'

They ran. Spanghero streaked ahead like a hunted stag. Harry Romaine was a close second, Nikki not far behind.

Ryfka was last. By then they could all hear the sound of the rapidly approaching plane. Harry dropped back, took her hand, pulled her along. She felt her arm was coming out of its socket.

They made it to the woods and flopped down as the Fieseler Storch swooped low overhead, engine howling, machine gun chattering. When they'd got their breath back they started off through the trees in Indian file behind Spanghero, who led them along paths and barely discernible tracks. Harry still kept hold of her hand, except when they had to crawl or wriggle through tunnels in the undergrowth used by foxes and other animals. Trying to protect her. It seemed ironic. Spanghero skirted clearings because of the plane, still circling overhead.

After about half an hour, Ryfka judged, though it seemed longer, the woods began to thin out and then, where the tree-line stopped, gave way to a field of young wheat rippled by the wind. A big rectangular field that sloped steeply down to the outbuildings of a farm. Spanghero called a halt and listened to the circling plane. 'He knows we're in here somewhere. And he's waiting for us to come out.'

At one side of the wheatfield was a hedge that finished about thirty metres short of the woods. Spanghero pointed to it. 'There's a ditch alongside it deep enough to give us cover if we crouch a bit. And it should be dry because of the slope. If we wait till he's over the other side of the wood we should make it all right.'

And make it they did, first moving along the edge of the wood till they were opposite the hedge, then waiting for Spanghero to give them the signal. Keeping their heads down, they followed the ditch for several hundred metres as it curved past the outbuildings, gradually growing narrower and shallower till it petered out near a lane lined with trees and matted hedges.

The lane was deeply rutted and the verges overgrown with couch grass and wild flowers. Many of the trees had intertwined overhead, like a tunnel with a leaky roof that let the sunlight in. It was deserted apart from a few sparrows and yellowhammers. And so peaceful even the buzz of the

Fieseler Storch, circling patiently over the wood, had the sleepy sound of a summer insect. Automatically they began to relax, their pace slackened – till accidentally they startled a partridge, which startled *them* even more, clapping up out of the wild flowers like automatic gunfire.

'Jesus,' said Nikki, 'I thought it was Gestapo.'

They followed the lane for a kilometre or so, then a metalled road that was badly pot-holed and finally a tarmac road in good condition.

'This bit's dangerous,' said Spanghero.

And it was. Twice in ten minutes they had to hide in a ditch as SS trucks roared by. Then they turned off into another rutted lane that twisted and turned for at least a kilometre before ending abruptly at the gate of a farm. The farmhouse, square and solid-looking, stood well back. A few chickens were pecking in the dirt beside it.

Spanghero pushed the gate open and signalled the others to follow. A big black dog rushed out of an open doorway at the side of the farmhouse, scattering chickens and barking furiously.

Spanghero spoke to him and he shut up and wagged his tail. Then a broken-nosed man who looked like a murderer appeared in the doorway and greeted Spanghero.

'You want something?' he said. 'Food? Drink?'

Spanghero shook his head. 'Thank you, old friend.' He put a finger to his lips. 'Understood?'

Broken Nose merely grinned, showing that some of his teeth were missing. Then he called the dog and went inside.

Mossop pressed down the switch of his intercom.

'Yes, sir?'

'Jean, 'as Smithy – Colonel Smith come in yet?'

'No, sir.'

'Christ Almighty, Jean, it's getting on for lunchtime. Ring 'im again.'

'I just have, sir.'

'When?'

'A few minutes ago. Still no answer.'

'What about whatsername, the one they call – you know, the Welsh one.'

'Warrant Officer Aeronwy Jones, sir? No answer from her either.'

Mossop flicked the switch to cut her off while he said 'Fuck' to the empty office, then pressed it down again. 'Sorry, Jean. Must've moved t'switch, accidental like.'

'Yes, sir,' said Jean, who knew all about that trick. 'That's the third time this morning.'

'Where the 'ell *are* they, Jean?'

'If they were looking for Pilot Officer Flynn, sir, they'd have been lucky to get home by dawn. Perhaps they're still sleeping.'

'Aye, well, that's the kindest interpretation. Get me Group Captain Burgess at Tangmere.'

'Just a moment, sir, I think we have Colonel Smith on the other line.'

'Thank Christ for that.'

Mossop switched off the intercom, picked up his phone. ''ullo? Smithy? 'ullo?'

Smith, propped up by pillows and wan as a ghost, said in a sleepy drawl: 'Morning, sir. Sorry I'm late reporting – '

'Where't bloody 'ell art tha'?'

'In bed, sir. Didn't get home till nearly seven – '

'Did tha' *find* 'im, Smithy?'

'Found him stoned out of his head. Looked to me as if he'd been on a three-day blind. Anyway, he refused. Said he was on leave. Then passed out. Not that he'd be in any condition to fly. We'd better get another pilot.'

'Jean's putting in a call to Tangmere now. And where's Blodwen Big Tits?'

'Also in bed. And no doubt asleep,' Smith yawned.

'Sounds like you'd better get some sleep yourself. See you later.'

'Yes, sir,' said Smith and hung up.

Then he turned over and put his arms round Blodwen.

'Group Captain Burgess on the line, sir,' said Jean.

245

'Put 'im through.'

After an exchange of greetings Mossop said: 'Bill, we must have an agent picked up tonight, in the early hours – '

'Another one?'

'What do you mean, another one?'

'We're already picking up Ryfka.'

'You are?'

'Didn't you know? One of your chaps asked Paddy Flynn to do it. Said Ryfka had asked for him specially. Paddy admits he was a bit sloshed at the time – '

'A bit?'

'And might have given your bloke some comic answers. He's a bit hazy on that point. Anyway, he rang me an hour ago to say he'd be reporting back for duty this afternoon.'

'Was 'e sober?'

'As a judge, old boy,' said Group Captain Burgess in slightly shocked tones. 'As a bloody judge.'

All that was left of the mine was a few dilapidated wooden shacks, sunk deep in brambles and bracken in a clearing at the foot of the hill where the trees were thickest. A chain-link fence had once enclosed the area, but most of it was missing, perhaps taken for scrap metal when war broke out. The only section standing was the entrance gates, still upright and firmly padlocked. They looked ludicrous and a bit sad, she thought, standing there all alone. Hanging on them was a lopsided notice, which said in bold lettering:

MINE WORKINGS
DANGER OF ROCKFALLS!
KEEP OUT

She'd always suffered from mild claustrophobia and felt a moment of panic at the thought of suffocating in the dark coils of a disused mine.

'Is there any real danger?' she said.

'Not much,' Spanghero said without looking at her. 'You might hear a few rockfalls, but they're usually somewhere

246

else. And if there's a fall in your gallery, it'll either be in front of you or behind you. So you go on – or you go back.'

'But we don't want to go back.'

'Not right back. Just far enough to find another way round. The place is like a rabbit warren.'

'But how can you tell where a rockfall is?'

'You listen,' he said. 'Unless it comes down on top of you. When all your worries are over.'

Her heart sank even more. 'Will the recent rains have had any effect?'

'Not much.'

All the time he was talking in his casual voice his eyes were scanning the tree-clad slopes of the surrounding hills. His big dark eyes remind her of a falcon.

Suddenly he froze. 'There,' he said, pointing to a stand of trees on a hillside about 400 metres away. 'Something moved.'

She focused her field glasses on the trees.

'See anything?' he said.

She panned right with the glasses, left with the glasses, tilted them up, tilted them down.

'Not a thing,' she said with obvious relief. She offered him the glasses.

'I can't see with those things,' he said. 'Maybe it's just a big bird. An eagle owl maybe.'

'They don't have eagle owls in these parts.'

'A buzzard then.'

'That's more like it.'

'Except it's not a buzzard,' said Spanghero. 'In fact, it doesn't move like any kind of bird.'

'Listen,' she said. 'No one can have known we were coming this way because we didn't know ourselves. Right?'

He shrugged. 'Let's go,' he said and led them past the main entrance of the mine, which had been blocked years before by a huge rockfall, now patched with moss and short wiry grass and clumps of globe thistles. A few more years and it would be indistinguishable from the rest of the hillside.

About fifty metres from the main entrance, and partly

hidden by a wooden shack and a heap of broken winding gear, was the entrance to what looked like a cave and turned out to be a tunnel. Spanghero produced a torch and went in, followed by Ryfka and Harry. Nikki, who also had a torch, brought up the rear. The roof was low and at first they had to crouch.

'Watch out,' said Spanghero. 'It's steep and littered with broken bits of the railway track they used for hauling the stuff to the surface.'

She held Harry's hand and that gave her some comfort. She hated the combination of darkness and dankness and the feeling of being shut in as they went down and down through a maze of galleries, sometimes splashing through standing water, sometimes stopping while Spanghero searched with the torch for the entrance to another gallery. Many of the galleries were blocked by roof falls, but Spanghero always seemed to know the way.

She held Harry's hand ever more tightly, trying to stem the feeling of panic that was threatening to overflow her. Perhaps he sensed something because he whispered to her: 'Don't worry. We're climbing up now. Can't be much longer.'

Then it happened. A dull crump, like an explosion. Then an earth tremor, then the sound of rock falling, falling, falling . . . He took her in his arms and held her. Or she might have screamed.

She gained control of herself. 'What was it?' she said. 'An explosion?'

'Could be firedamp,' said Spanghero. 'That could cause an explosion. Anyway, we better keep moving.'

Loubain saw the flashing of the signaller's lamp, but it was meaningless since he didn't understand Morse.

'What's he saying?' he asked the wireless operator.

'Four people in mine area. One could be female . . . Shall I send a signal to Standartenfuehrer Raab?'

'I suppose so,' said Loubain in a faraway voice, as if thinking of something else.

'And will you speak to him yourself, mein Herr?'

248

'Why not?' said Loubain.

Raab wasn't an emotional man and like all torturers had little imagination, but when he got the signal from Loubain a quiver of excitement went through him.

'Remember the airman is to be taken alive. The others are not important. If you have to shoot them, shoot them.' The quiver touched his voice. 'Though I'd prefer the girl to be taken alive, naturally.'

'Naturally,' said Loubain, whose replies were calm and concise, and Raab congratulated himself on choosing him for such a vital operation. He may have had doubts about Loubain in the past, but the Frenchman's common sense and cool efficiency had finally dispersed them.

Raab told his wireless operator to signal Blech to join him immediately. Then he got out of the command vehicle, which suddenly seemed small and oppressive, and walked up and down to wait for Blech, who arrived a few minutes later in an armoured car.

'We've got her,' said Raab, trying to keep the triumph out of his voice. 'The tiger cat's fallen into the pit.'

'And the airman, mein Herr?'

'Oh yes,' said Raab, 'we've got him too. We've got the lot.'

'Congratulations, mein Herr,' said Blech. 'And where is the, er, pit?'

'About half an hour away by road, plus ten minutes or so across country,' said Raab. He jerked a thumb at the command vehicle. 'Get in with me. We'll lead the way.'

They took a right-angled turn at the end of one of the galleries into a long narrow passage and for the first time since going underground saw light.

'Look,' she said in a shaky voice. 'The light of the world.'

The passage sloped up to a small ragged opening filled with blue. The sky.

'I'll go first,' she said, at once assuming command again. 'Give me a Sten.'

Nikki handed her his gun. 'Wait till I give the all clear,' she said. 'Then come up one at a time. You first, Harry.'

She was going to keep him as physically close to her as possible. Then, if they ran into an ambush and there was no escape, they'd die together. No surrender.

She made her way with some difficulty up the slope as the passage got narrower and the roof lower. For the last few yards she was on hands and knees. Just before the opening she stopped and listened. Nothing but the wind in the trees and the sleepy chirp of a bird. She put her head out. A sunlit clearing surrounded by trees and scrub. Straight ahead a path between the trees. She crawled out into the clearing and stood up. The warm sun flooding over her head and shoulders after the cold darkness of the mine was like a benediction. She took a great breath of fresh air, slung the Sten gun from her shoulder, leaned in the opening and called softly: 'All clear.'

She watched them come out, one after the other. First Harry, then Nikki, blinking in the sun. The last was Spanghero, who stretched himself like an animal, which made her smile. He started to smile back, then froze, staring past her. She whipped round.

Pointing straight at her from the path between the trees was the heavy barrel extension of an MG42.

Jesus, twelve hundred rounds a minute and a sound like tearing canvas . . . She could see the belt of ammunition snaking up from its box beside the tripod, the eye of the SS gunner, squinting at her along the barrel, lining up the notch of the back sight with the barleycorn front sight . . . And four SS men backing up the machine gunner with MP44 assault rifles . . . Jesus!

Then, from out of the trees stepped Loubain, also with an assault rifle, and started to cross the clearing. Much closer and he'd be moving into the SS men's field of fire. Her thumb was already hooked through the sling of the Sten. One quick movement – and she'd be killed, no doubt. But so would Harry, standing at her shoulder . . . No surrender.

Loubain stopped. 'Be careful not to give me an excuse to shoot you,' he said, cool and impassive as ever.

250

She took a deep breath and went for her gun, then momentarily froze as Loubain opened fire – on the SS. He'd swung round with the speed of a cat and cut down the machine gunner and two of the SS men in one burst. But by then the other two were firing back. Ryfka and Spanghero, firing almost in unison, cut them down.

Then she realized Loubain was lying on the ground, clutching his belly. Christ, a gut shot. She went to him, knelt down. His face was dirty white. Then she heard running footsteps coming down the path between the trees. She stood up.

'Wireless operator,' Loubain murmured.

Then she saw him. Young, plump, pale. Cap on the back of his head, SS jacket with lightning flashes on a collar too tight for the fat white neck. He stopped cold when he came upon the machine gun and the dead men at the edge of the clearing.

'Grosser Gott!' he said.

Then he saw Ryfka coming towards him with the Sten gun. He started to back away as she cocked it.

'Um Gottes Willen,' he said, voice breaking in fear, 'Ich hab' Kinder und – '

'Wir fuehren Krieg,' she said, giving him a burst of automatic fire that hurled him against a tree. He slid slowly down the trunk, chest torn open, mouth still agape with unspoken protest, eyes glazing in death.

She went back to Loubain. 'We'll carry you,' she said.

'Drag the machine gun over here,' he said. 'And turn it round.'

'We don't leave our wounded.'

'I'm too heavy to carry and I'm dying.'

'That could take days. And if you fall into Raab's hands alive – '

He pointed to the dead Germans. 'Leave me one of their stick grenades.'

She still hesitated.

'Listen,' he said. 'Raab's on his way. And he knows the airman has information about the Second Front. He also

251

knows you have a landing field north of Fougères – though he doesn't know where.'

She looked at his pale sweating face. 'You can handle an MG42?'

'I was a machine gunner at Verdun,' he said. 'It can't be that different.'

She took an MP44 and a stick grenade from a dead German, gave the grenade to Loubain, then knelt down and gently kissed him. 'Adieu, cher ami,' she murmured.

Then she got to her feet, slung the MP44 from her shoulder and said to the others: 'Let's go.'

Raab was worried about the sudden loss of radio contact with Loubain.

'Something's wrong,' he said. 'The last message was from the radio operator, who said he could hear firing. I told him to investigate and report back immediately. He hasn't reported back.'

'Maybe his set's broken down,' said Blech hopefully. Raab in a black mood was always dangerous.

'According to our own operator the set isn't dead. He just isn't answering.'

They were travelling in convoy on an unmetalled road, the command vehicle leading, followed by Blech's armoured car and two truckloads of heavily armed SS. The road ended in a field where the truck used by Loubain and his SS men was parked. Next to it was a one-ton half-track fitted with a 3.7 cm anti-tank gun.

'I ordered that,' said Raab. He waved a hand at the hilly landscape. 'I'm not walking over this sort of country. Besides, we don't know what we're going to meet at the other end. An anti-tank gun might come in useful.'

The SS driver of the half-track was asleep in the back. Raab, glad of an excuse to dissipate some nervous energy, gave him a roasting and threatened him with the Russian Front.

'Something's wrong,' he said to Blech. 'I know it.'

It was a long but not steep climb to the top of the hill,

252

which from the escarpment side gave a long view over farmland bisected by the N12 to Fougères. She turned and looked back over the hilly countryside they were leaving, wondering if Loubain was still alive and if he'd really be capable of handling an MG42. Then, carried on the wind, echoing in the hills, came an odd sound, like canvas being torn into strips. The MG42 was being fired in controlled bursts, the mark of an experienced gunner. There were heavy-sounding single shots in reply.

'Anti-tank gun,' said Nikki.

Then more firing, followed by a short silence. Then a muffled explosion.

'Stick grenade,' said Spanghero.

In the longer silence that followed, she blew him a kiss on the wind and murmured: 'Adieu, cher ami. Adieu.'

Raab stood among the German dead at the entrance to the clearing.

'Our machine gun's pointing at our own men,' he said, carefully stating the obvious. 'I suppose someone stayed behind to hold the pass . . . I wonder who.'

He walked over to the grenade-shattered body, knowing perfectly well who it was, and looked down at it as if it held the solution to a profound mystery.

'For a long time,' he said to Blech in a musing voice, 'I didn't trust him. But his efficiency, his reliability, and above all his judgment, finally won me over. In the end I trusted him completely. And that was when, with exquisite timing, he chose to betray me.'

He sighed like a man disappointed by human frailty. 'It is now obvious that he was simply biding his time.'

With an abstracted, almost absent-minded air, he took Blech's Schmeisser, released the safety catch, cocked it and emptied the whole magazine into the dead body, which jumped and flopped like a stranded fish.

Blech, who'd seen far worse sights on the Russian Front, was sickened by the pointless desecration of the dead.

*

Luc was waiting for them at the road junction with the N12, sitting in the van, dragging nervously on a Gitane.

'Hop in quick,' he said, 'the bastards are everywhere. Never seen so many black Citroëns and armoured cars. And a goddam' spotter plane buzzing around like a blue-arsed fly.'

They got in, Ryfka in the front, the others in the back. Traffic on the main road included armoured cars and SS trucks, she noted, travelling north and travelling fast. To set up new roadblocks, no doubt.

'Where to?' said Luc.

'We need somewhere to lie up for an hour or so,' said Ryfka. 'Till it's dark.'

'I have a friend with a cottage near a little place called le Breil-Renard,' said Nikki. 'We follow the main road to Romagne, then take a left turn. I'll show you where.'

'That means travelling *with* all this shit,' said Luc, referring to the SS and Gestapo traffic.

'Long as it's with you,' said Nikki. 'And not all over you.'

Luc let the clutch in and joined the main road traffic heading north. Several times he had to pull over to let black Citroëns, light armoured cars or SS trucks hurtle past.

'Never seen so much shit,' he muttered.

At Romagne they turned left and the traffic died away, and in no time at all they were driving along deserted country roads under a holiday sun. After the hectic rush of the main road it seemed like another world. An older slower world of meadows and orchards and grazing cattle. Ryfka began to relax. She saw a hedge starred with dog roses, smelt a bank of wild thyme ... It was almost June. The month of garden parties and strawberries and cream. She tried to imagine herself in a party frock, and couldn't. That was another world too. She felt in need of reassurance and turned to speak to Harry, who was in the back with Nikki and Spanghero, but couldn't think of anything sensible to say, except: 'Are you okay?'

'Yes,' he said, surprised. 'I'm okay.'

The light was beginning to fade when they got to the

cottage, which was more like a country house than a *chaumière*, Ryfka thought. And Nikki's friend, a handsome woman of about forty, greeted him more like a lover.

Nikki introduced her simply as Florence and the others even more simply as 'friends of mine'. Florence smiled, said: 'Enchantée,' and asked if they'd be staying for dinner. Nikki said he didn't think there was time, they had to be on their way within the hour. But perhaps some cheese and pâté and a glass of wine ... Served in the kitchen, preferably, since his friends liked to be near a back door.

'Of course,' she said, without turning a hair. And unobtrusively withdrew after serving them.

'That's some friend,' said Ryfka. 'One of your group?'

Nikki smiled. 'A warm sympathizer.'

Ryfka spread a map out on the table and pointed to a spot north-west of the Forest of Fougères. 'Our landing field. Codenamed Les Colombes. It seems that Raab knows we have a landing field around here. But he doesn't know where. So he'll try to cut the whole area off with a new line of roadblocks.'

She turned to Luc. 'We wait till after dark – in fact, till moonrise. Then you drive us up the N798 in the direction of Les Colombes, dropping us just short of where the roadblocks start. We should be able to spot them in the moonlight. The rest of the journey is across country.'

'And what do I do?' said Luc.

'Go through the roadblocks – you'll be clean without us – and contact Georges de Brissac, who owns the landing field. I'll give you his address. He'll give you whatever you need to set up the flarepath. In fact, he and his sons will set it up for you, if you don't know how.'

'Of course I know. Seen it done often enough.'

'Then tell me.'

'The flarepath must be more or less into the wind and start at least a hundred metres from the downwind hedge. Right?' said Luc. 'That's where I fix the first torch. Or lamp A, as you call it. And lamp B a hundred and fifty metres into the wind. And fifty metres to right of that, lamp C. Making an inverted L for the pilot. Okay, baby?'

'Okay,' said Ryfka. 'And check that the flarepath's level and firm with no obstructions and, of course, no trees in the approach funnel at either end. The code letter is U. You know what that is in Morse?'

'Do I hell.'

'Dot, dot, dash. Repeat it.'

Luc repeated it several times.

'And Paddy Flynn will flash the letter P in return. That's dot-dash-dash-dot.'

'What about weapons? I can't take any through a roadblock.'

'De Brissac has a small arsenal. So do the sons.'

'Sons? How many are there?'

'Two. Both troublemakers. And the old man's the worst of the lot. Vain as hell and quarrelsome as a cock. Good in a tight corner though.'

'They live together?'

'The sons and their wives share a big house together about a kilometre from Les Colombes. The old man lives a bit farther away, alone, except for a German Shepherd bitch called Lottie.'

'Listen,' said Luc, 'am I likely to have trouble with them?'

'The sons'll do what the old man tells them and he'll do what *you* tell him – because you're my representative.' Her mouth curved in a small smile. 'Unless he thinks you're talking balls.'

'Sounds like I'm in for a great time,' said Luc.

'If he has any suggestions, listen to him. He knows the lie of the land and the best places to give covering fire from.'

'Does Les Colombes have any special features I should know about?'

'It's a decent-sized landing field, about eight hundred metres long from hedge to hedge and almost half as wide. But dotted with clumps of trees and bushes.'

'That doesn't sound suitable for a landing strip.'

'That's what the Germans thought when they did a survey of the area some time ago and ordered some of the bigger fields to be ploughed up. In fact, if you look carefully, there's a clear strip about two hundred metres wide that runs right through the trees, almost from hedge to hedge. And the trees act as a kind of camouflage. That's why I chose it. It's the best I know. Anything else?'

Luc thought for a moment. 'Do you think there'll be trouble?'

Ryfka took a deep breath. 'Yes.'

Raab was a good organizer. After intensive study of a map showing the contours of land to the north-west of the Forest of Fougères, he had isolated an area large enough to feel reasonably sure the landing field would be within it. *Barrages* were set up on all approach roads. Then he put every available SS squad into the area. Each squad, of twelve men and a sergeant, were to patrol a specific section of the area. There was a common password in case one squad was challenged by another in the dark and the sergeants were issued with *Leuchtpistolen*, the equivalent of Very lights. These had a double function: to light up a suspect area and signal for assistance from other squads.

Raab himself would be on patrol in his armoured car and would respond instantly to any signal flare. He had also been promised a mobile searchlight from a local anti-aircraft battery. If they did locate the landing field they'd be able to flood it with light at the critical moment.

He explained all this to the sergeants and the commanders of the roadblocks at a meeting in a café he had taken over in one of the villages near the forest. When he'd finished he asked for questions and comments.

Von Heideck, who was in overall command of the road-blocks, said: 'What makes you so sure the landing field is within your designated area?'

'I'm not sure,' said Raab coldly. 'Any more than I'm sure she'll wait for nightfall before she moves. I'm simply making inferences from the evidence available.'

19

They reached the N798 without difficulty and headed north
till they sighted a roadblock, which Luc stopped well short
of. Roadblocks weren't lit, except by masked lights, because
of blackout regulations, but were visible from a distance by
moonlight. And the moon was up by then, though it had a
bad habit of disappearing behind patches of altocumulus to
drench the land in moments of darkness.

The others got out and Luc drove on. Ryfka watched as
an SS man with a masked lamp signalled him to stop. Other
SS men appeared and searched the van. Then Luc was
waved through. As easy as that. A good omen, she hoped.

She climbed a gate and started to cross a field. The
others followed in single file, Spanghero just behind her,
then Harry, then Nikki. The journey across country,
keeping to hedges and ditches for cover, wasn't too difficult.
The real danger lay in the narrow lanes and twisting roads
patrolled by the SS, though their jackboots could be heard
coming. And Spanghero's acute hearing gave them plenty
of warning anyway. But avoiding the patrols slowed them
down. They also had to stop whenever the moon went in
because darkness came down like a curtain. And they
daren't use torches.

Occasionally they heard patrols challenge one another
with 'Halt! Wer da?' Once the nearness of the challenge
made Ryfka jump. She had laid down a procedure to avoid
being surprised by a patrol. Whenever they came to a bend
in a lane or road they stopped and listened. Then she,
Spanghero and Nikki, automatic weapons cocked and at the
ready, moved round the bend in line abreast, with Harry
bringing up the rear.

'It should give us a couple of seconds' advantage,' she
said. 'Enough to wreak a little havoc.'

*

Luc banged on the solid oak door three or four times. The only response was the deep-throated barking of a German Shepherd dog. That's all I need, he thought, to be attacked by a savage GSD. He banged on the door again, then stepped back to check for a sign of life. A light blinked on in an upper window, then blinked off again, as if the house had momentarily opened one eye. No blackout, Luc thought. Callio bastard.

He went back to the door and waited. The barking continued. Then slippered feet flip-flopped down wooden stairs and a bad-tempered male voice shouted: 'All right, all right, I'm not fucking deaf.' Then it said: 'Shut up, Lottie.' The dog stopped barking.

The door was pulled open and Luc saw a big-shouldered man in slippers and trousers with a hairy chest and a belly ribbed with muscle only partly overlaid by fat. He had a shock of greying hair and a hard handsome face. And was holding a German Shepherd bitch by the collar.

'Who the bloody hell are you,' he said, 'waking us up in the middle of the night?'

'Middle of the night?' said Luc, to whom it was more like the middle of the evening.

'I go to bed with the chickens,' the big man snarled, 'because I have to get up with the bastards.'

'Monsieur de Brissac?'

'Yes, yes. Who the fuck are you?'

'I'm from Ryfka – '

'Then why didn't you say so? Come in, come in. This is Lottie,' he said of the dog and led the way through a half-panelled hall to a huge flagstoned kitchen. Luc noticed there was a mirror on every wall.

'Sit down, sit down,' de Brissac said. 'You too,' he said to Lottie.

Luc sat down at a pitchpine table covered with white American cloth. Lottie sat at his feet and looked up at him with big loving eyes. De Brissac sat opposite Luc, admired himself in a mirror and combed and patted his hair with his fingers.

'Now, what do you want?'

'To arrange a pick-up at Les Colombes – '

'To drink, idiot, to drink.'

'Well, a coffee – '

'With a little cognac. To warm you up. To warm us both up. Can get chilly out there in the small hours.' He got up and started to make the coffee. 'What time's the pick-up?'

'O-two hundred hours.'

'Not more than three passengers, I take it?'

'Just Ryfka and one other.'

'We packed four into a Lysander once. Terrible bloody squeeze.' He paused to admire himself in the mirror. 'There were plenty of Boche around earlier.'

'There still are. Let's hope they don't show up at Les Colombes.'

'Me and the boys'll hold 'em off if they do.' He made a grimace at the mirror to expose his teeth. 'All my own. Not bad for a man of sixty, eh?'

'You and the boys going to hold off an armoured car?'

De Brissac took a bottle of cognac from a sideboard and put it on the table with two *café filtres*.

'Or would you prefer armagnac?'

'Thank you,' said Luc. 'This is fine.'

De Brissac opened a cupboard, rummaged in it till he found a crowbar, then prised up one of the flagstones and brought out an oilskin bag from a cavity underneath. Inside the bag were two Sten guns and a dozen or more spare magazines. He laid them out on the table as if they were his best cutlery.

'One is for you,' he said. 'In case of trouble.'

Then he prised up another flagstone and brought out, two at a time, a dozen anti-personnel mines.

'Where the hell did you get those?' said Luc, shaken for once.

'I helped to clear minefields after hostilities were over,' said de Brissac. He gestured. 'Some stuck to my fingers.'

He found a pencil stub in a drawer, went back to the table and drew a rectangle on the shiny white American cloth. 'Les Colombes,' he said, then marked in some crosses. 'Clumps of trees.' Then he drew the letter L. 'The flarepath. You'll be here by the first lamp. I'll be here, in the trees. And my boys here and here. Anyone approaching over open ground gets caught in crossfire. All right?'

'Fine. But you didn't answer my question about holding off an armoured car.'

'Ah yes,' said de Brissac and made two more marks on the sketch plan. 'Gates. The only entrances for vehicles. Both locked.'

'An armoured car could crash through.'

'Well, we could try planting a few anti-personnel mines around the gates.'

'There are also hedges they could crash through.'

'Ah, but they won't think of that till they've tried the gates. Gates are official. And Germans love the official. And by that time our operation should be over. And we'll be off.'

'You have an escape route too?'

'An old culvert, its entrance masked by cow parsley and other stuff. Comes out in a dry ditch in the next field.'

'You've thought of everything.'

De Brissac shrugged. 'I'm not so sure. Those mines, for instance, I don't know if they're powerful enough to turn an armoured car over . . .'

'Be fucking interesting to find out though,' said Luc.

'You must meet my boys,' said de Brissac, brightening. 'You'd like them. Nice lads. Well brought up too.'

Progress was good. They hadn't come across a patrol for ages. Or so it seemed. Probably no more than ten minutes or so, she thought. The area was too big to patrol thoroughly, even with a battalion. It would need a small army . . . Perhaps Raab had overreached himself. Or the gods were smiling on them at last.

Then they turned a corner, from one lane into another, and ran slap into a patrol taking a break. Squatting by the roadside, smoking cigarettes in cupped hands.

They dropped to one knee and opened fire in short, controlled bursts. The SS men went down like ninepins in a bowling alley. Two or three managed to open fire in return, but their aim was wild. The SS sergeant, before he was nearly cut in half by automatic fire, managed to point his *Leuchtpistole* at the sky and pull the trigger.

The flare burst above them and hung in the air, illuminating the carnage in its ghastly light.

'Run!' she yelled.

They ran, following her as she swerved through the dead and dying. She cut across a field, into a lane, across another field . . . Flares seemed to be going up everywhere.

She stopped at a T-junction for a breather. Then Spanghero said: 'Patrol behind us.'

From the left she heard what sounded like a couple of heavy vehicles approaching . . . She went right. The narrow road twisted and turned – then stopped abruptly at the gate to a farm. A dead end. In more senses than one, perhaps.

She put a finger to her lips. 'Bound to be a bloody dog,' she whispered and carefully opened the gate. They crept past the farmhouse, a couple of barns and other outbuildings at the back and came to a paddock. Then she saw them. A line of SS men advancing slowly across the paddock towards them, assault rifles at the ready. Behind her the sound of the approaching vehicles grew louder.

'We'll have to hide,' she said. 'In one of the outbuildings.'

'No,' said Harry. 'There.'

He pointed to a haystack that had been piled up under a crude structure of four tall posts and a corrugated iron roof to keep the worst of the weather out. Except that most of the roof had been blown off, presumably in the recent storm.

'That's the place to hide,' he said.

She hesitated. A wrong decision could mean death or worse. Then a flare burst almost overhead, drenching the yard in ghost-green light.

Raab's armoured car pulled into the farmyard, followed by an SS truck. Raab and Blech got out of the armoured car, an SS sergeant and his platoon jumped out of the truck.

'There should be another platoon somewhere at the

back,' Raab said to the sergeant. 'Tell your men to start searching the outhouses. We'll join them in a moment.'

By now a dog was yapping its head off. The door of the farmhouse opened and the farmer, a bewildered-looking man still in night clothes, stood in the doorway, his young wife close behind him, peering fearfully over his shoulder. The dog ran out into the yard and stood yapping at Raab, who drew his pistol and shot it dead. The farmer's wife screamed, then burst into tears.

'Tell her to shut up,' Raab said. 'Or I'll take her down to Gestapo headquarters and give her something to cry about.'

She shut up.

'We're looking for three men and a woman. Criminals on the run. We think they came in here. Have you heard or seen anything suspicious?'

'No, monsieur,' said the farmer. 'We were asleep till you arrived, monsieur.'

'We're going to check every outbuilding. Even the henhouse. You'd better come along.'

'Yes, monsieur.'

'And remember there's a reward of two million francs for information leading to the capture of these criminals.'

'Yes, monsieur.'

Raab and Blech walked round to the back of the farmhouse. The farmer followed at what he judged to be a respectful distance.

SS men were already searching some of the outhouses.

'Have these two barns been searched?' Raab asked the sergeant.

'Not yet, mein Herr.'

'Bring half a dozen men and we'll do it together,' said Raab. 'Starting with this one.'

She and Harry had burrowed their way into the bottom of the haystack, while Nikki and Spanghero climbed into the top half. They spoke in whispers.

'Christ,' she said, 'it's damp as buggery and stinks.'

'All that rain we had must have rotted the straw. The

whole stack must have been soaked after the storm blew the roof off.'

'Why didn't the sun dry it out?'

'Not enough time, except to dry out the upper part.'

'Where Nikki and Spanghero are sitting pretty. Just my luck.'

Then she heard the heavy vehicles rolling into the farm-yard, orders being shouted in German.

Every barn and outhouse had been searched except one small hut, which stood near the haystack. Torches were playing everywhere and the farmer saw, with a mixture of shock and pleasure, that the haystack had been disturbed. And the stupid Boche hadn't noticed a thing. But to a farmer, especially one who'd stacked the hay himself, it was obvious.

'What's in there?' said Raab.

'In – in where, monsieur?' the farmer stuttered, wondering if Raab had noticed something after all.

'The hut,' said Raab. 'It's locked.'

'Only tools and things, monsieur. I'll get the key.'

'Don't bother,' said Raab, turning to the sergeant. 'Shoot the lock off, sergeant.'

The sergeant shattered the lock with a burst of automatic fire, then kicked the door in.

'Someone shine a torch inside.'

Half a dozen torches were shone inside the hut. Raab walked in, looked around. Broken furniture and other junk. Boxes with tools, screws, washers. Farm implements, some broken and waiting to be repaired.

Against one wall was a row of six petrol cans. He went to the door, beckoned the farmer, pointed to the cans. 'Petrol?'

'Yes, monsieur.'

'Where did you get it?'

'A friend, monsieur. He, er, had some over . . .'

'It's black market petrol, isn't it?'

The farmer was silent. Everyone bought black market petrol when he had the chance. And Raab knew it. He was just being bloody-minded.

'Isn't it?' Raab repeated.

The farmer jumped. 'Yes, monsieur.'

Raab took the sergeant's assault rifle, turned to the farmer.

'I could have you shot for this.' He moved back from the hut. 'But I'm a merciful man . . .'

Aiming through the open doorway he swept the petrol cans with automatic fire.

There was a whoosh as the cans exploded in a ball of fire. The little wooden hut went up like tinder, showering sparks everywhere.

The wind caught the sparks and blew them straight at the haystack. In seconds it was a mass of flames.

Raab stood back and laughed. 'Better than a firework display, isn't it?'

Then a figure leapt down from the haystack, clothes blazing. As he hit the ground his Sten gun was firing on full automatic. It was Spanghero. Then another human torch leapt down, Sten gun firing. Nikki. Both were cut down by a hail of bullets from thirty or forty automatic weapons.

'Stop firing!' Raab called out. 'I want the others alive!'

Silence, except for the crackle of flames devouring wood and straw. In the flickering light of the burning hayrick, Raab, Blech and the SS platoon stood round in a semicircle, waiting, watching.

At the bottom of the burning rick, in pitch darkness, Harry Romaine was fighting a desperate battle to restrain Ryfka. He was a strong man, but her fear of the fire, as it crept closer all the time, was even stronger. She bit, scratched, kicked, tried to knee him. He clamped his legs round hers like a vice, got his forearm under her chin and forced her head back to stop her screaming. But it was like trying to hold a wildcat. All the time he was whispering hoarsely: 'It'll burn itself out! The hay's too wet – don't you understand?'

In the end, as he felt his strength ebbing, he could only whisper: 'For Christ's sake . . . For Christ's *sake!*'

Suddenly she went limp and he thought she'd fainted. But

she'd simply stopped struggling as it began to get through to her that the fire was actually dying down.

In the darkness he felt her face against his. It was wet with tears. Of relief or perhaps remorse. Not that it mattered. Nothing mattered, he thought, as long as she didn't start fighting again.

'Hold me tight,' she whispered.

'I can hardly hold you much tighter,' he said, stifling a crazy desire to laugh.

Raab stared uncomprehendingly at the remains of the haystack. At least three-quarters of it had been burnt down. All that was left was a black smouldering heap.

Then the explanation hit him.

'They split up!' he almost shouted at Blech. 'The bitch went off with the airman and left these two behind.' He pointed to the bullet-torn bodies of Nikki and Spanghero. 'Come on. They can't have got far.'

Minutes later the yard was deserted. Only the farmer remained, suddenly feeling chilly in his night clothes. He shivered, knelt down by the smouldering remains of hayrick and said softly: 'If there is anyone still in there – the Boche have gone now. They really have. There's only me and the wife left. They shot the dog . . .'

There was a long silence and the farmer was about to give up and go indoors when two figures, black as chimney sweeps, rose slowly from the ashes.

Raab spent an hour in his command vehicle following the patrols as they swept the area round the farm. He then gave orders to widen the area of search.

'Where the hell's she got to?' he said to Blech.

'She could be lying up somewhere,' said Blech. 'She's still in the old Horseman territory. And she'll still have contacts.'

'Maybe, but she's got to move sometimes – if she's going to catch that plane.'

'Then why not forget about her,' said Blech. 'And watch for the plane. It shouldn't be too difficult with this moon.

It's bound to be a Lysander and the pilot's bound to be flying low – to avoid radar and to spot the ground signals.'

They were in the command vehicle and Raab turned to the wireless operator. 'Tell platoon commanders to be on the lookout for a Lysander. Description: a single-engined high-wing monoplane with fixed undercarriage and prominent wheel spats. Flying low . . . And find out where that mobile searchlight's got to. I want it here, with me. If I'm going to need it at all, it'll be in a hurry.'

The farmer's wife gave them bowls of hot water to wash in, then made coffee for everyone.

'Tell me,' Ryfka said to the farmer, 'what made you wonder if anyone was still hiding in the haystack?'

'When the Boche were searching I saw it had been disturbed and thought someone might be hiding there. I knew it wouldn't burn right down, and it's a good place to hide. Just bad luck it got set on fire.'

'You knew there was a reward for us?'

'The officer told me.'

She looked around at the shabby furnishings. 'You're not a rich man.'

'Or a traitor,' he said.

Dog minus 6

For a long time there was no sign of patrols and she was beginning to think the search had shifted to another part of the area. Then, when they were no more than two or three kilometres from Les Colombes, there were SS everywhere, on foot, in trucks, in armoured cars.

For the best part of a kilometre they had to use ditches and hedges as cover. Suddenly they were in the clear again, walking along a lane in the moonlight. Then they breasted a rise and there, spread out before them, was the landing field called Les Colombes, 800 metres long and more than half as wide.

She had a good view of the landing strip running between small banks and clumps of trees, which were well back from the flarepath. But the distance was too great to see the

267

torches tied to sticks that would mark the limits of the flarepath. Luc would be waiting for her in the bank of trees opposite the first lamp, and the de Brissacs, *père et fils*, waiting like brigands in whatever cover allowed them a field of sufficiently murderous crossfire.

'Come on,' she said and took Harry's hand and started across the field in the moonlight.

Raab was also waiting, with some impatience, at the crossroads where he'd arranged to rendezvous with the mobile searchlight unit. He was leaning against his armoured car, smoking a cigarette with Blech, when he heard the throb of an approaching engine.

'The searchlight truck,' he said. 'At last.'

Then he realized the throb was coming from the sky.

He looked up in time to see the Lysander swooping overhead, like a great dark bird. He felt he could almost reach up and touch her.

As soon as she saw the Lysander she started flashing her code letter, dot-dot-dash, dot-dot-dash. Seconds later Paddy Flynn flashed his own letter in return. She immediately switched on the first torch. Luc switched on the second, then raced fifty metres to switch on the third.

She had left Harry in the trees with instructions to wait till she signalled him with the torch.

'Then run like hell for the plane,' she said.

From about 500 feet Paddy Flynn did a descending turn through 180 degrees, throttling back and coming in over the hedge at 70mph, slats out, flaps down, flattening out and floating as little as possible, then putting her straight down on the flarepath, cutting the throttle and starting to brake. He raced past the first lamp but had slowed enough by the second lamp to do a U-turn and start taxiing back towards the first, when Ryfka was waiting.

He was about thirty metres from the lamp when a searchlight somewhere on the other side of the down-wind hedge was switched on, and shone straight into his eyes. A voice started shouting in German through a loud hailer. Paddy

Flynn braked, did another U-turn to get out of the blinding light and turn the Lysander into the wind, hoping there'd be enough of the landing strip left for a take-off. He kept the engine running and waited for Ryfka. He also kept one hand on his Smith & Wesson .38 in its holster on the port cockpit coaming above the throttles.

Luc, from the shelter of a copse, shot out the searchlight with a nicely judged burst of automatic fire. But SS troops were already advancing across the field in open order. Then they stopped, as if walking into an invisible wall. A wall of crossfire set up by the de Brissacs and Luc. They went down like corn under the scythe.

Raab's armoured car burst through an entrance gate and ploughed into one of Georges de Brissac's miniature mine-fields. The explosions didn't turn it over, but they wrecked the front suspension and the car ran round in a circle and jammed itself in the gateway. Raab climbed out, followed by Blech.

'Concentrate all your fire on this side,' Raab said. 'Above all try to take out the plane.'

'We can't get a clear shot at it from here because of the trees,' said Blech, 'and if we move we run into crossfire.'

'Never mind, we'll get behind them,' Raab said, and took a stick grenade from the belt of an SS man. 'Follow me.'

'I beg your pardon, mein Herr?'

'I said, follow me.'

'But you can't – I mean, there's no chance of getting behind them. I mean, they'll have someone covering the rear.'

'No they won't. They're too busy dealing with the frontal attack. Anyway, we've got to get that airman alive.' Without his smoked glasses Raab's pale eyes seemed to be glazed with moonlight and madness. 'I was a bombardier on the Western Front, Blech. I could land a grenade within a metre of the target . . . I won't kill him, you understand, just disable him . . . Follow me.'

He jumped into a ditch that ran along one of the boundary hedges, then made a right-angled turn behind the bank of trees that lined one side of the flarepath. Blech followed reluctantly.

Though the ditch was dry it was rough going and Blech soon began to limp – and lag behind.

'Come on,' said Raab. 'Come on!'

'It's my foot,' said Blech. 'The one I injured on the Russian Front.' Suddenly he stumbled, lurched forward and fell flat on his face. And groaned loudly.

'Sorry, mein Herr,' he called. 'Sorry.'

Raab stopped and turned. 'I'll have you sent to a penal battalion, you little shit,' he said. And disappeared into the night.

As soon as he was out of sight Blech sat up, dug a crumpled cigarette out of his pocket, lit it between cupped hands and said softly the German equivalent of 'Fuck you, Jack, I'm all right.'

Ryfka had manned one of the crossfire stations with Luc to help stop the SS flooding across the field. As soon as they stopped to regroup she slipped away through the trees and came out on the edge of the flarepath about fifty metres from the plane and almost opposite the bank of trees where she'd left Harry.

She flashed the torch on and off and yelled: 'Harry!'

A moment later he appeared on the other side of the flarepath, 200 metres away. She pointed to the plane: 'Run!'

They both ran towards the plane.

Something made her glance back over her shoulder.

She saw Raab step out of the trees about thirty metres behind Harry. He was holding a stick grenade, his arm pulled back to throw.

'Harry!' she shrieked involuntarily. A mistake because Harry stopped and looked back.

Raab flung the grenade.

She took careful aim with the assault rifle because she had only one bullet left. It hit him in the belly and he went down. A gut shot. For Gerard.

Then the grenade exploded. The blast picked Harry up and flung him backwards in a heap, like a rag doll.

'Harry,' she cried. 'Harry!'

And ran to him. Paddy Flynn had climbed out of the Lysander and was also running to him. Between them they pulled him to his feet and half carried, half dragged him to the port side of the Lysander, where the fixed metal ladder led up to the rear cockpit.

'You go up and get in,' Paddy said to her. 'I'll push him, you pull.'

She climbed the ladder, slid back the canopy cover and got in. She leaned out and heard Paddy say: 'Come on, me boy, I'll help you up the ladder.'

'What ladder?' Harry said.

She leaned down, grabbed his arms and pulled – as Paddy pushed from below – and got him up the ladder. She tried to pull him into the cockpit, but he seemed to get stuck.

'Jasus,' said Paddy, 'if the ould bitch is left on tickover much longer she'll oil up like a bastard.'

She gave another heave and Harry more or less fell into the cockpit.

'Okay, Paddy,' she called.

But Paddy was already climbing into the front cockpit. Seconds later she heard the Mercury engine howling up to maximum revs as they started rolling ... Sweet music. Then the first bullets thudded into the fuselage.

She looked out of the rear canopy and saw an armoured car coming down the flarepath, it's machine gun firing. She grabbed a helmet with its intercom attachment and shouted into the intercom: 'Bloody great armoured car behind us, Paddy.'

Paddy's voice crackled back over the intercom. 'Aye, and another bugger in front.'

Then, suddenly, they were airborne and climbing up to heaven.

Raab wasn't dead. The bullet had chipped one of the lumbar vertebrae, paralyzing him from the waist down. He tried to pull himself across the flarepath but progress was in inches. Then he heard the armoured car, then saw it, coming straight towards him, firing at the plane.

He shrieked at it to stop, clawed at tufts of grass to pull himself out of the way, but the grass came away in his hand.

He shrieked again, though he was too shocked to feel anything as it thundered over him. He would die later and in pain.

Harry was leaning back against the bulkhead. She shone a torch in his face to see if he'd react to the light, but he didn't. His face was torn and bleeding. She tried to clean it up with a handkerchief.

'Harry,' she said. 'You'll be all right.'

'It's my eyes,' he said. 'I can't see . . . I can't *see*.'

'I'll be your eyes,' she said, and put her arms round him and felt her love flow out like blood from a wound she could no longer staunch.

By then the whole plane was shaking and rattling, and the engine singing like a love song.